Treasure of the San Jose

Steve Higgs

Contents

The San José. September 1st, 1708

F leet Commander Admiral José Fernandez de Santillan looked up upon the sound of knocking at his door. A seasoned traveller, he was familiar with heavy seas and arduous journeys, but nothing could have prepared him for the storm his ship currently endured.

The news the person outside his door felt it necessary to deliver was going to be bad; Fernandez de Santillan felt certain that had to be the case. How could it be anything else?

He'd gambled and was about to lose.

"Come," he called, raising his voice to a bellow just to be heard above the creaking of the ship and the crashing of the waves.

The door swung open with a crash, the unpredictable surging shift in the deck wrenching it free from the man attempting to hold it. In the doorway, one of his most trusted lieutenants, his first officer Pedro Garcia Lopez, gripped the frame and tried to stay on his feet.

"We are losing her, sir!" he blurted. Water sheeted from his hair and clothing; the man was soaked to the bone. "I fear we have no choice other than to run her aground."

Fernandez de Santillan knew the man was not given to panic, so the worry tainting Pedro's voice was enough to cause double that to bloom inside the admiral's chest.

Rising to his feet, he asked, "Our current position?"

"Unsure, sir. There are too few hands to control the ship. We have been blown off course for sure and I can ill afford to spare anyone to take a reading even if the stars were visible."

Lurching in his attempt to cross his cabin, Fernandez de Santillan gripped his table, got his balance, and waited for the deck beneath his feet to even out before he pushed off on a run to get to the door.

Grabbed by his first officer when he almost fell, the admiral allowed his assistant to help him get steady before asking a question he felt most pertinent.

"Pedro, if you have no idea where we are, how do you propose to run the ship safely aground?"

"Land, sir. We can see land."

Only when he arrived on the deck, a deluge of seawater chilling him in an instant, did the admiral understand just how perilous their situation had become.

Together with a select handful of the ship's officers, he'd poisoned the rations of everyone else on board. They fed them gin and rum in celebration of making it safely across the Atlantic with the treasure in their hold and the sailors and unwitting officers, who were not part of the inner circle, drank it joyfully.

They passed out in a manner that befitted a night of drinking and the admiral's chosen tossed the bodies overboard the next morning.

It was then that the inner circle allowed themselves the opportunity to celebrate. They'd made it away cleanly, ensuring they would be reported as sunk by secretly delivering a message to the British. The message, delivered by a spy, gave a place where Spain's hated enemy would be able to hunt down and board the ship, seizing what they were falsely led to believe was a vast fortune in gold and jewels.

Of course, the San José *had* been loaded with a king's ransom in gold, silver, and gemstones, but once they put to sea the treasure was swiftly cross loaded. Taken from the pride of the Spanish fleet, the crew stowed it onboard a ship the admiral acquired almost a full year before his plan was put into motion. The decoy vessel was old and allowed to remain tatty-looking for the additional disguise that provided.

A small percentage of the treasure in the San José's hold was left behind with the skeleton crew assigned to sail it. They, and the young lieutenant commissioned to captain it, his chest swelling with pride, knew nothing of the plot to have the British catch them.

The admiral knew that to stand any chance of stealing such a vast fortune, they needed the world to believe they were all dead and the treasure claimed by the waves. That was why he had one man left on board the San José who knew the truth. One man who Fernandez de Santillan knew he could trust.

Francis Moreno was the son of a farmer; a poor child who would grow up to be a poor man had he not tried to steal from the young admiral when he happened upon him one day in the streets of Seville. The admiral, the third son of a count, could have had Francis killed for his crime, but chose to employ him instead.

Now Francis was dying, his body wasting away and wracked with pain. The admiral's personal physicians tried their darndest, but assured him there was nothing more that could be done to prolong the life of his oldest friend. For his part, Francis was ready to meet his maker, the rest that would follow, a blissful relief from the pain he daily endured.

When the British began firing upon the San José, Francis would light a fuse inside the ship's armoury, sending it to the bottom with all the remaining crew. No one would ever know the treasure was not on board.

The admiral believed wholeheartedly in his plan, so much so that he dispatched his crew to their watery graves a full week before they were due to sail quietly and discretely into a secluded port on the coast of Ireland. The treasure would be split between his inner circle, each man assured a fortune greater than most kings had ever possessed. What happened afterward would be down to each man to determine for themselves, but returning to Spain was off the table and they all knew it.

However, with another wave jolting the deck with such force the admiral would swear the hull had just struck the seabed, he questioned if there was any chance they would see the sun rise again.

Without the crew to trim the sails, when the breeze powering them contentedly toward their destination became a gale of unprecedented strength, they were at the mercy of the storm. The officers, less than twenty of them, were doing all they could to keep the ship afloat, but Pedro reported one had already been swept overboard and the rest had been fighting the elements for hours and were starting to flag.

"Land!" bellowed the admiral's first officer, angling an arm over the starboard side of the heaving ship.

Fernandez de Santillan had to squint to see it, but there between the thunderous sky and the mountainous waves, he caught a glimpse of a rolling hill when the lightning flashed to illuminate the grass and trees coating it.

It wasn't their destination, but they either aimed the ship hard for land or they went to the bottom where both they and the treasure would be lost for all history.

The admiral nodded, the only response his first officer needed.

It took three men to fight the wheel around, steering the ship directly for the land ahead and praying they might reach the shore before the water filling the hold overcame the remaining buoyancy to carry them all to their graves.

Slowly, inexorably, the prow forged its way through the waves. The ship was hard to control, the wind too strong for the amount of sail employed. There was nothing they could do to change that – the time to reduce the sails was before the storm hit and they would have struggled even then for there were too few of them to manage the ropes and sheets.

Battling against a surging tide, barely able to steer, and with giant waves constantly washing across the deck to add more water to the hold, the officers under Fernandez de Santillan's command said nothing. The howling of the wind and crashing of the waves made conversation all but impossible. However, it was the likelihood they wouldn't make it that clamped their mouths shut.

Despite their fears, the distant blob of land came ever closer. Was it Spain they could see? Was it France? Off course and floundering, it didn't matter too much. If they could beach the ship and survive the night, the storm would blow itself out and they could take it from there.

Positioned on the prow, Lieutenant Bernadino Alvarez watched anxiously. This close to an unknown shore the possibility of rocks that might tear out the bottom of the ship in a heartbeat was all too real.

He was half frozen and utterly exhausted. He couldn't guess how many hours might have passed since he last slept, but it was a lot more than twenty-four.

Jolting, a surge of fear gripped his soul when a flash of lightning illuminated something in the waves. They were closer to shore than he'd realised and ... was that a rock? Bernadino had a shout poised on his lips, his eyes locked on the patch of black where the roiling sea had just showed him ... something.

"Rocks!" The bellow left his lips with all the might he could muster. "Hard a starboard!" He screamed the words at the top of his lungs and indicated which way they needed to go. Why were they not turning?

The admiral and the other officers gathered on the ship's poop deck weren't even looking at Bernadino. Their attention was fixed quite firmly on the looming cliffs. Like Bernadino, they had failed to recognise how close the racing tide and gusting winds had driven them to the shore. Checking their relative position only moments ago, they were still too far away to be concerned. Now the high, rugged landscape loomed over them like a threat.

At the prow, Bernadino climbed so his crewmates and captain might see his frantic gestures. There were rocks ahead and they were going to hit them. By sheer luck they'd already missed jagged peaks to both sides. They needed to beach the ship and they were close to shore now, but that didn't mean they were safe. The ship's hull could tear out in an instant, being driven onto rocks they couldn't even see.

When the collision came, it jolted the ship with such sudden intensity Bernadino's grip would not have failed had he been fresh and feeling strong. With his fingers numb from the cold and the rope he held drenched and slippery, he tumbled from the ship with a startled cry to plunge into the thrashing waves below.

No one saw his fall and they would never be aware enough to notice their missing crewmember. Admiral Fernandez de Santillan and the rest were all too focused on aiming the ship at the black crack in the rock ahead.

They knew how much trouble they were in. The report from below was the water level had reached the galley. They were going to the bottom and the collision that threw them all to the deck just a moment ago could only mean the hull was breached.

A cave or a bay, that's what they all prayed the black slit represented.

Repenting the hubris that led him to believe he could get away with the greatest crime the world would ever see, the admiral begged the Lord to forgive his sins and deliver his officers, himself, and the bounty their ailing ship carried, to safety.

The ship jolted again, panicked cries coming from below that could only mean another breech. They were moments from sinking, but the intense wind, the very making of their defeat was also to be their saviour.

Wallowing, the ship wanted to move sluggishly, yet the power in her sails, holding together when the admiral was ready to bet they would falter and tear, powered them through the surf. There was no good reason to believe the dark hole in the cliffs would have a deep enough draught to allow the ship to sail inside, but it did. And there was no good reason to hope the hole in the cliff would be deep or wide enough to provide them with shelter, yet they passed easily through the entrance to find the wind dropped instantly.

Like a roar suddenly silenced, they could hear each other once again. What they could not do was see. The darkness inside the cave was absolute and the slim hope they each held that the gap in the cliff might lead to a secluded cove proved just a little bit too much to ask.

The result of a softer layer of sediment eroded over millions of years, the cave shelved swiftly upward, beaching the ship with a shocking jolt when it got far enough inside.

For a few seconds, the ship was stationary, unmoving for the first time since it left port on the other side of the Atlantic many weeks earlier. Then the next storm surge sent a wall of water into the cave. It lifted the ruined ship, but more than that, it forced the central mast into the roof of the cave.

The eroded rocks at the highest point might have held for another thousand years, or two thousand, or more. However, on that night, all it took to break it apart was a nudge at the exact right point.

The sailors below found themselves illuminated in a shaft of moonlight for the briefest of moments before the rocks above tumbled down upon their heads.

The rock walls, weakened by millennia of seawater and storms began a catastrophic collapse, sealing the entrance from the sea and trapping the ship inside a tomblike embrace.

Outside, the wind howled, the sea churned, and by the grace of God, Lieutenant Bernadino Alvarez washed ashore.

Present Day. New York.

C aptain Danvers did not sound pleased to hear from me, which was a little hurtful given that I'd just helped him close more than one major case, and rid the city of New York of an organised crime family in the guise of the Columbian Cartel.

"Patricia, I cannot act on this. You know that." He wasn't exactly whining, but the effect was much the same. I wanted something I knew he could give me, and he was trying to weasel out of it. "Have you tried calling her? Maybe she went on the metro, the signal can be patchy down there."

"Danny, her phone is disconnected, so it was either destroyed or someone removed the chip."

Undeterred, Danny said, "You said you only saw her a few hours ago. That's not long enough for me to even file a missing persons' report."

"I'm not asking you to file a report, Danny," I all but growled at the senior police officer. "I want you to start investigating what might have happened to her. I need officers and I need your clout to get me and my friends back inside the museum now that it has closed for the day."

If you are wondering what is going on, I'll take a few moments just to catch you up.

My name is Patricia Fisher. I have a job as a detective on board a cruise ship. You might think that sounds ridiculous because surely cruise ships are benign places where happy holiday makers sit around the pool all day sipping cocktails, and aren't most of them too old to get up to mischief?

Well, yes and no. The average age of the passengers on board is somewhere north of sixty with a lot of them counting eight decades or more to their name. However, a cruise ship is basically a giant floating city and thus attracts a criminal element who will prey upon the unsuspecting holiday makers. Remember the cocktails they were sipping? It makes them less alert, and the age demographic means persons inclined to steal, hustle, and generally rip-off, can find a worthwhile audience all gathered neatly in one location.

Hence the need for a detective.

The ship stopped in New York two days ago and ought to be leaving tonight, but a technical issue with a vital system dictates that it cannot. Regardless of that, I find myself outside the Metropolitan Museum in Manhattan where a friend of mine is supposed to be. Standing around, waiting impatiently for me to do my magic are more of my friends, and my boyfriend, Alistair, who just happens to be the captain of the ship.

"Patricia ..." this time Captain Danny Danvers *was* whining and I cut him off.

"No, Danny, this is real. I cannot talk about it over the phone, okay? You need to trust me that Barbie is missing, and that we need to act fast."

"Because of what she was researching?" Danny sought to confirm. I'd mentioned the subject already without giving him any details.

"Precisely," I agreed. "There is a lot of money at stake. The kind of money people kill for. Following a trail of bodies led us here, Danny. Barbie isn't just missing; she wouldn't wander off. Someone took her."

"The mystery man," Danny taunted me because I had no idea what to call the man who tried to kill me and Barbie when we failed to tell him what he wanted to know. That was weeks ago in the ladies' restroom in a bar on The British Union Isles.

Bored of discussing it, I chose a tactic I worried might not work.

"Captain Danvers, if I have to tear this town apart to find out what happened …"

"All right now, Patricia! That's enough dammit!" He was angry now. "I'm not about to start having you threaten me with consequences. I'll be there in ten minutes, okay? I owe you one, but don't fool yourself into thinking I'll go easy on you if I activate a squad of cops and she turns up ten minutes later."

I breathed a sigh of relief. Having a local police captain on my side would make all the difference. I thanked him only to get another terse reply. His hand was forced, and he wasn't happy, but I would upset every law enforcement officer in the nation if it meant I got Barbie back in one piece.

Putting my phone away, I climbed the steps to the front entrance where Alistair and the others were causing a scene.

Security at the museum wanted to close the building and lock up for the day, but there were enough of us to make that a problem for them. Most likely a mixture of failed or retired cops, they expected their threat of force to work. When it had no impact – they really were threatening the wrong bunch – they warned that they would call the real cops.

It was met by Alistair begging them to do just that. The museum's security team found themselves a little confused at that point and were still arguing when I got back to them.

"The cops are on their way," I announced, speaking more to my friends than the security guards who wanted to close the doors.

"Wait, what?" asked a burly man in security guard uniform. "You called the cops on us? Are you crazy?"

"No," replied Alistair, speaking in calm, soothing tones. "As we have explained multiple times, a friend of ours came here today to conduct research. We believe she met with Hugo Lockhart, an assistant curator in maritime antiquities. She is now missing and to find her the trail has to start here."

The burly man – clearly the senior guard present – waved a dismissive hand.

"Yes, yes, you said all that. There is no record that she bought a ticket or came into the museum today. We already went through that with him." The man locked eyes with Hideki, Barbie's boyfriend and the junior doctor on board the Aurelia. "Dude, she's stepping out on you. It happens to the best of us ..." The look he got from everyone in my group was enough to shut him up.

Trying myself, I squeezed through a gap between Alistair and Hideki, arriving just inside the doors where the impasse was taking place.

"Hello, we haven't met ..." I like to start by being polite in the hope others will follow suit, "my name is Patricia. What's yours?"

In the face of my engaging smile and pleasant demeanour, the burly, surly security guard withered. He exhaled in a resigned fashion, the air leaving his lungs to flap his lips on the way out.

"Mike," he muttered after a few seconds. The guard to his left and right – there were eight of them in total – all had panicked looks as though worried I might collect their names too.

"Nice to meet you, Mike. I'm sorry for the inconvenience this is causing, but my team and I are engaged in attempting to catch a serial killer wanted for dozens of murders across the globe."

That got their attention.

"The killer wants to find the whereabouts of a three-hundred-year-old haul of treasure worth approximately ten billion dollars."

The gum fell from the mouth of the man standing to Mike's left.

"Our missing friend came here today to inspect some artefacts that might assist in our investigation. This all came about when a man chose to stowaway on our cruise ship only to be murdered. Dr Nakamura's autopsy," I indicated to my right where Hideki stood,

11

"found priceless uncut gems in the man's belly. He'd swallowed them to avoid his killer taking them, you see?"

"Hey, man, I read something about that," blurted one of the guards. "Yeah, it was some English dame ..." his words tailed off when he realised what he was saying.

"Precisely," I agreed, making it obvious I was the English dame in question. Focusing my eyes on Mike's, I said, "Does it not strike you as worrying that Hugo Lockhart is missing and that there is no record of our friend coming here today even though we know she spent many hours inside this very building?" I jinked an eyebrow to encourage his response. When he just looked confused, I added, "It is as though someone wanted to keep her visit a secret."

Mike shook his head. "Or it means she was never here." He wanted to stick to his guns, and I could recognise that it was a good trait to have in a security team.

Giving diplomacy one last shot, I said, "Mike, all we need is a guide to take us back to where my team spent yesterday examining the museum's artefacts and to obtain some contact details for Mr Lockhart. This needn't take long. If you are not comfortable taking responsibility for that, please call the head of the museum or give me his number so I can do so. I'm sure we can have this straightened out in no time."

Actually, I didn't think there was going to be any straightening out. The nasty little man who pretended to be Professor Noriega was behind Barbie's disappearance, of that I felt certain. Professor Noriega was the world's foremost authority on the San José until he was murdered, and the San José once carried the treasure we briefly held in my safe until it was stolen. However, as these things always go, I had to prove my certainty before anyone with the authority to help would do so.

Mike laughed at the suggestion he call the head of the museum and wasn't about to give me the big boss's number even if he had it, which he assured me he didn't.

I was close to losing my cool when the police showed up. Mercifully, they were led by Captain Danvers and things went a mite smoother after that.

Yes, he needed a warrant to search the premises, as Mike happily pointed out, but that wasn't what anyone wanted to do. Mutual cooperation was all the situation required, and in the wonderful afterglow of this afternoon's many, many arrests, Danny had credit with his boss the chief of police who was, in turn, willing to use his credit to get someone to lean on someone ...

Refused entry in the same manner as my group, Captain Danvers had no probable cause to force entry and was happy to wait.

He didn't have to wait long.

"Um, Mike," hissed one of the men backing their superior. "What's Mrs Reeves doing back here?"

Mike squinted over my head at a woman in her sixties as she exited her car. She was parked at the curb behind the rearmost squad car and not looking at all pleased to be back at the museum.

"A work colleague?" I enquired.

"The deputy museum director," whispered Captain Danvers.

Mike swore under his breath, but held firm in his 'no entry' stance until Mrs Reeves got within shouting distance.

"Well? Don't just stand there. Open the doors. You're all on overtime until this is resolved." The overtime wasn't a gift, it was a blunt tool.

Mike muttered something to one of the men in his shadow and the welcome sound of doors being unlocked met my ears a moment later.

Mrs Reeves closed the remaining distance to find me waiting to greet her.

"Thank you for this," I began to say.

She stuck out her hand for me to shake. "Think nothing of it. When I heard the great Patricia Fisher needed to look for clues inside the museum, I knew it was a chance I couldn't miss."

No one had ever referred to me as 'the great' anything before. I wasn't sure what to say, and mumbled a few words of thanks.

"I've always thought of myself as something of a detective," she carried on talking. "Of course, the mysteries I try to solve are hundreds or even thousands of years old and have nothing to do with catching criminals. If you will allow me, I would love to observe. I promise to be quiet and stay out of the way."

How was I supposed to say no to that? If her words were not enough, I was being melted by a hopeful gaze a puppy would struggle to match.

Moments later, and inside the museum where Judy Reeves – it didn't take us long to get on first name terms – proved to be an excellent guide.

"Now, I must say that I do not know Hugo all that well. He's been with us for many years … at least five, I would say. I can look that up if it's important, but he's the kind of man who keeps to himself. Very quiet. Does his work and goes home again. Of course, most academics are like that." She broke off what she was saying to point the way to go. "It's just down here."

Judy was leading us to the research rooms where she believed Hugo and Barbie would have spent their time today. It wasn't where Hideki had been with Barbie and others the previous day; then they were escorted to a library where they were able to examine some of the manuscripts and artefacts, all made possible through Barbie's early contact with the museum.

At the same time, Mike, his attitude now adjusted, was taking my security team to review the camera footage for the day and find contact information for Hugo Lockhart.

I have a large team of people around me, all of them capable and each possessing different skills. Martin Baker, his wife, Deepa Bhukari, Schneider, the giant Austrian, and Anders

Pippin are all members of the onboard security detail who worked with me before I took the job as ship's detective.

They were joined by Sam Chalk, an assistant I took on when I briefly ran my own private investigations agency in England. That particular venture had recently been taken over by Mike Atwell, a former police detective now retired. I hoped to look in on him when I next found myself in the UK.

Next to join was Molly, another one from England. Molly Lawrie used to be my house-maid, but was far happier as a junior member of the ship's security detail.

That was the official roster for my team, but I am lucky to boast two good friends, of whom Barbie is one and Jermaine is the other. Jermaine is my butler according to his job title on board the ship, but he is so much more than that. Through Barbie the team gains a doctor as her boyfriend, Hideki, is never too far away, and Alistair joins in whenever the limitations and demands of his role as captain permit.

Certain the team would find the information they required, I hoped to be as lucky.

I wasn't.

Barbie told me Hugo called to say he'd uncovered some additional artefacts and I knew from our conversation that one such item was the diary of the captain of the San José. Through research already conducted I knew that man to be Fleet Commander Admiral José Fernandez de Santillan, a fine seaman by all accounts, but one unlucky to have run into unfavourable numbers against the British in 1708. He was supposed to have perished that day, yet Barbie told me the document she was reading earlier today included entries dated after the ship was supposed to have been sunk.

Perplexingly, the museum had no record of such a document. Trying her hardest, Judy roused more than a dozen scholars from their beds, bringing them back to the museum or talking to them over the phone to determine if they could shed any light onto our quandary.

They could not. Even Hugo Lockhart's immediate supervisor, the curator of marine antiquities, knew nothing of such an artefact and denied it could exist. Had such a document been found, it would have called into question everything that was known about the San José and created a swarm of discussion that would have kept the academics arguing its authenticity for years.

Fearing his subordinate must have lured my friend to the museum under false pretences - I admitted she was an attractive and desirable woman - Hugo's boss wanted to know what he had to say for himself.

That led us right back to one of the first questions: where is Hugo Lockhart?

Where is Hugo Lockhart?

The museum had a dead end feel to it, but I left Alistair and Hideki there along with half the security team to keep digging. More of the academics on the payroll there, were on their way at Judy's insistence. Her willingness to help was shortcutting the process significantly, but I held reservations about what, if anything, we might be able to find.

If forced to guess, I would say that the captain's diary that got Barbie so excited was the real thing and that it had never been part of the museum's inventory. The fake Professor Noriega believed the treasure was out there to be found and though I was only guessing, I believed the diary had come into his possession – it would explain why he was so convinced the treasure could be found. To anyone who was able to identify the diary's significance, it would act as the first step on a treasure trail to find a haul far greater than had ever been witnessed.

The man pretending to be Professor Noriega believed in the treasure. He put a knife to Barbie's throat when he demanded I tell him all that I knew. Whoever he was, I was convinced he was still after the treasure and most likely behind Barbie's disappearance. In many ways I hoped that was the case. Otherwise, I had no clue what might have befallen my blonde friend.

That changed when my phone rang.

"Alistair?" I prayed he was going to say she'd been found alive and well, but that wasn't the case.

"I think I found something," he revealed, his voice cagey like he wasn't sure if his information was going to be any good or not. "Or someone, I should say."

Curious, I prompted him to say more.

"The man from the ship. The one who broke into your safe and fought off both me and Jermaine."

A ripple of anger crossed my butler's brow at the reminder.

"What about him?" I begged to know.

"I think he was here. Sorry, I know that's not exactly the solid evidence you want. I'm going through CCTV footage – they have a few cameras aimed outside the museum – and a seven-foot-tall giant with a bald head walks by one. That was three hours and thirteen minutes ago. The angle doesn't show his face, and I know I fought him in the dark, but I swear it's the same man. I'm sending you a still frame now."

My phone pinged, and I tapped the icon to open the message. Leaning closer to Jermaine so we could both see the image, I squinted at my tiny screen.

Next to the bald-headed man was another person. They both had tan skin that suggested Mediterranean or South American heritage, but the shorter man was largely obscured by his tall companion.

Obscurely, the shorter man wore cowboy boots and a Stetson hat, his wavy blonde hair trailing from it to almost touch his shoulders. The Stetson hid his face and the bald man's head was turned away from the camera.

"This is the best shot?" I asked.

"The best we've found so far," replied Alistair, his voice sounding full of apology.

I didn't know who they were, and I knew it was a bit of a long shot, but when Jermaine confirmed what I was thinking – that the giant was the same man he and Alistair fought, I accepted the lead for what it was.

"Thank you, Alistair. Please let me know if you find anything else." With the call ended and the slightest smidgeon of a clue to help guide us, I turned to Captain Danvers. He was impatiently waiting to knock on a door.

Hugo lived with his mother we discovered upon arriving at the address the museum's HR department listed for him.

A short woman with her light brown hair turning grey, she peered around the edge of the door to her apartment in Yonkers.

"Yes? Can I help you?" she asked, concern at finding the cops on her doorstep instant and obvious.

Inside her place, we learned that she did not know where her son was. Not returning after work was most unusual behaviour for Hugo, if his mother was to be believed. She'd called his number and sent him messages advising the brisket she'd cooked was going to ruin.

There was little to learn other than he'd been acting a little strange for the last day or so.

"How so?" I tried to clarify.

"Well," Hugo's mother looked down at her hands where they were clasped in her lap and then back up, "he was excited about something, but he wouldn't say what."

Probing to get more from her, I asked, "Did he mention treasure at any point?"

Her eyes registered surprise. "Treasure? Oh, no, nothing like that."

"How about a ship called the San José?"

This time she shook her head back and forth, her eyes unfocused as she consulted her memory.

"Artefacts? Did Hugo mention any exciting new artefacts in the last few days?"

Now I got a wry smile. "All Hugo ever talked about was artefacts. He spent half his time at the museum sorting through and cataloguing ancient something or others some diver had found at the bottom of an ocean. Sorry, I'm not being very helpful." Her features took on a concerned expression. "Has something happened to him?" she asked. "Is Hugo in trouble?"

We got the answer to that just less than an hour later.

According to Captain Danvers, New York averages a couple of murders a week. Some of that is gang related, but they get the same level of household violence, vengeful lovers, and oops-I-didn't-mean-to's as anywhere else.

However, called to investigate a report of a body in a dumpster, two patrol cops found Hugo Lockhart's body. He had cocaine on his clothing, and his wallet was empty though left nearby for handy identification.

Responding to the call, I went with Danny to the scene. Jermaine insisted on coming with me and I did nothing to deter him – I always feel safer when he is by my side.

"Seems you were right again," Danny remarked, his tone devoid of emotion as he crouched next to the body. EMT's had taken it from the dumpster to check for any sign of life. He'd not been dead long; a couple of hours perhaps, and the scene was staged to look like he'd been buying drugs and fallen foul of his dealer.

No one was buying that story.

"How did he end up way out here?" asked one of Captain Danvers' detectives, there to take over the meat of the investigation.

At the edge of an industrial area in New Jersey, the colder air blowing in from the Hackensack River chilled me, though I did my best to ignore it. I'm not familiar with New York, but looking at a map on Jermaine's phone, it was clear Hugo was a long way from the museum and nowhere near home. Whether that was significant or not I would need to figure out.

Touching my hand to Captain Danvers' arm, I took him to one side.

"Danny, this is exactly what we found in Rio."

He frowned a little, wanting me to explain.

"The San José and its treasure ..." I wanted to keep all that a secret and had done so until today. We were past that now though and my only aim was to find Barbie and get her back. "When we found gold coins on the ship ..."

"In Finn Murphy's backpack?" Danny wanted to confirm he had the story straight before I went too far.

"That's right. When we figured out what we were looking at and where they could have come from, we tried to contact a professor at a museum in Rio de Janeiro. He was dead, and I'm fairly certain he was killed by a man who came to the ship in the Canary Islands posing as the professor. He tried to kill me and Barbie when he didn't get what he wanted."

Looking a little lost, Danny said, "I'm sorry, what has this got to do with Hugo Lockhart?"

"The professor in Rio had a research assistant who was murdered a day or so before the professor was also sent to his grave. Just like Hugo, the assistant was found miles from where he should be with his death staged to look like he was buying drugs or something."

Danny nodded along. "And you think it might be the same man. The same man who came on board your ship posing as the professor from Rio."

"Precisely. How quickly can you get a forensic accountant involved?" When Danny's right eyebrow took a hike toward his hairline, I explained, "I'm just guessing, but if I'm right ..."

Danny interrupted to snigger, "What are the chances of that?" He was paying me a compliment. Sort of.

I let it pass and pressed on. "If I'm right then he is a man of means. He has money ..."

"Then why is he after the treasure?"

21

I shrugged. "There is money and then there is MONEY. This is the latter. When I spoke to one of Professor Noriega's colleagues at the museum in Rio, he told me the gold, silver, and gemstones that went in the San José's hold would be worth close to ten billion dollars at today's prices."

"US dollars!"

I shot him a look. "Yes. US dollars." *I mean, what other currency would I be talking about?* "Can you get someone to take a look at Hugo's bank accounts?"

Danny is bright enough to guess what I was thinking.

"You're hoping the man behind it was paying for Hugo's assistance. You think maybe Hugo is dead because he helped out and in doing so exhausted his usefulness."

"Or came to know too much," I added. For now, all I could do was guess why Hugo's life might have been deemed forfeit. "My point is that I'm hoping there might be a trail of money."

"It's worth looking," Danny agreed.

My next comment was drowned out by the sound of a plane flying overhead. The commercial airliner – I'm not educated enough to be able to tell you what model it was, but it was big and displayed a British Airways logo, was coming in to land, its landing gear down already.

"Are we close to an airport?" I asked.

Jermaine said, "Teterboro is just a mile or so from here, madam." Our eyes met and a worrying thought bit into my soul. If Hugo was here, so far from where he should be, was he dropped off en route to the airport? If someone had Barbie, they couldn't very well take her out of the country against her will using a regular passenger jet. But maybe the man behind it all was even better resourced than I had previouslyimagined.

Jolting when my brain supplied a possible answer, I grabbed Jermaine's arm. "They might be trying to take her out on a private plane!"

He shot his cuff to check his watch. "We don't know what time she was taken. How long would they need to take off from such a large airport?"

I had no idea what the answer to that might be, but pointed out, "They estimated that Hugo could only have been dead for a couple of hours. They still have to pass through security though, right? Even being clever because they've got a kidnap victim with them, they would still get tied up doing pre-flight checks and waiting for runway clearance, right? I was asking questions, but I wasn't looking for anyone to answer. This was nothing more than an exercise to get it straight in my head.

I saw the change in Jermaine's expression. His best friend in the world was missing and he'd been keeping a lid on his emotions until now. However, the chance that I might be onto something combined with the opportunity to get her back galvanised him into action.

Facing Captain Danvers, he said, "How quickly can your officers get us to Teterboro airport and talking to someone who can help us?"

Danny's eyebrows formed ridges above his eyes; he wasn't used to having demands placed upon him by anyone other than his boss.

Before he could snap a terse response, I jumped in with, "We really need your help, Danny. Reacting swiftly now might catch Hugo's killer and return our friend."

Unable to argue, though he still didn't look happy about it, he shouted at one of his officers and thirty seconds later we were hauling butt across town again.

Hugo was dead and we would get nothing from him. Maybe the autopsy would turn up something, but I didn't have the time for that. More pertinently, Barbie didn't have the time for it. It was time for action. I just hoped we were not too late.

Barbie

"Ah, I see you are awake, Miss Berkeley."

Barbie stared at the man looking down at her. Coming to on what was unmistakably a plane, she had found herself in a storage compartment, her hands and feet bound with plastic ties. Groggy from drugs administered while she was already unconscious, the effects were wearing off, but she was yet to try to move or stand up. Not that she could get far with her ankles bound.

Time had passed; how much she could not know for there was no clock and she was without her phone or any other device that might prove useful in such a situation. Cursing herself for being so easily duped, she made a mental vow to hurt Hugo Lockhart when she got the chance.

"Who are you?" she asked the man now filling the doorway that led to the passenger compartment. It was hard to judge his height from her position sitting on the floor, but he was on the short side. His features and skin tone made her think he might be South American, and his accent, though his English was flawless, carried a trace of Spanish in the background.

He looked down at her with dark eyes, assessing and calculating, but not answering until he was ready.

"My name is not important," the man replied. "However, since you will be in my company for some time, you can call me Xavier."

For once Xavier Silvestre wasn't concerned about giving away his name. Normally, he was extra secretive in all matters – it was the prudent thing to do. In regard to Miss Berkeley, who was quite possibly the most attractive woman he had ever met, he was less bothered for one simple reason: he was going to kill her as soon as she helped him find the treasure.

"How about if I call you something else?" Barbie asked, following her question up with a few suggestions that turned the air blue. She was not happy about being kidnapped.

Silvestre smiled down at his captive.

"I believe that would be counterproductive. I apologise for the theatrics of my decision to abduct you. I felt it to be necessary."

"And you had Hugo help you lure me into your trap? Where is that little weasel? He needs a kick in the pants for starters."

Silvestre smiled, recalling Hugo Lockhart's face when he realised what was about to happen to him.

"I'm afraid Mr Lockhart will not be joining us. I killed him and left this body for the police to find." Being sure to hold Barbie's gaze when his words hit her, he said, "I believe he was my seventeenth victim, Miss Berkeley. They were all necessary kills, you understand. It is my destiny to find the San José and the treasure it carried. No one will get in my way, and should they do so ... well, I'm sure you get what I am saying."

Barbie swallowed hard, gulping down rising bile and fear. Her life since she met Patricia Fisher could be described as risky and scary on many occasions, but there had always been friends around to make her feel safe. Quite often, if they were on the ship, those friends were armed. Right now, though, she felt very alone and tied up as she was, if her captor chose to hurt her, defending herself would be difficult.

Swallowing again to force down her fright and working her mouth to rid it of the dryness she now felt, Barbie sounded timid to her own ears when she asked a question.

"What do you want?"

Silvestre came forward, noting that the blonde woman didn't shy away at his approach as he expected she would. He didn't like that; she was supposed to be afraid – fear is a useful tool. He would break her spirit soon enough if it proved necessary.

Crouching, so his head was closer to the height of hers, he said, "I want to find the San José. I know that you and Mrs Fisher discovered details that I have not, but I am willing to believe that you do not yet know the exact location of the San José. You would all undoubtedly be there already attempting to recover the treasure for yourselves were that the case."

"We have no interest in the treasure," Barbie blurted, telling the truth, but instantly chastising herself for giving away information. She needed to do better than that.

Silvestre narrowed his eyes at her. "Don't lie to me, Miss Berkeley, especially when your falsehoods are so blatant. You have all gone to a lot of trouble to learn more and to keep the information you have secret. You could have announced the treasure you took from Finn Murphy, but you did not. You chose instead to secure it inside a safe. We both know that Finn Murphy found the treasure and together we are going to find out where it is. Do you know who killed him?"

The question surprised Barbie. To her the identity of Finn Murphy's killer was of interest, but only because it was a piece of the puzzle and because Patty was desperately trying to solve a murder on board the Aurelia. Barbie's claim to have no interest in the treasure was true. They wouldn't be permitted to keep it even if they were to find its location, and the only reason they chose to investigate came from obligation on Patty's part.

Seeing the quizzical expression his captive now bore, Silvestre chose to keep talking.

"It was a Spaniard by the name of Carlos Ramirez. He was a low-level crook who Finn made the mistake of approaching. He wanted to turn some of what he found into cash, but Carlos was nothing if not a swindler and a cheat. Before I killed Carlos, he told me he met Finn in Morocco, but I suspect now that he was lying, unable to find the truth even in the last moments of his life."

Barbie watched and waited. And she listened. There was a mystery to solve here, that part was for certain. Barbie had no interest in the treasure, but that didn't mean she wanted the man she now knew as Xavier to have it. In fact, she would do anything she could to deny him his prize and see he came to justice. However, she recognised that her position was unfavourable and told herself to wait for the right moment before attempting to escape.

Silvestre glanced down at the swell of his captive's chest and the toned skin so tanned and smooth above the muscle beneath. Her youthfulness was attractive in and of itself, but as a package, she was something else.

"Together," he continued, "we will find the final resting place of the San José and I will share with you the enormous wealth it represents." Idly, and unable to resist doing so, Silvestre allowed one hand to drop from where they were folded on his knee. Gravity carried it to her right leg where he caressed her thigh.

He did not see the two-footed kick coming.

Barbie had a simple rule about men getting handsy: if you let any of them get away with it ever, they will think it is ok. Not just with you, but with other girls too. Therefore, on principle, and because she'd had to do it a hundred times before, she reacted the instant he touched her without invitation.

Pulling her knees to her chest while rolling onto her back, Barbie reached over her head to brace against the floor when she unfolded her legs in a single explosive movement. Her feet, tied at the ankle and therefore working in tandem, struck Silvestre in the face, lifting him off the floor and driving him back as though he'd been hit by a car.

His skull smacked into the bulkhead between compartments on his private Gulfstream jet and he came to rest in a crumpled heap.

Barbie, fired up and angry, pulled her legs back to her chest and threw herself upright in a fluid move that took her from prone on her back to standing. It also succeeded in breaking the tie around her ankle. The plastic had cut into her flesh, drawing blood before it snapped, but now free to move she felt imbued with fresh energy and the drive to escape.

Maybe there was a weapon she could grab in the next compartment. Maybe she could get to the cockpit and convince the pilot to land, but Barbie knew for sure that whatever opportunities there might be, she wouldn't find them staying where she was.

Her legs were just a little wobbly from hours of inactivity, but she leapt over Silvestre's arms when he flailed them in the air in a feeble attempt to stop her.

Landing on the other side of the bulkhead door, Barbie darted forward, getting some distance between her and the man who was already clambering back to his feet. Should she have followed up with more blows? Should she have done something unthinkable under any other circumstances and tried to kill him?

Barbie wasn't sure she had it in her to go through with such a barbaric act. Not unless she could know for certain it was a choice between that person's life and her own. It was a moot point, of course, for the opportunity was already lost.

Searching frantically with her eyes, she spied a cocktail bar. Set against one side of the plane and near to the entrance for the cockpit, it had to contain something she could use as a weapon ... something she could employ to get her hands free.

Commercial airlines are thoroughly strict about knives and cutting implements making it on board, but privately owned jets have no such rules. There was no aircrew to serve drinks, and so far as Barbie could see there was no one else on board save for whoever was flying the plane.

Racing to get there, a rage-filled cry driving her to go faster as her kidnapper came through the bulkhead door to join her in the passenger compartment, Barbie found what she needed. It was a tiny knife compared to what she wanted, but the blade lying next to the slices of lime was good enough for what she wanted – to cut through the remaining plastic tie and free her arms.

Silvestre ran across the cabin, his features contorted with fury.

"Don't look at him," Barbie chastised herself. "Look at what you are doing." She said the words in a calm tone, wishing she felt anything of the sort. Her heart thumped in her chest and her breath came so fast from the situation's adrenalin that Barbie worried she might pass out.

The knife, however, was not only sharp enough to cut through the tough plastic pinning her wrists together, but she managed to complete the cut without opening her flesh and before Xavier could close the distance between them.

Brandishing the blade, Barbie made her limbs loose. She would never think of herself as a fighter, but had been taking lessons from Jermaine and was confident she could overpower the man now looking unsure about how to proceed. Men are considered to be stronger than women, and Barbie knew that in general terms it was true. However, years of training with weights ensured the muscles she possessed were capable of lifting more than her frame might suggest and she was taller than her opponent with a reach advantage of several inches.

"I want you to take me back to New York," Barbie demanded, trying to make her voice sound calm and in control though she felt neither.

Silvestre smiled. "I don't think so. Why don't you put down the knife, little girl?"

Talking tough, Barbie sneered, "Why don't I cut you open in a few places and see if you fancy getting some medical help, say, maybe back in New York?"

Silvestre shrugged, an exaggerated gesture to indicate he was giving up.

"Ok. I tried."

Barbie saw his eyes flick up and got a fleeting sense of someone moving behind her.

"If you will, please, Gomez."

Silvestre's words rang in Barbie's ears, but only for the briefest moment before a huge fist delivered a hammer blow to the top of her skull. Her consciousness swam for a second, her knees disobeying her instruction to work. The knife fell from her hand, and she collapsed.

Looking down at the inert form, Xavier Silvestre sighed. He needed her cooperation. Oh, he could torture her to extract what she knew, but as Carlos Ramirez proved, information gathered under duress could be unreliable.

Gomez knelt to scoop Barbie's unconscious body. Fetching fresh ties from a pack in the cockpit where he'd been watching the pilot fly, he retied her hands and feet, this time adding extra ties around her knees and elbows after pulling her arms behind her back.

She would have a headache when she awoke, and it would be the least of her worries.

A Fond Farewell

Teterboro Airport is smaller than I am used to, and that is both a good and a bad thing. Good because finding someone in authority wasn't buried behind as many layers as it might be at a much larger facility, and because they were not as busy. However, it was bad because they had fewer flights to manage, and their turnaround time was significantly swifter.

That we might already be too late and find that Barbie had left was a very present fear. The biggest hurdle though came in the shape of having no idea who we were looking for.

Until I was in the presence of the head of security and given the chance to explain, it had not once occurred to me that in order to ascertain if Barbie's kidnappers might have come through the airport, I needed to, at the very least, provide them with a description.

My suspicion was that the giant who broke into my cabin on board the Aurelia and stole the jewels we found in Finn Murphy's backpack was somehow involved. How confident was I? Not very.

I asked about men over seven feet tall to which the answer was a resounding no. They hadn't seen anyone like that this evening.

In the last six hours – a bigger window than I felt we needed to check – twenty-seven planes had taken off, all bound for different destinations. The flight plan for most was internal to the US, but beyond that, no one was giving us any information without appropriate warrants through which we could demand it.

Captain Danvers assured me that shouldn't be a problem, but it wasn't going to happen until the morning when he could get the right people to sign off on it.

The airport people weren't being obstructive; they were just doing their jobs, but I wanted to wring their necks anyway. Barbie could be anywhere, and truthfully I had no idea if she might have been taken onto a plane or smuggled away in a boat. For all I knew, whoever had her could be holed up a hundred yards from the museum.

We had no evidence to guide us and painfully, I was forced to acknowledge that New York has multiple airports and the wider state area yet more that could easily be reached in a couple of hours.

Dejected and disappointed, I called Alistair back at the museum. They'd had no better luck there either. It wasn't time to call it a night – I wasn't sure I would sleep until we had Barbie back – but it was time to regroup.

With Captain Danvers graciously helping, we were heading back to the ship. We rode in silence, each holding our own thoughts. Barbie was missing, the trail going colder by the hour, and to me it felt as though I was missing a limb. I could only imagine how Hideki and Jermaine were taking it.

The giant structure of the ship filled the view long before we pulled up alongside the awning for the royal suites entrance. Sitting in the back of Captain Danvers' car alongside Jermaine, I didn't move when he came to a halt. Over the last two days, Captain Danny Danvers had come to be someone I thought of as a friend. It was the second time we'd met, both times fraught with danger and such circumstances create a bond.

I reached forward to touch his arm as he unclipped his seatbelt.

"Danny, I need to thank you for helping us this evening."

"I was just doing my job," he replied dismissively.

"No," I argued, "you were doing far more than was required. Earlier, you went against your chief and trusted me when it would have been safer to refuse to help."

Danny twisted in his seat to meet my gaze.

"Are you getting out, or what?" He said it with a smile - he didn't want to hear how wonderful he was. "This is New York, Mrs Fisher, I've probably got another ten crimes to solve already."

Opting to stay serious in the face of his flippancy, I said, "If you ever need to escape the city and want to take a cruise ..."

"Ha!" he choked out a laugh. "On a cruise ship with you? I value my life a little more than that."

I nodded and closed my mouth. He didn't want to discuss the way he'd put his career and his life on the line to follow my lead. Or maybe it was that he also felt the developing kinship and knew that he could go no further while I had no choice but to continue pursuing the trail of my missing friend.

Patting Jermaine's thigh – it was time for us to go – I thumbed the button for my seatbelt and waited. Jermaine likes to get my door and I have learned that it irritates him when I fail to act like the upper class lady he wants me to be.

Accepting his hand, I slid out and onto my feet as though I were a princess in a dress that made horizontal movement difficult.

Danny was on the dockside to bid me goodbye.

"I hope you find your friend," he said, "If the forensic accountants turn up anything, or we get a lead on Hugo Lockhart's killer, I'll let you know." He offered me his hand and I dodged it, pulling him into a hug and kissing his cheek.

I whispered, "Thank you," one more time and let him go. My friends were inside the ship already, assembled in my suite where we were going to figure out what we knew and pull together a plan to find Barbie.

A Plan

I took the offered gin and tonic with just a tinge of guilt. I was drinking and would enjoy the relaxing effect that came with the alcohol knowing Barbie was most likely unable to partake in such luxuries.

Feeling bad about it wasn't going to get her back, so I took a gulp of the near-freezing liquid and put my glass to one side.

In my suite, which is large enough to house a decent sized party, all my friends had assembled. Jermaine was handing out drinks, Alistair was talking with Deepa and Martin, and Sam was looking over the shoulders of Hideki and Schneider while they scoured information on a laptop. Molly and Anders were on a couch, sitting next to each other, their faces aimed my way.

"What's the plan, Mrs Fisher?" asked Molly.

Her question caused a hush to descend on the room and everyone turned to face me. Did I have a plan? Was I capable of coming up with a way to find Barbie.

With every ear attuned to hear what genius idea I might have cooked up, I felt the pressure of the situation and almost crumbled. Truthfully, I might have done so, submitting to my desire to sob uncontrollably were it not for the fact that Barbie needed me to be the best I could be.

Flicking my head to get a loose strand of hair from my eyes, I let my gaze rove around the room. They were great people, every last one of them, and willing to put their lives on hold if it meant our little family could be whole again.

"So," I began with a stuttering start, "we don't know much. I believe Barbie was at the museum today and that Hugo Lockhart lured her there so she could be taken. She called me to say she was reading the diary of Fleet Commander Admiral José Fernandez de Santillan, the captain of the San José. If we assume that much is true, and we know the museum had no such artefact in its catalogue, then it's not much of a leap to believe there is another player involved."

"The fake professor?" questioned Sam. It pleased me that he was keeping up and I shot him a smile.

"Yes, Sam, very possibly. So far, he is the only person we know to be actively after the treasure."

"What about the giant who cracked your safe and stole what you recovered from Finn Murphy?" asked Alistair.

I began to pace; I find it helps me think. "My current theory is that those two men are connected. The fake professor had all manner of questions and got to scope out my suite before the robbery occurred."

"He tricked me into showing him Finn Murphy's body," growled Hideki who looked to be barely holding it together. "I told him about the gemstones in Finn's belly and showed him the autopsy report."

Attempting to soothe his mind, I said, "We had no reason to suspect him at the time, Hideki. Recrimination now will gain us nothing. Let's keep moving forward."

Jermaine said, "We know the giant was at the museum today. If we are working under the assumption that he is an accomplice to the man who came on board posing as Professor Noriega, then they must be behind Barbie's disappearance. That's helpful, but what can we do? We don't know who they are or where they might be, right?"

"That's right," I agreed, trying to not sound negative. "Approaching this from that angle won't work."

Molly raised her hand before saying, "What other angle do we have?"

It was time to lay out the road ahead. Taking a deep breath, I started to talk.

"I believe we know almost as much as the fake professor and his giant ..."

"We need to give them names," Deepa interrupted. "The fake professor and his giant is too unwieldy."

"How about Professor Death and Lurch?" Martin suggested with a chuckle.

Sam chipped in with, "How about Scooby and Doo-doo?" which made everyone laugh.

It was good that people could still find some humour in our current situation, but I wanted to keep moving and had names of my own.

"I'm calling them Dr Disguise and Hench." A murmur crossed the room, my friends repeating the names to see how they felt about them. Each name described the individual in question well enough for there to be no confusion as to who we were talking about.

"Okay," Alistair spoke for everyone, "Dr Disguise and Hench it is. You were saying you think we know as much as them? How does that help us?"

"Because we know they are after the treasure – that must be their guiding motivation behind taking Barbie – but they don't know enough to figure out where it is. They took Barbie because they think she ... or rather we as a team, know something that will take them to the next step or maybe get them all the way to where the X marks the spot. Barbie is bright enough to make herself of value. She will help them," I was certain she would do what she could to stay alive and would know we would be trying to find her, "but she will drag it out, hoping she can find a way to communicate with us."

Hideki frowned at me. "We're going to wait and hope that she calls to tell us where she is?"

"Nope." I looked him dead in the eye then turned my head to slowly meet the gaze of just about everyone else in the room before delivering my plan. "We're going to find the treasure first."

Silence settled over the group. They could all see it. If we had what Dr Disguise and Hench wanted, we could use it as a bargaining chip to get Barbie back. If, along the way, she managed to escape, or we figured out Dr Disguise's real identity, so much the better. For now though, this was all I had.

Hideki broke the silence, clapping his hands together and coming to stand in front of me.

"Okay, Patricia, where do we start?"

September 3rd 1708.
Bernadino Awakens.

B ernadino woke with a jolt, roused from his exhausted slumber by a horrifying dream in which he was underwater and couldn't breathe. Sitting upright in bed, every muscle in his body protested and pain from a thousand bruises drew a gasp from his lungs. Even they hurt, but as he settled back down onto the bed in which he strangely found himself, he detected movement across the room.

"He's awake," said a woman, her voice carrying the tremble of old age.

"I'll take him some bread and soup," replied another, younger woman.

Bernadino recognised the language as English, the tongue of his nation's sworn enemy. He knew it well enough to communicate with his ... captors? Bernadino wasn't sure how to label them, but knew his accent would give him away even if his features didn't.

Opting to stay quiet and observe – he felt too weak to think about overpowering the two women and escaping – he watched the younger of the two cross the room with a small wooden bowl on which he could see a torn piece of bread balancing. Steam rose from the bowl; the soup of which she spoke.

"Can you eat a little something?" the woman asked, settling at the side of his bed.

Rather than speak, he gave a quick nod of his head and let her spoon a little of the hot liquid into his mouth. He dribbled some, the woman mopping it up with a finger as it ran over his rough beard.

The soup was hot and though it didn't taste of much and the bread was stale, Bernadino knew he needed to eat if he was to regain his strength.

Fleeting memories returned as he continued to swallow the almost scalding broth. The ship? What had become of the ship and the treasure in its hold? He recalled seeing the rocks in the water and shouting to get the attention of those on the poop deck. He remembered the sting of cold water against his already numb skin when he plunged into the roiling waves and the terror he felt knowing his life was lost.

Between then and waking up was a mystery, yet somehow he survived. The question firmly at the forefront of his mind was whether anyone else had.

The woman, in her very early twenties and quite pretty, with bright blue eyes and a pale complexion, filled in some of the blanks as she fed him.

"Found you in the surf we did when we went collecting cockles. Do you know what ship you were on? Discovering you on the shore, I expected to find a shipwreck after the storm last night; that would have been a boon to the village, I can tell you."

Bernadino understood what she meant. Shipwrecks could deliver fortunes if the goods in their holds could be recovered or were washed ashore. It was why wreckers led ships onto the rocks, killing the crew and plundering the hold.

Saying nothing, he allowed her to continue talking.

"My name is Mary." She looked over her shoulder to the older woman still tending the stove. "That's my mum. Dad is at market today, but will be home later. Do you have a name?"

Bernadino stayed silent, his eyes locked on the young woman's.

"Can you speak English?" she questioned and again he chose to keep his silence.

When he had his strength back, he would leave. In the dead of night or when no one was watching, it didn't matter which. But where would he go? The question surfaced like a spear to his heart. He could never return to Spain; that bridge was burned the moment they agreed to steal the treasure. They could go anywhere with that haul of gold and live like kings. Women, feasting, and merriment would be known for the rest of their lives. But without the treasure, he was not only penniless but trapped by his own sins.

The world would know he was dead; drowned on board the San José when the British sank it. And where were the admiral, the other officers, and the ship? Had they managed to weather the storm? Surely not, but the girl, Mary, said there was no shipwreck. Had it gone to the bottom then? Bernadino thought that unlikely. With the rocks around it would have broken up and there would be flotsam all over the coast. Mary would have seen it for certain.

He could not fathom what that meant. The ship was doomed, of that he was certain, so it could not have sailed to a safe port or outrun the storm, and it couldn't have sunk either. Bewildered by the mystery, Bernadino found himself too exhausted to fight his body's need for more sleep.

No sooner had Mary returned to the stove to fetch him some more of the shellfish broth, than he was asleep again.

What he could not know was that he was not the only survivor. One more member of the San José's murderous crew lived to tell the tale. He was being nursed back to health a few miles away, his broken bones reset by those who in the wake of the storm found a mysterious hole in the ground. Close to the edge of the cliffs, it led into a dark hole below where a sorrowful voice demanded they investigate.

A Decision to Act

I n my cabin, the team got to work assembling what we knew into categories. To start with there was Finn Murphy. The Irishman's body was found in the hold when the ship was about to leave the Mediterranean.

Then there was the San José itself. The Spanish treasure ship had not been sunk by the British, despite what history chose to record. How the error in records came about I could not guess and would waste no time considering. What we needed to figure out was where it went.

Deepa pulled up a map of the world in 1708. Produced by a German called Hermann Moll, the outline of the continents was not too far off what we know it to be today. I wanted to see it because I could not, off the top of my head, tell you when Australia was discovered or how developed America was at that time.

Through a process of elimination, we discounted any British territories because the Spanish were at war with the British at that time. We also ruled out Spanish territories under the assumption the crew of the ship would be arrested the moment the supposedly sunken ship sailed into port. The letters Barbie found, written by Lieutenant Bernadino Alvarez, said as much – he could not return home and wanted his love to join him in England.

Here it became sticky because we knew one member of the San José crew found himself in England, one of the first places we ruled out.

"Hold on," said Martin. "What if the British boarded the San José and took it back to England? They could record the ship was sunk and who would be any the wiser?"

His wife, Deepa, pointed out the flaw in his theory. "Seizing a ship from a rival nation and claiming the contents of its hold as booty was a legitimate act. The captain of the British ship would have received a huge payout, so too his officers and even his crew would get a handsome windfall, I believe. The Brits would have nothing to gain by stealing it all. Besides, where is it all if it went back to Britain and how did Lieutenant Alvarez survive?"

Huffing a defeated breath, Martin asked, "So where did they go?"

Studying the map made us none the wiser so it was a good thing we had Finn Murphy to explore.

"I think we need to go to Asreb," stated Jermaine firmly. "The beetle," he referred to the carcass of a bug found in Finn Murphy's matted hair, "only exists on one island on the whole planet. Melilla is a Spanish enclave off the coast of Africa of which the uninhabited island of Asreb is a part. Maybe that was the San José's destination and maybe it wasn't, but we didn't find Barbie's laptop at the museum so it's a safe bet the same people who have her have it too."

"They already know about the bug from my autopsy report," Hideki pointed out.

Jermaine asked, "Did your report point out the significance of the bug? Did it highlight it?"

Hideki shook his head, unsure why Jermaine was asking. "No."

Jermaine continued to press, "Were there lots of other things listed in the report? Other odd bits of detritus you found in his hair and about his body?"

Hideki could see where Jermaine was leading us.

Shifting his position to look at me, my butler said, "I'm not sure they will have picked up on its significance, madam."

Hideki agreed. "It was just one of four different bugs I found on his body or in his clothing. Barbie knows what it means though."

Jermaine added, "Barbie might even steer them toward it." He looked at me, "She'll be playing along and buying time if she can, waiting for us to show up."

It was decided in an instant; we were all going to Melilla, a little-known city on the northern coast of Africa where it was surrounded on all other sides by Morocco. If we were incredibly lucky, we would find Barbie there and be able to rescue her. That was a long shot. Our aim, really, was to try to find clues to the location of the ship.

With my entire team tuned in to follow every single lead that anyone had ever explored, I hoped we might discover something no one else had ever found. I would confound Dr Disguise by finding the ship first if that was all I could do.

Captain Danvers would work on the New York end of things, and maybe that would yield a result. In the meantime, I went back through my records to find the next of kin information for Finn Murphy.

Obtaining it had not been the simplest thing and only occurred when we were able to get an Irish Embassy involved. Unlike the passengers, whose emergency contact details are recorded even before they step on board the ship, no such information is gathered for stowaways.

Nevertheless, we had it and once I found it, I dialled the number from the phone in my suite. More than half the team had drifted away, taking a break to get food and to pack for we were leaving soon. It was nearing midnight in New York and there were no commercial flights out until the morning.

That didn't matter because I had no time for the restrictions an airline would impose. One of the most remarkable parts of my life story, should anyone ever care to tell, is to do with the Maharaja of Zangrabar. Through fate or a quirk of circumstance, the planets aligned to place me in the right location to find a priceless sapphire the tiny Middle Eastern country treasured, but had lost to thieves more than thirty years earlier.

Upon returning it and subsequently meeting and then saving the Maharaja from being assassinated by his uncle who wanted the throne, I gained a benefactor. Not just any benefactor though, for the Maharaja is one of the richest people on the planet.

He gave me a house, he gave me cars, he gave me a credit card that appears to have no limit, and he bought the royal suite on board the Aurelia for me to live in for as long as I wanted.

So if I wanted a private jet to fly me around the world in pursuit of my friend, I was going to have one and felt secure in the knowledge the Maharaja wouldn't bat an eyelid at what it cost.

What did it cost? I didn't ask and was probably happier in the dark. Jermaine chartered it and we had less than three hours until it would be ready to leave from Newark Liberty International Airport. To get there we were taking the ship's helicopter.

With Jermaine busily packing my clothes, I was fussing with my mother and daughter over a pair of dachshunds. I couldn't take them with me and was sad to be leaving them behind. They would be safe on the ship and were to stay with Alistair who was also unable to come.

As captain of the ship, his job was to remain with it, not least because it was broken and waiting for parts, stuck in New York until it could be fixed. That was due to happen in the next day or so, but fitting the new parts led into a series of tests and only once they were complete could the ship sail.

My heart felt heavy as I cuddled Anna and Georgie, my dogs able to tell there was something going on and giving me odd looks. I tried to explain though I'm sure they didn't understand a word of what I said.

The phone kept ringing at the Irish end, Finn Murphy's mother failing to answer. The time difference made it around five in the morning there, so it came as no surprise. It frustrated me as you might imagine, but accepting I wasn't going to get through any time soon, I stabbed the red button with my thumb and went to see if there was anything I could do to help Jermaine.

Melilla

"Where are we?" Barbie asked, blinking in the harsh sunlight as she stepped out of the plane.

"In Melilla, my dear," Silvestre replied with a smile.

"Why?"

Silvestre walked away from his plane. A car was waiting twenty yards away, a Mercedes S class in sleek black with darkened windows.

Before Barbie could begin to follow, Xavier's giant wrapped a giant hand around her right bicep, clamping it in a vice grip as he marched her across the tarmac.

"Hey!" she complained. "I can walk myself!"

Gomez released her arm, doing so with a rough shove that almost threw her to the ground. Stumbling, she shot the bald behemoth a hate-filled glare, but kept moving, staying ahead lest he find more reason to hurt her.

Massaging some life back into her bruised arm, she looked around.

It was hot, that was the first thing to note. Shimmers rose from the runway where the sun beat down on it. Looking up at the sky, she noted the position of the sun – it was high in the sky and therefore nearing noon. When she was taken in New York, it was mid-afternoon and cold outside as the year rolled into winter. Now she was in North Africa and wishing she had different clothing.

A change of panties would be nice for a start. How long had she been on the plane? Could such a small aircraft make the journey in one go? She'd been drugged for a portion of her ordeal, that much she knew, the effects skewing her perception of time.

There was no one in sight around the runway; it wasn't a municipal airport, more like a length of tarmac in a field. There would be chances to get away from her captors later, she was certain of that, but this was not the time to start running for the horizon for there was nowhere in sight to run to.

Approaching the car, where Xavier was opening the trunk to fetch something from inside, she told herself to be patient and play along. Xavier's henchman was only too happy to hurt her if given the slightest reason. Her neck still hurt from the hammer blow he landed on her skull.

This was her first time in Melilla, but Barbie knew it to be densely populated. The moment they came near people, especially if she spotted law enforcement, she was going to make a break for it.

Xavier lifted something from the trunk, a cruel smile on his face when he turned to face her.

"Just in case any foolish ideas about escaping creeps into that pretty blonde head of yours, Miss Berkeley, I have something for you to wear."

Barbie's blood ran cold. She didn't exactly recognise what she was looking at, but she could guess.

"This is an explosive cuff," Xavier boasted proudly, brandishing the plastic and leather device. "I have two." He reached into the trunk to produce another. "One for each arm," he explained with a smile. "I control them with an app on my phone." He demonstrated by tapping the screen to open the app. "I would have put them on you in New York, but explosives and aircraft do not good bedfellows make."

Barbie closed her hands, forming fists and flexing her muscles.

"You're not putting those things on me!" She meant it. She would fight. No! She would run! Wherever they were, somewhere outside of the city, there was nothing in sight, but she could outrun the pair of them and if she was fast enough, she could get to rugged ground where their luxury Mercedes couldn't follow. It was a complete flip from the plan she had thirty seconds ago, but back then no one was threatening to turn her into a human bomb.

Gomez threw a hand around her neck, yanking her roughly just as she started to move. Thick fingers dug into her throat, cutting off her next breath.

The crushing grip cut off the blood flow to her head, her vision dimming almost instantly as her pulse began to hammer like a claxon in her ears.

"Yes, I think unconscious might be better for this. Thank you, Gomez."

Barbie heard Xavier talking and knew what he was going to do. She wanted to fight, willed her body to rally, but there were sparkly lights clouding her eyes. She flailed a swinging leg, hoping Gomez might release her, but it was harmlessly batted away and for the third time since Hugo Lockhart led her from the museum, she lost consciousness.

A few minutes later, the Mercedes pulled away. Barbie was loaded into the back next to Xavier Silvestre, secured into her seat with a belt. On each forearm, the explosive cuffs, controlled by an app on Silvestre's phone, sat snugly against her skin. They were tight enough that she would have to cut off her hands to remove them, and utterly tamperproof.

It was the first time he'd used such a device and had to admit he was impressed by the workmanship. His years of ignoring laws and rules to pursue the San José's treasure without care or thought for human life created a network of contacts among which was a team who were thoroughly proficient at making things to order.

Confident his new 'assistant' would not now try to escape, Silvestre was heading for the city and its port where he would take a speed launch across to the island of Asreb. Like everything else in his life, the launch was already organised. Gomez was nothing if not efficient.

In the back of the car, he gently pushed Barbie's head until it was resting against the window on her side, not lolling in the centre where she looked ready to dribble onto his shoulder. Silvestre didn't like that she was so tall. Why were women allowed to grow taller than men?

His issue, of course, stemmed from being below average height himself, a genetic curse caused by his father marrying a petite woman. His mother had been attractive in her youth, Silvestre understood his father's choice, but his father stood over six feet tall even when age had withered him. Why could height not be one of the traits he inherited?

Pushing the irritating thought to one side, he opened Barbie's laptop. Collected from the museum before they departed, Silvestre was pleased to find Miss Berkeley's notes regarding the San José. He'd made a copy of Finn Murphy's autopsy report and read it thoroughly more than once, hoping he might glean some vital piece of information that would tell him where the Irishman had been.

He'd even read the note about the insect found in his hair. However, it was only when he read Miss Berkeley's note that he discovered its significance. Lucanus punctatum was about as rare in the insect world as one could get. It existed in one place only – the uninhabited island of Asreb.

It was a breakthrough of sorts. He wanted to see the island for himself, not that he expected to stumble upon the three-hundred-year-old wreck of the San José with the gold spilling out to twinkle and sparkle invitingly in the sun. No, to find out if it had ever been here, Silvestre knew he was going to have to do some investigative work.

When he got the call from Hugo Lockhart, Silvestre had been ready to head to Ireland where he planned to torture Finn Murphy's friends and relatives. Someone had to know where the Irishman was before he boarded the Aurelia. Discovering the significance of the bug in Finn Murphy's hair changed Silvestre's priorities.

Now there were agents on their way to Ireland where they would complete the task in his stead. Quite why he hadn't thought to take this step sooner, he was unable to articulate even to himself. No matter, the task was now in hand.

Closing the laptop – reading in a car always made him nauseous – Silvestre settled in to enjoy the ride.

Luxury Travel

"Patricia, I think we've got something."

"Already?" I questioned. "That was quick work."

The call from Captain Danvers came as I made my way to the ship's helipad with the rest of the team. We all had backpacks rather than suitcases, the nature of our adventure to come so unknown, we all wanted to be able to move with ease.

I'd kissed Alistair goodbye with a tear in my eye and pushed away from him before I had too much time to think about how long I might be gone for. Walking away from him made me feel a little empty inside, but I would fill that void with outrage and a need for justice.

Whoever he was, the man who had Barbie was going to pay. She had better be in one piece when we got to her, or I could not predict what Jermaine and Hideki might do. Or maybe I could, and that was what worried me.

Mercifully, Danny's call broke my unhealthy focus on retribution.

"Well, don't get too excited yet, I'm not calling to tell you we've cracked the case," he grumbled.

"What did you find?"

"Well, it triggers my ulcer to say it, but you were right about Hugo Lockhart's bank accounts."

I wanted to punch the air with a fist, but to do so would be unladylike and it wasn't enough of a victory to get that excited.

"Ten thousand dollars was deposited two days ago. You're going to ask me who the money came from and I'm going tell you we don't know."

I frowned. "They can't figure that out?"

"The forensic accountants? Well, yes, probably, is what they are telling me. There are a whole bunch of monthly payments going back years, all from the same account. I am given to understand the person sending the funds has routed it around the world through a series of transactions so it will be difficult if not impossible to trace back to its source."

"But your chaps are on it, right?"

"Naturally. However, I must pass on their warning that the money may originate at an untraceable source."

"Such as?"

"A Swiss bank account. There are other places where a person with money can hide their transactions, but Swiss seems most likely according to the boffins. They can get to the source if that's the case, but all they will find is a number for the account. If they are right, then getting a name will be impossible."

"Then if it cannot be traced back to a person, why go to all the trouble of routing it around the world?"

"Ah, yes, I asked the same question. The answer, I'm afraid, is so anyone attempting to trace it will trigger an alarm. In all likelihood, the person behind the money already knows we are looking for them."

I gritted my teeth. He had been one step ahead of me from the start. Dr Disguise, as I chose to call him, came into my world pre-armed with knowledge about the San José. Indeed his interest in me came about only because we stumbled across Finn Murphy and came to know more than we should.

He was steps ahead of me when he was attacked on the British Union Isles, and again in Rio. Now he'd tracked us to New York and taken Barbie – a prize far more valuable than all the treasure the San José might hold.

I had to take a deep breath to calm myself.

"Okay, thank you, Danny. Please let me know if your people have a breakthrough."

He wished me luck, expressed that he didn't hold out much hope of success in this case, and let me go. Above me on the helipad, I could hear the rotors beginning to turn. Jermaine was waiting for me, helping me in before the heli-crew made sure we were secure.

A short, thirty-minute hop later, we were boarding the chartered jet. It was a Bombardier Global 7500, a new model only recently introduced, the captain proudly boasted, as he welcomed my team on board. There was an open bar and three aircrew in the central cabin to provide for all our needs.

None of us were interested in the bar. It was late and we needed sleep as much as anything. Thankfully, as one might expect from a luxury private jet designed and built to accommodate the world's super rich, the seats folded into beds, and they had pillows and blankets on board to make us all comfortable.

Sleep came, but was fitful, my head too full of questions without answers to let me rest properly. At some point after four in the morning on New York time, where my brain was still operating, I fell into a deep slumber and was awoken to find everyone else up and about.

"Sorry, said Deepa." Crouching so her head was down almost next to mine. "We were all trying to be quiet."

I fought a yawn that split my head in two and stretched, pushing my arms and legs out to scare away the kinks from sleeping on a seat. It was comfortable, but it's not really a bed.

"Where are we?" I asked, swinging my legs around to sit up. "What time is it?"

"Local time is just coming up on four in the afternoon," said Hayley, a member of the aircrew. There were two women and a man acting as our hosts for the duration of our charter which was open ended because we had no idea how long it would take us to find Barbie and end our nightmare. I don't want to say they were picked for their looks, but all three were stunningly attractive.

"We should land in an hour," added Deepa.

"Coffee, madam?" asked Jermaine, appearing at my side to offer his arm when I got ready to stand up.

"Hey, that's my job," teased Hayley, smiling at my tall Jamaican butler as she moved to the bar area where a coffee pot sat on a hot plate keeping warm.

I nodded and had to stifle another yawn.

When the yawn finally subsided and I could talk, I asked, "We're landing in Melilla? I thought we needed to stop and refuel." Before we set off the captain told us the distance was too far to achieve in one hop.

"We stopped in Ireland, madam," Jermaine explained. That was three hours ago.

Ireland.

"Where's my phone?" I looked about for it was not where I left it.

"Charging, madam," Jermaine advised, crossing the cabin to where it sat in a charging cradle.

I thanked him as I accepted it and flipped to my call log to redial the number I had for Finn Murphy's next of kin.

Accepting a mug of steaming coffee from Hayley with thanks, I listened to the phone ringing and wished somebody would answer. They didn't. A quick check confirmed the battery was almost fully charged, so I dropped it onto my seat and used both hands to sip at the dark liquid.

"Madam, if you would like a few moments to freshen up I have laid out a selection of outfit choices in the bathroom."

How do people manage without a Jermaine in their lives? How had I ever managed to get dressed before I met him? I was being flippant of course, and though I loved having him around to care for my every need, usually before I thought I needed it, I was able to function perfectly well on my own.

There was indeed a selection of outfits waiting for me to choose from and the bathroom was precisely that, not the tiny cubicle one gets on board a commercial aircraft where they pack the passengers in like cattle.

Looking in the mirror I was dismayed to see that I'd been drooling in my sleep. The whole of my left shoulder was damp, and I had a damp chin, both of which I'd been too drowsy to notice at any point in the last five minutes. It was nice that my friends are all too polite to point such things out, but I'm not sure that's for the best.

A knock at the door came just as I was applying a little makeup to hide the bags under my eyes.

"Mrs Fisher," it was the male steward, Raymundo, "We need you to retake your seat now, please. We will begin our descent in just a few minutes."

I promised to be out momentarily, packed my toiletries into one bag, my makeup into another, and rejoined my friends in the main cabin.

The plane landed so smoothly I hardly noticed, and it taxied to the tiny airport terminal where we departed directly into a small bus that took us to immigration. The unavoidable processes over, we spilled onto the street outside where the heat was oppressive but a welcome change to the cold of New York.

Sam came to stand beside me. "What now, Mrs Fisher?" It was a good question, and precisely the prompt I needed.

We had, of course, discussed what we were flying to Melilla for. In many ways the destination was a wild stab in the dark, yet I couldn't fault Jermaine's logic in wanting to come here. Unless Dr Disguise had already visited and dismissed this location, the autopsy report for Finn Murphy would give him a new place to explore.

That Finn Murphy was here at some point in the days prior to his death could be in little doubt. The dead bug proved it. The question now wasn't so much whether Dr Disguise was here or not, but whether the San José ever had been.

Asreb

- -

B arbie woke when the car hit a pothole on its way through the ancient city. Coming to, she was disorientated, but as the fog cleared and she saw Xavier idly watching the world go by as though he hadn't a care in the world, her rage kicked in. She had explosive cuffs around each forearm, extending from her wrists almost to her elbows. The leather outer had been customised and decorated so they looked more like fashion accessories than the constant threat they represented, but Xavier wouldn't detonate them if she had her hands around his throat.

Launching herself across the dividing space on the backseat, Barbie felt certain that Gomez, in the driving seat, would be unable to stop her until he brought the car to a halt. By then she would have wrestled the phone from Xavier's grip and be able to run away with it, fleeing from whichever side of the car Gomez wasn't covering.

The sharp point of a knife pricked her skin before she could get to her target – Xavier had been ready for her attack! How on earth did he get the knife into his hand so fast? Where did it come from?

Turning his head to face Barbie, Silvestre looked at her with emotionless eyes.

"I grow bored of your resistance, Miss Berkeley. I am keeping you alive because I believe you will be of use in my quest to find the San José. However, if you do not desist with these pointless attempts to overpower me, I will simply kill you. Which would be a shame.

Few women are ever as beautiful as you. You have youth on your side and your beauty will fade, but for now you are quite exquisite."

Barbie lowered her hands and sank back into her seat.

Silvestre folded the knife away. Stowing it back inside his sleeve where he always kept a blade to hand, he continued talking.

"As things stand, Miss Berkeley, I have no intention of ending your life. If we find the San José, I will not only remove the explosive cuffs from your wrists, I will send you away with all the gold you can carry in your hands. You will be a rich woman and what I give up will be insignificant when the remainder is counted. I implore you to see reason and behave from now on."

Barbie refused to allow herself to believe his promises. He boasted about killing people who got in his way but intended to let her live? He would kill her the moment she outlived her usefulness and nothing would convince her otherwise – certainly not his words.

She would, however, play along. Thus far, her attempts at freedom had all resulted in injury. She felt her abdomen now, her fingers coming away with a spot of blood staining them where Xavier's blade penetrated.

"I need fresh clothes," she said.

"And you could already be wearing them had you chosen to act more reasonably on the plane."

"You drugged and abducted me," she pointed out.

Twisting to face her again, Silvestre asked, "Would you have come otherwise?" he gave her a moment to acknowledge his point. "Now, no more senseless discussion. We are at the port. Please be assured that if you run, I will detonate the charge in your left arm. I will then have Gomez kill anyone within sight and will take you, complete with whatever bloody stump is left from your left arm, and we will continue. Am I understood?"

Barbie broke eye contact, staring straight ahead when she said, "Yes."

The Museum

J ermaine, Sam, and Hideki came with me when we split at the airport. It was necessary to hire two cars anyway, and made sense to make that three so we could spread ourselves over a wider area.

Melilla isn't a big place, but it is still a city. The population is less than a hundred thousand, and it has an ancient feel to it that reminded me very much of Valetta in Malta. If Dr Disguise was here, our chances of finding him were slim, but we were going to do the very best we could. That meant a visit to the police headquarters to circulate pictures of Barbie. Deepa and Martin were going to handle that. They were also armed with pictures of Finn Murphy in the hope he might be known here. I wasn't sure what kind of person Finn was – until now it hadn't crossed my mind to question it. Now I wondered if perhaps he was hiding on board the Aurelia and stowed away there because he was on the run. From what or who I could only guess, but being able to confirm he did visit Melilla would go a long way to proving we were looking in the right place.

Molly and Anders were heading to the port with Schneider to keep a close eye on anyone heading out to Asreb or coming back. They also had pictures of Barbie and Finn which they would show around to see if anyone had seen them. Finn was unlikely to be remembered; it was almost two months since his body was found, but if Barbie *was* brought here then it had to be today, and she was the kind of woman men remembered seeing.

With the others departing to complete their tasks, it was just my party left. We were heading to what passed for a museum and maritime centre here. I wanted to pick the brains of whoever knew most about the history of shipwrecks in these parts.

Jermaine drove, acting as chauffeur with Hideki in the front passenger seat and Sam in the back with me.

I wasn't sure what to expect of Melilla, and spent the ride through the city observing the sights outside. Like many places, it had areas where money had been spent, and other areas where it most definitely had not. I saw kids in scrappy clothing out playing in the street. They had shoes and clothes and looked well fed, but two miles later we were driving past boutique shops and swanky hotels with expensive cars parked outside.

The land sloped down to the sea where the map app on Hideki's phone promised we would find the maritime centre.

Inside, we were forced to wait for someone to fetch the curator. Yet again, I elected to employ my quasi-celebrity status to get things moving, and it worked, the young man behind the reception desk becoming flustered under the intense stares aimed his way.

The museum was little more than a tourist attraction, intended to make a few bucks from those with nothing better to do. It wasn't a big place, so I considered it a mercy they could boast a proper academic in the form of a professor as their head person.

Professor del Castillo turned out to be a woman in her sixties. Slender and with a sense of energy in her every movement, she was just the right person to help us.

"Shipwrecks in 1708?" she frowned as she repeated my question. "I'm not sure we have any recorded."

From my handbag I withdrew the one remaining gold Escudos coin in my possession - Dr Disguise and Hench got the rest.

"Has anything like this ever been found on or near the island?" I pressed.

She took the offered coin, testing the weight with her hand. Her lips were skewed to one side and her frown deepened when she inspected it more closely and found the date.

"Can you tell me where you got this?" the professor asked.

I gave a short shake of my head. "I would rather not, sorry. I'm afraid I have a mystery to solve and a friend in danger." I could sense Hideki tensing at the mention of Barbie. "We have reason to believe this came from a treasure ship called the ..."

"San José," The professor completed my sentence. Watching my face to see how I might react, she knew she had guessed correctly. "Oh, goodness," she gasped in surprise. "Really? The San José?"

Unsure what to say, I went with, "How did you know?" hoping she was going to reveal that she believed it was in the water near Melilla or that she knew Finn Murphy. I was not to be so lucky though.

"I studied the San José as part of my thesis. My professor at the time liked to talk about what would happen to the global economy when it is finally found. The treasure will be worth billions on today's market. Depending on where it is found the fight for ownership could rage for years." Looking up from the coin she still held, the professor said, "You came here asking about shipwrecks. Surely you know the San José was lost off the coast of Columbia?"

Now was not the time to keep secrets. Not if I wanted Barbie back.

"Professor del Castillo, it would take too long to explain everything, so here is the short version. Whether the San José sunk or not, some or possibly all of its treasure survived." I got a sceptical eyebrow in response. "A man called Finn Murphy found it and was subsequently murdered. We found a fortune of uncut gems in his gut and then a backpack containing an even bigger fortune of these gold coins along with intricate pieces of jewellery and even more gemstones."

The professor's expression shifted to shocked disbelief.

Hideki grabbed her attention. "We are not interested in the treasure. There is another party trying to find it and they took my girlfriend because they think we might know something they haven't figured out."

Shaking her head as if to clear it, Professor del Castillo said, "Wait, what? Someone has been kidnapped?"

"That's right," I confirmed. "We are just trying to get her back and the best way for that to happen is by finding the treasure first."

Her eyes glinted with excitement. "You really think the San José's treasure might be out there?"

Hideki pulled out his phone, showing her a photograph of the gold and jewels from Finn Murphy's backpack. These were laid out across the floor in my suite and had both of my dachshunds in the frame where they were sniffing the coins out of curiosity.

She uttered something in Spanish that had to be an expletive for her cheeks turned red and she apologised.

Hideki said, "The man who found the treasure had the dead body of an insect in his hair. The only place on earth the insect can be found is on Asreb."

Seeing not only the truth of it, but the implied possibility, the professor looked about ready to faint.

"This is all so incredible. I mean ... I've heard wild theories over the years. People have found artefacts from the San José, but they could all be explained away one way or another." Nodding her head, she said, "You think the ship could be here?"

I shrugged. "I think it is somewhere. Finn Murphy found the treasure. I would be a lot less certain if the other interested party were not so willing to kill, steal, and kidnap."

"Wait! Kill? Someone has been killed?"

Sam frowned. "Yeah, that Finn Murphy bloke for one," he said, like it was patently obvious.

Acting embarrassed, the professor said, "Of course. You did say that."

I could have added that there were several other murders, including Hugo Lockhart only a day ago, but she did not require the full picture.

"Professor, I have to take you back to the purpose of our visit here today. Were there any shipwrecks recorded in the waters around Melilla in 1708 or have there ever been any reports of treasure found here?"

Jolted into finally giving me an answer, all I got was disappointment.

"No, sorry, nothing like that. I can pull up the database and show you, if you wish, but there were no shipwrecks of note in 1708. The war between Spain and England and the wars that preceded and followed did not take place in these waters. Naval battles in the Mediterranean were rare at that time. Most took place in the Atlantic and there were no shipwrecks due to weather either. Not around that time."

It felt like a big dead end. How could this be where Finn Murphy found the treasure if no one knew about it? Could it have been here all this time and he was the only one who ever found it?

I thanked the professor for her time. She apologised for being unable to help, and just when we were about to leave, she asked, "Do you want to get out to Asreb? I have a boat."

Barbie Goes to Asreb

Already in the waters off Asreb, Barbie, questioned what they were doing there. Four miles across from north to south, and three miles from east to west, it was a flat, featureless lump of rock. Home to millions of seabirds due to the food-rich waters surrounding it, there was nothing to see and no reason to believe they were about to stumble upon the wreck of the San José.

Playing her part, she said, "Your efforts would be better spent exploring on land. If Finn Murphy was here, he must have chartered a boat or hired some diving equipment. The San José is not going to be found like this."

Silvestre turned to face the blonde. She was right. He was so desperate to find what he believed was rightfully his, that he'd become blinded by the need to move forward.

"Also," Barbie continued, "the captain's diary – how did you come by it? If it is genuine ..."

"It is," Silvestre was quick to reply.

"Then, who had it? Are they related to the captain? Did he survive and if so were there any other artefacts left behind that could provide some kind of clue."

Silvestre knew precisely where the diary came from. It was discovered in a library in England more than one hundred years ago. No one knew where it had come from, and it had languished unloved until just less than a decade ago when technology finally digitised the library. The librarian, bored with her job inputting data in a dark room in the library's basement, nevertheless took the time to figure out what the leather bound and very old document was.

It was some time after that when Silvestre became aware of it. His regular custom of searching for any reference to the San José produced a new hit, and he almost wept with excitement when he discovered what it was.

He had Gomez steal it, of course. It wasn't safe to have any record that he was ever at the library or registered as an interested party – he'd made the mistake of using his name when he first started to chase the treasure. That was before he thought to disguise himself, before he found Gomez.

Instead of talking to his captive about the captain's diary, Silvestre focused on where they were.

"That is for another time, Miss Berkeley. Right now I wish to explore the possibility that Finn Murphy was here. "Gomez!" he shouted, "Turn the boat around. Let's head back to shore."

He got no reply, but the boat shifted almost immediately, the prow swinging to port when the silent giant spun the wheel. Barbie had to hold on, the change in trajectory causing the ship's hull to skip and bounce over the waves when it turned.

"Finn Murphy was here," Silvestre stated confidently. "The bug tells us that. Carlos Ramirez said he met him in Morocco and perhaps he was telling the truth after all. Finn Murphy left Melilla and perhaps he went to Casablanca. He could have boarded the Aurelia there and met with Ramirez. If the San José isn't here, then perhaps it is somewhere along this coastline. I shall find out soon enough."

The powerful twin-engined launch leapt forward once more when Gomez pulled the throttle back to its stop. Barbie thought the experience to be exhilarating even though it was completely ruined by her company.

Nearing shore, they saw another ship passing to their starboard side. They were too far away for her to see, but there was something about the tall, black man at the helm that caught her eye. Looking away quickly lest the man she knew as Xavier noticed, she felt certain it was Jermaine going by. That had to mean it was Patricia too and that being the case the whole gang was probably here.

It gave Barbie the lift she needed, and now she was motivated to keep her captor and his henchman in Melilla. If Patricia could track her across the world in less than a day, she could find where she was being held and a rescue would come.

But what about her explosive cuffs? Barbie knew Xavier would detonate them if he thought she might escape.

Things were looking up, but she was a long way from being safe.

Proof of Life

Martin and Deepa had drawn a blank looking for traces of Finn Murphy. If he had ever been to Melilla, he kept a low profile. He hadn't rented any diving equipment as we hoped might be the case, and there were no boat hire places with a record of his name. It was conceivable he operated cash-in-hand or even stole one, but the more likely conclusion was that he'd never been here.

It failed to explain the bug in his hair, which was perplexing. However, the dead beetle thingy was also the only reason we had to think the Irishman was ever in Melilla. If it was a red herring, then we were looking in very much the wrong place.

Showing the photograph of Barbie drew interest, but not in a good way. Schneider and co showed it around, but despite the lecherous comments, no one had seen her.

Going out to the island of Asreb did not feel like a worthwhile next step, but it would give me time to think. Just three miles off the coast, it was a short hop in Professor del Castillo's motor launch. When she said boat, I figured she was talking about a little thing with a sail, but it belonged to the university back in Barcelona. The outpost in Melilla was, rather like the city itself, an enclave of something bigger. Bigger in this case, meant a proper budget and a motorboat at her disposal so she could study and produce academic papers – a key facet of any academic's working life, she assured me.

"There is a jetty off the western shore," she raised her voice to be heard over the rushing wind as she ploughed through the waves. "It's in the lee of the island and quieter there."

She instructed Jermaine to coax the boat in slowly due to seals in the area though I suspect the true reason was as much to do with nervousness over his ability to control the vessel. She usually had a pilot take her out, but at such short notice he was not available, and we were not going to wait.

Much as I suspected, there wasn't a whole lot to look at. Asreb is a rock. Grass and shrubs and a few short trees grow on it to give the island a green top to contrast with the rocky sides, but the professor assured us there had never been humans living on the island.

It took Sam all of about thirty seconds to find one of the insects.

"Look at this, Mrs Fisher," he called me over.

Sure enough, Hideki confirmed, we were looking at a living specimen of Lucanus Punctatum. It was an odd-looking thing. Sort of like a cross between a woodlouse and a beetle. It wiggled two antennae in the air, balancing on the tip of Sam's thumb.

What did it tell us? Well, not a lot. We already knew Finn Murphy came here, we just didn't know why or when or even whether this location had anything to do with the San José. Heck, he could have been here months before he was found dead below decks on the Aurelia. The little insect might have found its way inside his sleeping bag and died there, becoming matted into Finn Murphy's hair only in the hours before he died. Worse yet, it could have been transferred to him from someone else in which case it really was a red herring.

There was just no way of knowing.

Swivelling around to let Professor del Castillo know I wanted to return to Melilla, I found her to be missing. So too was Hideki.

Jermaine explained, "They went to collect data, madam. It would seem the professor has a series of cameras located on the island."

"Cameras? How far does she have to go? How long is she planning to be?" I asked the questions with the frustration I felt. It was unfair of me and I apologised to Jermaine immediately. There was no time to be wasted on such trivia and had Hideki not gone with her, I might have given serious thought to leaving without her.

As it was, I needn't have worried. Almost before I could start to complain, she reappeared, Hideki by her side as they came back down from higher ground.

"It's all part of a shipping survey," she explained. "There's something wrong with the link so I'm not getting the data automatically. I've been meaning to come out here and have a look for days. I can fix it, but for now I've got a download directly from the cameras."

Hideki was good enough to explain why I should care.

"The cameras record vessels going by in the shipping lane, but anyone walking close by would also have triggered the lens. If Barbie came out here ..."

"Also," Professor del Castillo remarked on her way back to the boat, "we can go back and look at the historic data. If your Murphy fellow walked by one of the cameras, we might see what he was up to."

"He might have the treasure in his backpack already," said Hideki, sounding hopeful.

"Or we might see him going diving from a boat," suggested Jermaine.

My eyes flared at the possibility, and I was overcome with a sudden need to get back to the little museum in Melilla so we could see if the cameras recorded anything worthwhile.

"Oh, we don't have to go back to find out," said the professor, pulling a laptop from a backpack.

We crowded around her, holding a blanket over the screen to keep the glare off. Don't ask me what technology underpins how the cameras know to take a picture, but there were still frames of us approaching the island, each one dated with a timestamp. In the minutes before our arrival, a tanker had gone by and more than two dozen other vessels on the other side of the island where ships from all around the Med were heading back toward Gibraltar and the Atlantic Ocean beyond.

Explaining as she clicked through the frames, we learned there were students in Spain who were collating the data as part of their post graduate degree programme. It had been going on for years, hence not only the age of the cameras but Professor del Castillo's need to get out here to fix it.

When Jermaine barked a command to, "Stop!" I almost fell overboard such was the shock of it. I wanted to whack him on the arm, but found myself overcome by curiosity because Sam, Hideki, and Jermaine were all getting very excited.

"What?" I asked. On the screen was the hundredth photograph of the sea around Asreb. It looked like all the others.

Hideki pointed, his index finger picking out a fancy power launch turned broadside to the island.

"Barbie," he stated, his voice filled with triumph, concern, and a need to hurt someone.

Sure enough, at the wheel stood the enormous man I'd come to refer to as Hench. There was a second man behind him sitting in a comfortable sofa style chair at the back of the boat. He wasn't really visible though because a blonde woman obscured him. She was wearing the same thing I last saw her in and there was no question it was Barbie.

I flicked my eyes to the corner of the screen and jolted.

"That's ..." I checked my watch. "That's less than an hour ago!"

Needless to say we were tearing through the surf moments later, Jermaine pushing the engine to its maximum and the professor wise enough not to challenge him since Hideki was at his side questioning whether he could make it go any faster.

I was on the phone to Martin.

"She was here!" I blurted the moment the call connected, yelling my information before he even had a chance to speak. "We have a photograph of her in a boat in the water off Asreb. That giant was driving the boat!"

"You're sure?" Martin questioned. "We must have spoken to a hundred people and none of them have seen her. I don't think there is a boat hire and charter company on Melilla we haven't visited."

"It's her all right. Her and the giant, and the man who's behind it all. The one who pretended to be Professor Noriega. There's no chance we're wrong."

Martin accepted I was right without further comment.

"What can I do?"

"We're on our way back to you now. If you look out toward Asreb you can probably see us."

"I can!" he replied. "That is, there's a speedboat heading this way at crazy speed."

"That's us," I confirmed, holding on for dear life as the boat bounced and bucked over the waves. "Get the rest of the gang together. She's here somewhere and people must remember a seven-foot-tall giant walking past them. They must be staying somewhere ..." I gasped. "They must have landed somewhere! Maybe we can cut them off before they get back to the plane."

"I can talk to the police again," said Martin, but his tone was less than hopeful.

"Were they helpful?" I asked.

"Not even slightly. They have enough of their own crimes to deal with, it would seem. I managed to make enough noise that they gave up trying to send me away and brought out a detective to speak with me. That didn't really get me anywhere though. If Finn Murphy was here, then he kept his head down. There's no record of him, but all that means is that the police didn't have to deal with him. To find out if he came through Melilla, our best bet is to speak with immigration, but I don't see them giving up information when we have no right to demand it. Should we speak to Interpol?"

The same question crossed my mind the moment I realised we were going to be chasing Barbie across multiple time zones and around the world. However, even though they might help us, getting them to do so would require a lot of explanation and interviews and there wasn't time for it. The trail might go cold while we tried to convince them to help.

We were on our own and probably better for it.

Nearing land, I would be out of the boat soon – good thing because I was beginning to feel quite queasy from all the bouncing about. A new strategy was needed, and it was going to take all of us.

"Martin, please contact Schneider, Molly, and Anders, get them to stop what they are doing, and switch to visiting the high-end hotels. There can't be more than a dozen of them. It's a long shot, but if Dr Disguise is staying here tonight, I'm willing to bet he is going to do so in luxury. They can ask about the giant. Just make sure they know not to approach. If they find where he is staying, have them call it in."

"Okay, Patricia. What about me and Deepa?"

"Can you get to the docks? We are about to arrive. I want to see if you can find anyone who knows the boat Barbie was on."

"On our way. ETA five minutes."

He sounded out of breath when he ended the call and was likely running already.

My heart banged around inside my chest, beating out its desperation to find Barbie. She was here somewhere, and I was going to find her.

Dr Davis

D r David Davis, aware that he was abruptly left to manage the ship's sick or ailing passengers and crew with just one other doctor and a small team of medics and nurses, prayed he wasn't going to have a sudden outbreak of ... well, anything.

The rotation of on call doctors only really worked when there were three of them. Unexpectedly down to two, they could call in somewhere else to cover – the cruise line had lots of doctors employed and there would be someone prepared to cut short their leave – but whoever chose to volunteer wasn't going to arrive in the next day or so.

He knew it was a little uncharitable, but felt glad Patricia Fisher was off the ship too. Her presence always had a 'hard to define' likelihood of mayhem multiplying. Not that he blamed her exactly, but there were never any shootings, stabbings, poisonings, or deaths in general when she was not around.

Bored, because he was covering Hideki's shift in the medical centre and had no patients (thank goodness), he chose to look back at the case that demanded his junior's absence.

Well, sort of.

Hideki was with Patricia Fisher, undoubtedly getting into hot water in their pursuit of his girlfriend, Barbara Berkeley. Silently, Dr Davis acknowledged that he would also willingly race around the world to recover his girlfriend if she looked like Barbie. However, in his late fifties, twice divorced, and with an ample roll of unnecessary extra meat around his middle, he knew he was lucky to have a girlfriend at all.

As he understood it, Miss Berkeley's disappearance was all to do with Finn Murphy and the uncut gems Hideki found in the man's gut. Like everyone else on board, Dr Davis had no idea Patricia and friends subsequently found a backpack full to overflowing with gold and jewels, and knew only that Hideki had been helping to investigate something to do with the Irishman's death.

Following that line of thought, and largely because he had nothing better to do, he navigated to the computer file for Finn Murphy and started to poke around.

Getting Somewhere

Deepa and Martin appeared just as I accepted a helping hand from Jermaine to get out of the boat. They were just coming into the dock area, descending from higher ground along the road leading in.

The midday sun beat down to make it hot and I was glad to be wearing shorts and a stretchy top. Even so, now that the sea breeze was gone, I was starting to perspire. Arriving in the airconditioned car hired at the airport, Deepa and Martin looked cool and collected.

I took a moment to thank Professor del Castillo; she'd been good to us and was hanging around now so she could transfer the one good picture she had of Barbie on the speedboat. We were going to need it. Her own boat, or rather, the one belonging to the university, needed to be docked elsewhere, but she offered to leave it where it was in case we needed it. We could collect the keys from her in that eventuality. She even gave us her phone number.

Jermaine received the photograph to his phone and sent it to everyone else. Our singular task was to find someone who recognised the boat.

We split into pairs, Jermaine with me, Sam with Hideki, and Deepa with Martin. We could cover more ground this way, but it added an element of risk none of us were happy about, so it felt like an overdue mercy when Hideki and Sam found someone who knew the boat in the photograph less than ten minutes after we spread out. Jogging to get to their location, I found them still speaking with a local charter operator.

Hector Ruiz was in his mid-fifties and growing a paunch that sat atop his belt. A faded cloth ballcap covered his hair, and that which peeked out was grey and turning white. More grey hair showed in the vee of his equally faded polo shirt. His arms were thick with muscle, the result of hauling boats or fishing nets I assumed and his business – the boat, the signs, and the equipment - which must once have looked new and pristine, bore the signs of no further investment since opening many, many years ago.

"Yes, I know this boat," he repeated what he'd already told Hideki. His English was broken but passable. "It belongs to a hire company at the far end of Melilla."

"How did we not find it," cursed Martin. "There were five of us scouring the dock, asking about Barbie and the giant."

"No, not on the dock," Hector corrected what I too had assumed. "At the far end of Melilla. It is not available for general hire to anyone. Only those who fit the right ..." He struggled to find the word he wanted which led to the rest of us guessing.

After a minute of everyone getting it wrong, Hector snapped his fingers.

"Rich. That's it. Money. You have to have money. It is very exclusive. Part of a club."

"Like a country club?" asked Martin.

Hector shook his head. "No, Senor, for yachts. They use this boat to take people out to their yachts."

Hideki and Jermaine had their fingers flashing over their phones in the next second. Hideki won, finding the name, address, and website for the yacht club a fraction faster than Jermaine.

We thanked Hector and hauled butt.

We had two cars, and needed them to cross town unless we wanted to play sardines. Hideki jumped in with Deepa and Martin just to even things up and on the way I called Schneider.

"No luck so far," he reported. "We have twelve hotels that might be worth checking, but only four that look likely. Those are the nice ones according to all the review sites. After that, the quality diminishes fast, but if they haven't checked in yet …"

Then making enquiries using just a description of the giant and a photograph of Barbie wasn't going to work. Not knowing the name of the man behind it all was infuriating.

To kill time in the car, I called Captain Danvers back in New York.

"What?" he growled down the phone. "Do you know what time it is here?"

"Did you get anywhere with the money?" I asked, completely ignoring his bellyaching. He'd probably worked late last night and didn't deserve to be woken so early – I figured it was either five or six in the morning there, though I honestly wasn't sure what time zone we were in. Regardless, time was of the essence.

"Lady, I was asleep. I'm yet to have my first cup of coffee. I could do with a shower. I know your friend is missing, but if I had anything to report, I would have called you."

"How soon can you find out?" I pestered.

"Good morning, Danny," he mimicked my accent and made a weak attempt at sounding like a woman. "I'm so thankful for all the extra work you are doing for a case that is so far outside of your jurisdiction. I do hope you had a decent sleep last night."

Taking a deep breath, I said, "Danny, I'm sorry if I woke you, but I need to know if there is any update. We've flown halfway around the world while you were sleeping, and we've found her."

"Really?" He did nothing to hide the shock in his voice. "You got her back already? Are the perps in custody?"

"No, we haven't got her back, but she was here," I tried to provide a little clarity. "We think we know where she might be and that's our next destination, but we don't have a name and that's crippling us."

Captain Danvers dropped his hurt and offended act. "Okay, Patricia. I'm up. I'll make some calls and push some buttons. But listen, there's no point chasing me. I will let you know the moment I find something worth telling you."

We ended the call and I was putting my phone away when Jermaine announced that we were arriving.

The Melilla City Yacht Club was the kind of establishment that catered to the superrich. Not that it was in the league of Monaco, but there were some impressive yachts parked beyond the gates at which we were forced to stop.

The gates were, in fact, barriers, the red and white kind that swing up from a pivot point at one end. There would be a button to control it inside the little shack. The shack was a flimsy thing made of powder-coated sheet metal and Perspex. While I was certain we could back up and drive straight through it and thus avoid the barrier, the ornamental wall of rocks two feet beyond it would stop our car dead. The wall continued on both sides of the road, and filled the gap in the middle where the shack sat on a small island.

All around was planted with flowers, shrubs and trees, the gardeners clearly working hard to make it all look pristine.

"Are you members?" asked a security guard with a sidearm. There were two of them, both of whom looked confident and capable.

Jermaine flicked his eyes to the rear-view mirror where they met mine. He didn't say anything, but I believe he was asking for permission to 'take care' of the guards. This was tricky. If I gave them a sniff of the truth, it was my guess that they would choose to defend the members of the club since that was their job.

We wouldn't get in and would need to either force entry – not a palatable option given they were armed and we were not – or sneak in via another means. The first was messy and even if we succeeded it would bring the police. The second option would simply take too long.

A third option presented itself while I debated, and though you might think I would be glad for such an unexpected bonus, it came in the very worst form.

From the front passenger seat, Sam pointed.

"Hey, look, there's Barbie!" His usual goofy grin was in place, but it fell when he saw how Jermaine and I stiffened.

Driving up to the exit of the other side of the road was a sleek black Mercedes. In the rear window, we saw a shock of blonde hair that could only be Barbie. In front of her, a man who filled the driver's seat and was so large he was forced to lean slightly to one side to fit the width of his torso. His seat had to be cranked back as far as it would go and lowered to its full extent.

I'd forgotten just how massive he was.

They swept past us with a wave from the second security guard who lifted the barrier upon their approach so they didn't even need to slow down.

Yet again, I failed to get a decent look at the second man who was sitting on the opposite side of the back seat, next to Barbie where I imagined he must have a gun on her.

Jermaine hit his horn and slammed the car into reverse. Martin was at the wheel in the car behind us, effectively blocking us in. The barrier prevented forward movement and we couldn't go backward until Martin started to move.

Thankfully, he got the message and Deepa phoned me as their car shot backward to perform a swinging J turn so their nose was pointing the other way and their car was on the other side of the road.

Deepa's voice burst out, "Was that Barbie?"

"Yes! Get after her. Ram them off the road!" I had to hold on tight in the back of the car, flung around by the changing forces of inertia when Jermaine also performed a reverse turn at speed. The stench of rubber from the car ahead filled my nostrils to the accompanying sound of our tyres doing much the same.

A glance behind me showed the security guards jabbering into their radios. I could only guess who they were talking to or what they might be reporting, but I doubted it was anything good from our perspective.

However, if they were calling the police, I was fine with that. Some armed officers would be helpful when Barbie told them all she'd been kidnapped.

In the car ahead, Martin, Deepa, and Hideki needed very little time to catch up with the target vehicle. It was cruising through the streets in no particular rush. Of course that changed when Martin tried to get alongside them.

At the wheel, Hench floored his accelerator and I saw Barbie's shocked face appear in the rear window.

She saw us and knew the rescue was on. The only question in my head was what she would now do. Barbie is tough and resilient. She looked unharmed though I was conscious I only caught the briefest glimpse of her face. Would she dive from the car? Would she overpower the man in the back because Hench had to drive and couldn't get involved?

As Jermaine closed the distance, all I could do was watch.

The Chase

In the back of the black Mercedes Silvestre swore, and turning to look at Barbie he asked, "Is she always this doggedly persistent?"

Barbie shot daggers with her eyes. "Yes. She won't give up. Patricia Fisher doesn't know how to lose. You know she took down the Godmother, right?"

"Yes," Silvestre smiled. "A most impressive feat, but she will find me a little less easy to pin down."

A horn blasted, the oncoming traffic on the other side of the road forced to mount the curb when Martin refused to yield. He was right alongside Silvestre's car, but could not get in front. Sooner or later a truck would come, and the chase car would be forced to swerve or crash.

"Really?" Barbie snorted. "You flew from America to the north of Africa, and she found you in less than a day." She saw a flicker of rage behind her captor's eyes and chose to soften her voice. "She's not after the treasure, you know. None of us are. She's only here because of me." Barbie made the claim with utter confidence.

Silvestre spat, "You've done nothing but investigate the San José since you discovered Finn Murphy's body. You expect me to believe you are not after the billions in gold that went into the San José's hold?"

They were thrown hard to the left, Barbie almost spilling into Silvestre only to be held in place by her seatbelt. If he had a weapon, she would be able to use the confusion to grab for it, but his phone with the app to blow her arms off was safely in one of his pockets.

Barbie nodded, her eyes imploring Xavier to see the truth. "Yes. Patricia's job is to solve crime on board the Aurelia. Finn Murphy was murdered onboard the Aurelia. It really is that simple."

A grinding of metal came when Martin slammed his car into theirs. Barbie swung her head to see the face of her boyfriend looking back at her from less than a foot away.

He mouthed something, or maybe he was shouting. Over the roaring engines and grinding steel, she couldn't tell.

Silvestre didn't believe her claim. What fool would refuse the chance to obtain billions of dollars' worth of treasure? Normally, a finder would get to keep only a fraction, the rest being claimed by the country from which it originated, the country where it was found, or a mix of the two in most cases following a lengthy and expensive legal battle. In his case, though, Silvestre planned to keep it all.

Depending on where it was found, and he believed it had to lie in shallow water where Finn Murphy must have dived to recover that which he once had, Silvestre had all the resources to conduct a covert operation. No one would know what he'd found, and the treasure would all be his. He felt a little displeasure at the knowledge that he would have to kill Miss Berkeley. If he let her go, with or without a small portion of the treasure in her possession as he promised, the truth would emerge.

He could not allow that.

"Miss Berkeley, I believe our visit to Melilla is at an end," he announced calmly. Ideally, he would kill Mrs Fisher and all her friends. That would stop her pursuit *and* her interference. In practice, he believed he was unlikely to succeed. The police would be drawn by their insane car chase, and he had no time to explain who he was or why he was in the Spanish enclave.

Therefore it was time to leave.

"Where are we going next?" Barbie asked, keen to know anything that might aide her escape. Information could be a powerful ally and the more she knew the better she could prepare herself.

"That is none of your concern," replied Silvestre, his focus elsewhere. "Your friends are proving to be a nuisance so we will regroup. I shall divert resources to eliminate them, and we will begin again. I fear Melilla was a red herring, as you like to say in English."

Lifting his phone from an inner coat pocket, he made a call.

In the car behind Silvestre's, Jermaine was doing his best to remain calm. Breathing exercises were part of his daily routine and something he learned long ago in his martial arts training. Focused breathing helped to deal with stress and dissipate anger, both of which he could feel edging into his consciousness.

Martin was doing his best to get around the car in front, but was unable to do so for a variety of factors. The engine in the black Mercedes was more powerful than those in their hire cars for a start. If the road was clear and straight, it would probably leave them for dead.

It also had command of the road. Martin had to keep swerving around oncoming traffic and each time they approached a turning, he had to fall back or risk shooting past if the giant at the wheel chose to take it.

The chase had covered several miles already, and they were entering the most densely populated part of the city, close to the port. There were mopeds everywhere; the citizens of Melilla favouring them for their compact size and frugal running costs. The pedestrian traffic forced all three cars to slow while beeping their horns feverishly to clear the route ahead.

Turning his head slightly, Jermaine said, "Madam, I am going to attempt to ram them. If I am able to perform the manoeuvre correctly, I should be able to create a spin that will take them off the road or kill their speed.

He never got a chance to try.

From a side street, a garbage truck stuck out its nose. The red light holding it back had just turned to green and he wasn't looking for there to be cars approaching at speed. Too late, he saw the chase heading right for him and froze.

Gomez mounted the curb with his employer barking commands from the back seat. That he narrowly missed pedestrians and people riding their mopeds was not by design – Silvestre ordered him to plough through them if he must – mercifully, they managed to get out of the way as he whipped down the side of the truck and shot out behind it.

Martin was not so lucky. With almost no notice and given nowhere to go that wouldn't result in multiple civilian casualties, he screamed a warning and hit the truck head on. The air bags went off inside, protecting the human cargo from serious injury though bruising, wrenched joints, and more would plague all three for weeks.

In the car behind Silvestre's, Jermaine likewise yelled a warning, but with an extra second of notice was able to slow their car. They saw Martin crash, Deepa and Hideki thrown about inside, but they were all wearing seatbelts.

Unable to slow completely, Jermaine was through the gap and past the garbage truck in the blink of an eye.

Certain his friends would be hurt, but not in any real danger, he pressed his foot back down on the accelerator and continued the chase.

However, the lead car had gained vital yards and when it reached the end of the congested city centre first, it left them behind. With it's more powerful engine it was able to pull away, the distance between them now insurmountable.

Jermaine continued to give chase, egged on by Mrs Fisher and Sam who both wanted to get Barbie back as badly as he did. Inevitably, the gap between them allowed the car in front to lose them when it took a turn Jermaine could not see.

Sirens filled the air. The police, slow to respond, but clearly closing in, would prevent them from catching up to Barbie and her captors if they were able to spot her again.

Choosing side streets, since that was clearly what the target car had done, Jermaine, Mrs Fisher, and Sam all scoured the city for any sign of the black Mercedes. There were cars all around them, but nothing like the one they sought. It could be called a game of cat and mouse, but what did that make the police?

Turning yet another corner, his breathing exercises beginning to fail in their ability to keep him calm, Jermaine saw they had come to the edge of the city. Ahead of him if he kept going, the houses and developed area ceased, giving way to the scrubby grassland and desert they flew in over.

With a surge of excitement, he hit the accelerator forcing his passengers back into their seats.

When asked what he was doing, he explained, "They must have landed at a different airstrip, madam. With a kidnapped passenger in tow, they wouldn't have landed at the same municipal airport as us. That would involve immigration and passports and security. Our interference here was not expected, so if they are choosing to flee ..."

"They'll be heading for their plane," Mrs Fisher completed his sentence.

Bursting from the end of the street and on to the hard, compact dirt beyond the last house, they all saw the plume of dust following a black spec as it raced into the distance. The black Mercedes was on a road which had to start somewhere to their right.

They could cut directly across the desert and scrubland but the likelihood of a puncture or driving straight into a gully or ravine was far too high. Reluctantly choosing caution, Jermaine angled the car to the right, driving parallel with the houses until he found what he hoped was the right road.

Not that it could really be described as a road. There was no tarmac, no white line up the middle. It was, however, flat and intended to be driven on by cars.

Wasting no further time, Jermaine once again floored the accelerator.

In the backseat, Mrs Fisher was talking on the phone with Deepa. She and Martin were unhurt and while Hideki had a cut to his head, he wasn't suffering anything worse. The police were with them, and it looked like they were going to be detained for questioning.

The situation was going to take some straightening out. For them too, Jermaine accepted, when a slurry of flashing lights filled his rear view. The cops were behind him now, but he wasn't about to stop. Barbie was just ahead. If he could get to her, this could all be over. The giant might be armed, but he'd been shot before. It didn't bother him that the giant had beaten him in their last fight, this time he was motivated.

He would get Barbie back or he would die trying.

The cop cars continued to gain, eating up the space behind him but the plume of dust following the black Mercedes was gone and that could only mean one thing: they had stopped.

Through the heat haze, the outline of a small plane emerged. Was it starting to move?

There was no more acceleration left in the pedal, the car was doing close to one hundred and forty miles per hour and the temperature gauge was showing red. The car couldn't take much more, but Jermaine never considered letting up.

If he had to ram the plane's undercarriage, he would.

Mrs Fisher agreed. If they could stop the plane or damage it, the police would sort out the rest of it. In many ways the very fact they were being chased by the Melilla cops worked in their favour. However, even as they sped across the compacted dirt, it became obvious the plane was getting further away not closer. It had built up speed as it raced to take off.

The black Mercedes had been abandoned where they boarded the plane. Jermaine stole a glance at it when something bright orange inside the car caught his eye. A further glance confirmed it was on fire. No one was getting any evidence from it today.

They saw the runway only moments before their car reached it. Like the 'road' to get to it, the airstrip was nothing more than compacted dirt, but it was good enough for the plane they so desperately wanted to stop.

Its wheels left the ground just as they swung around to follow it down the runway.

They were too late.

Cursing, a completely uncharacteristic thing for the Jamaican-born butler to do, he punched the steering wheel with enough force to leave it buckled.

The cops were pulling alongside as he eased off the pedal, finally allowing the car to slow. They were barking instructions in Spanish, their voices loud over their cars' external address systems. Jermaine knew he would have to obey and stop the car, but his attention was not on them but on the plane.

It was banking to the right, climbing still as it clawed at the sky for altitude. In so doing, it exposed the tailfin and plane's designation. It wasn't much, yet in theory at least, it could be used to trace the aircraft and discover who owned it.

A Little Help, Please?

That we all got arrested came as no surprise. The cops were reacting to reports of numerous traffic violations, so it came as a welcome surprise and a relief when we were released less than two hours later. I didn't even have time to arrange a lawyer.

The police were not interested in charging Patricia Fisher with motoring offences – they didn't have anything else on us and miraculously, nobody got hurt during our chase through the town. Apparently, I was considered a political hot potato and the mayor wanted the chief of police to let me go. Thankfully, that meant my friends too.

I believe it helped that we had been to the police and attempted to secure their help in the hours before we found ourselves chasing Barbie and her kidnappers through Melilla. We all heard the mayor bellowing at someone – possibly the chief of police – and a door slamming before he appeared beaming a politician's smile.

The mayor, a handsome man of about sixty, with greying hair and whiter than white teeth, shook the hands of everyone in my party, apologising that his city's officers hadn't been more willing to assist when we claimed to be searching for a kidnapped woman.

Grumbling in the corner, the chief of police pointed out that many women go missing every year, the port a known hive for human trafficking. The mayor ignored him or, at least, ignored his comment. He wanted them to assist us in finding the origin of the aircraft we almost caught and in our enquiries regarding Finn Murphy.

Through the mayor we were put in touch with immigration, and finally got some answers. Unfortunately, they were not the ones we wanted.

There was no record of Finn Murphy ever visiting the Spanish enclave and I was beginning to think the bug in his hair was a false lead of the worst kind.

The license plates on the black Mercedes were fake, most likely swapped out when they stole it, hired it, or otherwise came into possession of the vehicle. The police could probably figure out who owned it, but the VIN under the bonnet had been ground off, so identifying it was going to come down to the owner stepping forward.

If the man we were chasing paid for it – I believe he is seriously rich and the plane he left in was probably his own – then the owner would stay quiet and that line of enquiry was also a dead end.

That left only the plane's tailfin.

FG425-H didn't mean a whole lot to me. However, the mayor, like a superhero without a cape, swung in to help save the day again. One phone call later and I was talking to the head of the airport.

The aircraft had landed at the remote airstrip without appearing on their radar which meant it had to have come in low and to have flown that way for many miles upon approach.

The mayor, who was still arguing with the chief of police about his men being used for such trivia when they had 'real' crimes to solve, took a moment to gloat. We were clearly dealing with someone whose plans were nefarious.

It was only when the aircraft left that the Melilla airport authority spotted it. When it climbed hard and fast to get away, it appeared as an unexpected blip on the control tower's screens. Attempts to contact the aircraft all failed and they lost it somewhere over the Mediterranean Sea fifteen minutes later. Not because he had dipped back below the radar – they were tracking his aircraft at thirty-six thousand feet – but because his transponder shut off. There were only two reasons for this to happen, according to the expert giving me advice: either the plane exploded in mid-air, or they manually switched it off. The former sounded unlikely, and the latter was a highly illegal thing to do and would get the pilot banned from flying for life plus severe repercussions for the company behind it.

Regardless of that, they were taking Barbie somewhere and there was no way for us to see where that was.

The tailfin was the one ray of light in an otherwise dismal day. It was registered to a corporation in Spain. That didn't tell us much and a quick internet search returned almost no information. I knew what that meant because I'd seen it before: the registered company was a dummy corporation. There would be layers of confusing information to wade through to find the real people behind it, but the back of my skull itched when I thought about Spain.

The San José was a Spanish ship. The man pretending to be Professor Noriega had distinctly Spanish features. Was he Spanish? Had we just figured out a country of origin for all our woes?

The answer was a resounding maybe, but what did that do for us? A city is a big place if you are trying to find one person. A country ... well, looking with eyeballs wasn't going to get it done.

What did that leave us with?

Irish Countryside

The pilot and cabin staff were on board the Bombardier private aircraft and waiting for us when we arrived. It was late afternoon by then and I was feeling tired. There hadn't been a lot of food since we arrived in Melilla, which is to say there had been some pre-packed sandwiches the police obtained at the mayor's insistence.

Back on board our fully fuelled plane we could indulge in restaurant level catering. I chose a fillet steak with peppercorn sauce, asparagus, new potatoes, and watercress. I ate every last morsel and felt guilty the whole time, worrying Barbie might not be eating at all.

In all honesty, I thought that unlikely. Barbie was a survivor and would be sure to look after herself. She might be in poor company, but if they intended to kill her, they would have already done so. Keeping her alive indicated she had a purpose.

I slept for much of the five-hour flight, unsure when I might next get a chance and was awoken by Jermaine to be told we were on final approach.

Before settling in to sleep, I'd placed yet another call to Finn Murphy's next of kin with the same result as all my other attempts. Why were they not answering the phone? Were they in trouble? Concern ticked away at the back of my mind, but that wasn't why we flew to Ireland. No, the bigger driver for this trip was the hope we might discover something of value.

That and because I didn't know what else to do. A mystery man, possibly from Spain, elected to kidnap Barbie in his bid to recover a fortune in lost treasure. My involvement with the case started when Finn's body came to light in the bowels of the Aurelia. It was always my intention to see his case through and find the killer. Until now it was just for completeness – tying up loose ends. However, with Barbie missing her rescue might hinge on me figuring out a truckload of unknowns and I worried I wasn't good enough for the task.

Trying the number for Finn's next of kin once more now that I was awake, I yet again got no answer and cursed under my breath. I had enough time to brush my teeth while the plane taxied to the terminal at Cork airport and that gave me a few minutes to think about what we had achieved in the previous twenty-four hours – not a lot – and what we might hope to achieve tonight. My mood was gloomy which wasn't going to help to move things forward, yet I couldn't shift the feeling that this trip might be a dead end.

We almost caught up to Barbie in Melilla – she was right there! But she slipped through our fingers and now we had no way to know where she might be.

Martin and Deepa arranged for hire cars during the flight so paperwork at the Alamo desk was a mere formality. Just a little more than forty minutes after touching down, we were on the road and heading into the countryside.

With the change in time zones and the five-hour flight, it was early-evening when we set off and the two-hour drive was going to make our arrival a late one and still there was no answer to the mobile phone number. Despair crept over me like a cold, damp blanket.

All the way to Kenmare in Ireland; what if Finn's family were not there? Had they changed their phone? Was it going to be that simple?

Breaking my train of thought, Jermaine spoke for the first time in more than an hour, "Madam, the satnav shows that we are five minutes from our destination."

"Really?" I questioned, levering myself forward so I could see past his shoulder. "There's nothing here."

Jermaine aimed an index finger at the satnav screen. "We should find a collection of houses just over this hill."

More than two hours into the journey, I needed a pitstop to pee if nothing else. That was going to be hard if we arrived and there was no one home.

The screen did indeed show a collection of houses, what might be called a settlement elsewhere in the world, but to me was a hamlet. Smaller than a village, which needed a post office to qualify as such in my opinion, a hamlet was nothing more than a few farmhouses thrown together at a crossroads.

It didn't look like much more than that on the display and when we broached the hill and could see a few lights ahead, it didn't look like much more than a few houses in real life either.

"This is where he lived?" asked Sam, curious as ever.

"It's where his parents are listed as living," I corrected him.

Jermaine was already slowing, the two cars behind us doing likewise. From the gloom the car's headlights picked out the wooden post and the sign of a public house appeared. There were lights on inside and given the state of my bladder, popping in to ask questions there first was thoroughly enticing.

I touched a hand to Jermaine's shoulder. "Pull in there, please, sweetie."

"The pub, madam?"

"Yes, please. I need to use the facilities before we do anything else."

Jermaine did as I asked, angling the car off the road and into a carpark to the side of the building. A large, backlit Guinness sign on the side of the pub cast odd shadows. It was a touch of modernity that seemed out of place with the 19th century look of everything else.

We were in rural Ireland, a country I'd visited before but only once when the ship docked in Dublin - a modern metropolis. Out here in the countryside Ireland is a whole different thing, like a land that time forgot. That said, there were modern cars parked in the carpark including a rather nice BMW 5 series and the carpark looked to have been tarmacked in the not too distant past.

Everyone clambered out of the cars, my friends all twisting and stretching to relieve aching joints and numb posteriors.

"Any idea which of these houses we want?" asked Hideki, his eyes roaming the dark landscape punctuated only by the light shining out from a few sporadic windows and the dozen lampposts that illuminated the strip of road a hundred yards in either direction.

I needed the restroom too urgently to give it any consideration, and voiced my intention to rejoin them shortly.

The toilets were not just inside the door as I prayed they might be – sometimes that's where you find them. Forced to enter the bar of the public house itself, I braced myself for the inevitable looks I knew I would get. The opposite of a tourist mecca, the people inside probably hadn't seen a stranger in months. Possibly years.

Gentle conversation coming from inside ground to a halt the moment I stepped through the door and six men perched on barstools swivelled their behinds to see who might be coming in. Behind the bar, a woman with flaming ginger hair and a fair complexion jinked an eyebrow.

Pinned in what felt like a spotlight, I gulped nervously. I wanted to use the ladies' and return to my group, but meeting so many anticipatory gazes, it felt rude to ignore everyone.

"Can I get a large gin and tonic, please," I managed to croak through dry lips. "A Hendricks if you have one. I'm just going to use the ladies first, if that's okay?"

"It's fine by me," replied the barmaid. "You'll need to turn around though, the bogs are outside."

Super. Not a restroom so much as a bog. I hoped to heaven the 'bog' was more than the title suggested.

Arriving back outside in the carpark, I was greeted by Sam, who said, "That was quick."

"Yes," I agreed, scouting around and spotting the outbuilding I needed in a dark corner behind the pub. "Won't be long." Over my shoulder as I hurried away, thinking I needed another layer for it was anything but warm at this time of the year in Ireland, I said, "There are locals inside. I'm going to question them when I get back." It had nothing to do with the gin and tonic awaiting me at all.

When I returned a few minutes later, Jermaine was waiting for me, keeping silent vigil as always.

"Where is everyone?" I asked.

"Sam went into the pub with Schneider, madam. The rest set out to see if they could find the Murphy household."

I could hear, but not see Deepa, Martin, and the rest. Wherever their search took them, they were out of sight for now.

Jermaine opened the pub door for me. Inside I found Schneider and Sam at the bar where they were already in conversation with some of the locals.

Sam, gregarious and without guile, had chosen to announce who we were and why we were here. In a sleepy Irish hamlet, that was enough to get everyone talking.

"To be sure, it is her, Young Neil," said one man, nudging the fellow sitting next to him as I came back through the door. He had his phone in his right hand and looked to be comparing me to a photograph on his screen.

Young Neil was sixty if he was a day, but that made him a good decade younger than the other men lining the bar.

"Here's your gin and tonic," said the lady behind the bar, her tone hard to read. She placed the glass on a bright blue bar mat advertising *Sharp Lager – Polish off a Sparkler*. "You'll be wanting to know about my brother then."

My hand was reaching for the temptingly cold drink when she made the remark and it stopped me dead in my tracks. She didn't say who she was, but the inference was obvious.

"You're Finn Murphy's sister?" I asked, collecting my drink but doing nothing more than breathe in the scent rising from it while I waited.

"Aye," she nodded, pulling a glass from above her head and filling it with coke for Sam. "He died on board that ship of yours, didn't he." She was speaking to me without making eye contact, her focus on her job though I couldn't tell if that was deliberate or not.

I wouldn't call the Aurelia 'My ship', but I got what she was saying.

"That's right," I replied. "I'm sorry for your loss."

My condolence brought a half smile to her mouth. "Losing Finn wasn't that much of a loss, truth be told."

"Shame on you, Ruby," said one of the men seated at the bar.

"Oh, hush your mouth, Bertie," she snapped in response. "My brother was a no-good layabout thief, swindler, and cheat. There was never a day he made an honest buck. He got what was coming to him and the only shame here is what it did to me poor mam."

She said 'mam' not mum or even 'mom' as Barbie would say and for a silent second I pondered how it was that the same word came to be said so diversely in the same language.

Pushing the idle thought from my mind, I sipped my drink and looked squarely at the woman behind the bar. Ruby was a flaming beauty with youth on her side. I placed her in her late twenties; twenty-seven or twenty-eight maybe. Her flawless skin was as pale as can be and her green eyes looked to have been borrowed from a Disney princess. At five feet and eight inches, she was slender and attractive. A damp patch stained her top where the material stuck to her left breast. She either hadn't noticed or it happened so often she'd stopped bothering to care.

"I hate to take you away from your work, but I desperately need a few minutes of your time, Miss ... Murphy, is it?" I hazarded a guess. There was no ring on her finger that I could see.

"You can call me Ruby," she replied, handing a fresh pint of a dark ale to the man at the far end of the bar. "But I'm working until closing time and then I'm up early in the morning to tend the livestock, so I'll not want to be kept up tonight when I do finish. Where are you staying?"

She was being a little dismissive. She didn't want to talk to me and probably believed she had nothing much to say regarding her brother even though I doubted she had any idea what I was going to reveal.

"Our friend was kidnapped."

The shocking statement came from Sam, and it changed the attitude of everyone present. It was not my intention to reveal the nature behind my urgency; not to everyone, but too late now.

Ruby looked from Sam, who I believe she was scrutinising to see if he was making a joke or telling a lie, and found my eyes.

"This has to do with my brother?" she questioned.

I nodded to give confirmation and said, "I came here to find your parents. Time is short and I hope they or you can tell me something that will help us."

From the far end of the bar, the man said, "Oh, Ruby, you can leave us to mind the bar for you. It'll not be the first time."

She swung her head around to pierce him with a laser-eyed look. "Aye, Greg, and what happened the last time I left you reprobates alone?"

The men burst out in sniggers.

"Oh, we were just having a little fun," Greg tried to defend himself though he did so while laughing.

Ruby's teeth were gritted, like she was trying to reach a decision. Before she got there, the pub door opened again, the rest of my friends coming to join us.

"Did you find the house?" Jermaine asked.

Hideki replied. "Yes. It's not a house though. It's a pub."

Momentarily confused, when my brain caught up with me, I turned to ask Ruby, "This is your parent's pub?"

"Aye, it is. They nearly lost it trying to pay off Finn's debts a few years back. He ripped off the wrong bunch and would have ended up dead or worse if mam hadn't stepped in."

I began to see why she didn't have a whole lot of love for her sibling.

"Are they here?" I questioned, wondering why she was so reluctant to leave the bar and the old men alone if there were other persons here who could help out. I didn't need to quiz all three of them at the same time.

Greg, the man at the far end of the bar, who seemed to be the most talkative of the group, remarked, "What's with all the sudden interest in the Murphy family?"

Ignoring him, I pressed, "Look, I'm sorry to push, Ruby, but Sam wasn't wrong about our friend. I don't think you want me to explain it all in front of your patrons," I used an arm to indicate the line of men at the bar. "We aim to get her back and I need to ask you and your parents some questions about where Finn was in the weeks leading up to his death."

Hideki stepped in to reinforce how urgently we needed her help. "Seriously. Anything you can tell us will be of help. You might know more than you realise."

"About my brother? I don't think so. I don't know where ..." She stopped talking mid-sentence, a thoughtful look claiming her features. She'd just remembered or realised something; I would bet my life on it.

I was going to push her, but she twitched her head around to look at me and my group.

"There was a postcard."

Gilded Cage

B arbie looked at herself in the full-length mirror. Two days in the same clothes wasn't a terrible torture to endure, but she was happy to get a shower, wash her hair, and dress in something clean.

Xavier, as he insisted she continue to call him though she suspected it wasn't his real name, had done as promised and provided her with new clothes. A wardrobe of them, no less. It was all the right size, including the selection of bras which made her question if Xavier measured her or checked while she was unconscious. The creepy thought made her shudder.

The selection of clothes were hardly what she would normally wear – she lived in sports-wear most days – but it was all designer labels and really rather nice.

She gave the dress another swish. Printed with bright flowers, it was a quintessential summer wardrobe item. It didn't go with her running shoes, but the selection of shoes, some jaw-dropping brands among them, were impractical if she needed to run anywhere and escape was still number one on her list.

It was dark outside, but it had been light when they landed, and she was certain they were in Spain. Her belief was based on a list of clues: the amount of time they were in the air, the direction in which they flew, and the look of the land outside when they came down. She also saw a few road signs as they drove from the private airstrip to wherever they now were, but the place names were not ones she recognised. They did provide another clue though: the distances were listed in kilometres.

Xavier's accent was hard to place, but it was obvious he spoke Spanish. That could have meant any one of a number of South American countries, but they were in his home now, of that she was also certain, so he was Spanish too.

She needed a lot more information if she hoped to narrow down their likely current location. Ultimately, she doubted it mattered where she was. With no means with which to communicate her position to anyone else, and with no option to escape without losing her arms, she was going nowhere unless Xavier took her.

Wherever she was, she was here because Xavier had more evidence and artefacts to show her. They left Melilla in a hurry, Patricia, Jermaine, and the others giving chase. It enraged Xavier, who swore and shouted in Spanish.

Did he realise she understood every word he said?

Xavier wanted to kill Patricia Fisher in the most awful ways he could imagine. It was further proof, if she needed any, that he was never going to let her go. She knew too much about who he was.

Hungry, and convinced keeping her strength up was in her best interest, Barbie went in search of Xavier and his giant goon, Gomez.

The house felt like a palace. Barbie found marble floors and ornate furnishings in every direction. High ceilings and big windows gave a sense of space along with wonderful views over the lush countryside beyond. Barbie ignored it all. She wasn't here for the views.

"Xavier?" she called when she failed to find him or Gomez in the first two minutes. The house was vast and it spoke of the arrogant confidence he possessed that he chose to let her wander around unguarded. Or perhaps, she mused, he was certain she wouldn't risk him setting off the charges in her cuffs.

The threat was proving enough to make her behave, and once she'd eaten Barbie knew she would commit to research and help him find where the San José might have gone.

"Xavier?" she called again. Now at the foot of a curving set of marble stairs, she spotted movement and started toward it. She'd caught sight of a shadow passing by a hallway, and found a woman in casual clothes when she entered the passageway herself.

That the woman was a housekeeper or cleaner of some kind was in little doubt. She wore rubber gloves and carried a square, plastic bucket filled with sprays, liquids, and cloths. Her head bopped along to the sounds coming from a pair of earbuds.

Barbie closed the distance, certain she could quiz the woman and get some information. Just knowing where she was might make all the difference.

"Miss Berkeley?" Xavier spoke from behind her, spinning Barbie around before she could get to the maid.

Exhaling her frustration, Barbie pushed a thin smile onto her face.

"Yes, Xavier. I've been calling your name. I thought perhaps your cleaner could tell me where to find you."

As though he had not heard what she said or chose to ignore it, he said, "I see you found the clothes my housekeeper provided for you. I trust you have everything you need."

Barbie nodded. "Yes, thank you." She was being polite and cooperative and would continue to be so until she could figure out how to escape. She didn't want to kill anyone, but was coming ever more to accept that taking Xavier's phone from his dead hand might be her only hope of escape. Such a feat would require some planning or the ability to react when the right opportunity came along.

Until then, she recognised her situation for what it was: a gilded cage. There was no option to flee, and it seemed that so long as she played nice, she could expect clothes, and food and a nice room to sleep in. It was better treatment than she had expected.

"Very good," Silvestre began to walk away. "I have much to show you, Miss Berkeley. Together we are going to solve the mystery of the San José and find the location of the treasure it held. First, perhaps something to eat?"

He was acting as though he was her host and addressing her as if they were old friends or respected colleagues.

Barbie was opening her mouth to express how ravenous she felt when Xavier's phone rang. Impeccably polite, he apologised before answering the call.

"Yes, you have them?"

Barbie chose to mimic Xavier's courteous behaviour, strolling away a few paces so his conversation could be more private. She did not, however, move out of earshot.

Silvestre had been waiting for the call. Waiting significantly longer than expected, truth be told. Reaching out through his contacts to find someone capable of a simple 'locate and take' task more than twenty-four hours ago, it ought not have taken this long to find Finn Murphy's family. Chances were that they didn't know anything of value, but he wouldn't know until they were questioned.

Expecting to hear they were en route to his location, Silvestre was most disappointed to be told that was not the case.

"We have been unable to locate the targets thus far, Senor Silvestre."

"Then why are you calling me?" he questioned. They were supposed to be good at what they do. How hard could it be to grab an unsuspecting, unprotected couple in their sixties?

Certain an excuse was coming, Silvestre was shocked by what the caller said next.

"Patricia Fisher is here."

Silvestre absorbed the news and licked his lips, a nervous, unconscious action.

"You are sure?"

"It's her all right. She's got a bunch of friends with her. You want us to take her as well?"

The man was calling to renegotiate, Silvestre recognised the unspoken subtext of his question. Taking extra people meant extra pay and Silvestre was fine with that if they could get the job done.

However, what he said was, "No. She will lead you to Finn Murphy's parents. Watch her. Follow her. Strike when you can get them all and I will double your fee."

"Double?"

"Yes, double. Now get it done."

Three yards away, Barbie stood with her back to her captor while she pretended not to listen. She couldn't hear what the person at the other end of the call was saying, but would bet her life they were discussing Patty.

When Xavier ended the call without another word, Barbie turned to face him.

"You won't win," she stated simply. "Patricia is too good. You can score a draw though. She's not coming after you."

Silvestre cocked an eyebrow.

"Well, she wasn't. She is now but that's because you have me. Let me go and you can continue searching for the San José. We were never after the treasure, just the truth about Finn Murphy."

Silvestre tired of discussing the same subject. They had been over this already. He refused to believe Patricia Fisher and her friends were motivated only by the need to solve a murder. To claim such a thing was infantile.

Taking two swift paces forward, he dropped his friendly act and snatched hold of her right bicep.

"Patricia Fisher will shortly be my guest, Miss Berkeley. Just like you are my 'guest'. Everything she thinks she knows, any advantage you believe she may have, will shortly evaporate. Pray that I do not decide that I only need one of you."

Barbie allowed the awful man to drag her along. She could have fought him, she was quite certain she was stronger, but until she had a plan to escape his clutches permanently, Barbie saw no point in risking injury.

It was time to see what research material he had for her.

Keeping the Magic Alive

R uby's postcard or, more accurately, the postcard from her brother Finn, which she mentioned wasn't on the fridge where she expected it to be.

"This is where I last saw it," she claimed, her lips pressed tight as she questioned the accuracy of her memory. Her mother would know where it was, but neither of her parents were at home. "They're looking after the McCaffrey's farm," Ruby revealed. "It's on the other side of the hill. Tom McCaffrey's wife insisted he take her on holiday."

"Aye," sniggered Bertie, "It's their honeymoon. They've only been married for twenty-eight years. She said he either took her to the Maldives and to hell with his sheep or she was leaving."

Tuning Bertie out, Ruby said, "That's where they are. Mum won't have thrown it away, so you'll have to go there to ask her where it is."

"Can't we call them?" I pressed, wanting to get the information quickly. "I cannot sufficiently stress the urgency."

Ruby just sniggered, a response echoed by the gentlemen lining the bar.

"You can. Just don't expect to get through. The signal where they are is even worse than it is here."

"No signal at all," agreed Young Neil.

The news provided an explanation for why I'd been unable to raise them at any point since I started trying.

"I can take you," said Ruby, "but you'll need to make it worth my while."

She was asking for money, which felt quite mercenary. I wasn't about to argue though, and she *had* made it quite clear she needed to be up early in the morning. On the cusp of negotiating a price for her assistance, I was beaten to the punch by Jermaine.

"One moment, please, madam." He held a hand aloft to beg a few seconds' grace. To my surprise, he didn't have a question for me or for Ruby, but addressed his next question to Greg at the far end of the bar.

"Sir, earlier you said something about there being a lot of interest in the Murphy family recently? Has someone else been asking after them recently?"

Now that Jermaine had raised it, I could remember Greg's comment, but hadn't thought to question it at the time.

Greg took a swig from his pint; it was already in his hand, and he wanted to quench his thirst before he placed it back on the bar.

"Well, there were two fellas outside the pub this morning when I came past. They looked lost so I offered to help. They told me they were after finding Mr and Mrs Murphy and asked if this was the right place. I told them it was and that they were away."

"What did they say to that?" asked Deepa.

The man gave a half shrug. "They asked where they could find them and that's where I got a bit confused."

"Easily done," joked Bertie, grabbing the chance to throw some banter at his friend.

Greg fired back, "Speak for yourself," and flicked a few drops of beer from his glass.

I thought I was going to have to ask Greg to focus but he returned to his story unprompted.

"Now, where was I?"

"You were just ordering a round for everyone in the bar," said Bertie, barely able to get the words out without laughing at his own brilliant sense of humour.

Electing to ignore him, Greg said, "No, I was talking about the two men. So, they said to me they were relatives of the Murphy's, but their parents moved away years ago when they were little boys. Said they were the sons of Cathy and Michael Flannery."

His statement caused a susurration of conferred whispers to pass between the other men at the bar.

Ruby frowned. "Did you tell them where my ma and pa are, Greg?" It was a warning that he'd better not have.

Greg cocked an eyebrow. "Not after that I didn't."

Jermaine said, "I'm sorry. I'm not following. Were they related to Ruby's parents or not?"

All ears turned to hear Greg's next words.

"Well, Cathy Flannery used to be Cathy Brennan." He paused for effect. "Helen Murphy's sister and Ruby's aunt. Cathy and Michael did indeed move away when their children were kids, but unless their eldest boy, Liam, made a startling recovery, I would expect him to still be dead."

Inside my head, alarm bells went off, but Greg was still talking.

"The boys were red heads too, and the fellas this morning both had dark brown hair and they didn't look all that much like brothers to me. Also, they ought to have recognised me since I'm their uncle."

It was a small, close-knit community where everyone knew everyone. Whoever Greg met this morning had done their research. Just not quite enough of it.

Ruby got her question in first.

"Who were they, Greg?"

He jinked an eyebrow at her.

"I don't know, Ruby. I wasn't about to call them liars and see what they chose to do about it. I'll not be called a coward, but there's a big difference between that and picking a fight with two fellas half your age."

"They looked like they were in good shape?" asked Martin. "Like they could handle themselves?"

"They sure did," confirmed Greg, picking up his pint again.

Jermaine swivelled around so he was facing me, and Sam pivoted on his heels to turn away from the bar. We all looked at each other for a moment, no one saying what we all had to be thinking.

Hideki broke the silence, "We need to get to them fast." It wasn't a suggestion.

Ruby snapped, "Hey! What's going on? Who were the two men Greg met this morning? Is this something to do with my brother?"

I doubted she was going to like the worrying theory in my head, but I needed her to come with us, so she got it all in lurid detail.

"Ruby, your parents are probably in terrible danger."

"What!"

"I'm sorry. I'm don't mean to panic you, but the person who has our friend has killed several people that we know about and probably a lot more that we don't. He's after the same information as us, but for a very different purpose. We need to get to it first so we can force him to hand our friend back. The men who came here this morning knew enough about your family history to play the part of two men who could credibly be related. They were after the kind of personal information strangers wouldn't be able to demand."

I checked around, meeting the eyes of my friends to make sure I wasn't out on a limb. They all nodded. "I believe they were mercenaries sent to grab your parents. The man we are chasing wants to know what they know."

"About what?" Ruby demanded to know, anger and worry making her voice sound edgy.

I beckoned for her to come with me. "I'll tell you on the way. It's imperative we don't delay. Okay?"

"We'll look after the bar," said Greg. "Won't we boys?"

He got a round of approval from everyone except Ruby who reached above her head to grip the rope attached to a bell hanging from the ceiling.

Ruby gritted her teeth and groaned. "Do you promise?" she asked, her question aimed at all the men seated along the bar. "I remember what happened last time I left you in here."

"Ruby, we need to go," I warned. My gin and tonic was yet to be finished; I'd taken only a few sips, but as I backed toward the door, gesturing for Ruby to follow, I laughed at myself and reversed course - no chance I was letting good gin go to waste.

Greg offered Ruby a sombre look, attempting to impart his ability to take the situation serious.

"You should go, Ruby," he encouraged. "Me and the boys will leave in a few minutes. We'll just finish up and go, won't we boys?"

A chorus of agreement echoed as the old men enthusiastically assured Ruby there would be no silliness this time. Reluctantly, Ruby accepted that she didn't want to wait around to turf them out and pausing only to grab a jacket, she ran out of the pub on my heels.

It came as no surprise when Ruby insisted on travelling with me and demanded I tell her everything I knew and why I believed her parents might be in danger. The McCaffrey's farm might have only been on the other side of the hill, but that turned out to mean a twenty-minute drive around the country lanes.

I told her about the treasure, leaving very little out. I told her how we found her brother in the hold of the Aurelia and that he had in his possession enough gold and jewels to make him a very rich man. She heard about our encounters with the mystery man still known only as Dr Disguise, and how I believed he would stop at nothing to find the San José. When I finished, I didn't give her a chance to ask questions because I had some of my own.

"Where was he, Ruby? Where was your brother before he boarded the Aurelia?"

Ruby repeated the claim she made earlier. "I have no idea. I haven't spoken to my brother in years. Dad hasn't either. Mam didn't exactly forgive Finn, but she wasn't prepared to cut him off. He would send letters every now and then and she would write back. I don't think she'd heard from him in months though, except for the postcard. I only know about that because ma and pa were rowing about it when I came in one day."

"They were fighting?" I questioned, just to be sure I understood her turn of phrase.

Ruby nodded. "They sure were. Ma put the postcard on the fridge door and da found it. He flipped his lid, shouting about never letting that 'boy' darken the door again. Mum went straight for the bible, beating him back with the tale of the prodigal son. That's been a favourite of hers since Finn first started to get into trouble."

"You really think she will have it with her? The postcard, I mean?"

"It's not on the fridge any longer, so it either went in the bin, which I doubt, or it's in ma's handbag because da knows better than to go poking around in there."

The conversation reached a natural lull, and I was left to my thoughts. In many ways I'd hoped the Murphys knew about the treasure, but if Ruby was bluffing her ignorance, she had me fooled. The postcard would show where it was bought – there would be a picture on the front and on the reverse it would list where the photograph was taken. It would also show where it was posted though the two places might not be the same. Whatever it showed would give us a new reference point and, critically, a date.

The date would tell me when he was in the place where he bought the postcard and I had to hope that made all the difference. If I could backtrack from when we found him to where he was, it might be possible to figure out when he got on board the Aurelia.

Maybe. If it hadn't been dumped in the trash.

It still felt like I was scrambling in the dirt and very much like I was trying to find Barbie by looking for someone else.

Driving along the dark country roads, there was no sense in asking Jermaine to go faster, he was already driving above the posted speed limit and pushing the car as hard as the road conditions would allow. Any faster and he risked crashing.

Nearing the destination, and with Ruby giving directions, I could feel the tension building in her. Getting there and finding armed assailants had already stormed the McCaffrey's farmhouse or were attacking when we arrived would prove me right, but that wasn't what I wanted. I wanted to be wrong.

I was holding my breath when Jermaine crested the final rise and the lights of a farmhouse appeared before us. The road had no streetlights and was lit by only the moon and our headlights. Pulling off the road and up to the front of the property there was no sign of anything going on, but I wasn't exactly expecting to see a gun battle in progress.

"Mam!" Ruby had the car door open before Jermaine could stop and began calling before she was out of the car. "Mam!"

Her voice was lost to the breeze and no response came. With me chasing behind, Ruby reached the farmhouse door and hammered on it. Not that she waited for an answer. Ruby barrelled through the door and inside still shouting for her mother.

"Mam! Are ye deaf?" She turned right inside the house and kept going, heading for the illuminated rooms. Mam! Oh, um, wow," she gasped.

I wasn't far behind her and got to hear a woman's voice respond.

"Ruby! Get out! Get out, get out, get out!"

I was just stepping into the room and too close behind Ruby to avoid seeing the adventure going on inside.

"Mammy!" gasped Ruby. "What are you doing?"

About five and a half feet tall with bright ginger hair the same as her daughter's, Mammy was wearing a business suit that was many years out of style and reminded me of a young Margaret Thatcher. Matched with sensible heels and a plain handbag, her outfit was completed by a foot long wooden rule which she was slapping into the palm of her left hand.

However, Ruby's mother was on the periphery of my vision because my eyes were locked on the other person in the room.

Ruby's father (I hope) was attired in a lacey, black and white French Maid's costume. The dress fit him, which denoted it had been made to be worn by a man because he was twice the size of his wife. Coated in black hair along his chest, back, arms, and legs, he had very little left on his head and what was there had turned to grey.

He wore black ankle boots in a style more commonly associated with women, and held a feather duster in his right hand.

My eyes were about as wide as they could go and though I knew I was supposed to be averting my gaze and reversing course to get back outside, I couldn't quite convince my feet to move.

Ruby's father looked mortified and said, "Um.'

The wooden rule slapped into Helen's palm with a resounding, *whack!*

"I didn't say you could stop cleaning," she growled, her husband instantly attacking a shelf with his feather duster, his cheeks still burning scarlet.

"Mam, what is going on?" Ruby had both hands gripping her head. "Is this why you told me not to come to the farmhouse?"

Helen Murphy gave her daughter a sympathetic look.

"Your father and I have been married a long time, dear. Sex gets a bit samey after a while. We like to spice things up sometimes."

"Spice things up?" Ruby echoed, horrified and possibly scarred for life by interrupting her parents' nocturnal activities.

Placing a hand on Ruby's shoulder, her mother said, "You will too if you ever give in and marry one of your many suitors."

Ruby shot a glare at her mother, but offered no argument which I suspect was more to do with wishing she could gouge out her eyeballs and wash them in bleach to remove the images now locked inside her brain.

Behind me, the rest of my friends were filing into the house. Heading for the sound of conversation, they all had a gasp and something shocked to utter when they saw Ruby's parents.

Jermaine did the sensible thing and closed the door, leaving only me and Ruby in the farmhouse's living room.

"Anyway, young lady," Ruby's mother changed the subject. "What are you doing here? Who is minding the pub? Please tell me you didn't leave Greg and Bertie in charge again."

"I locked up early, mam," Ruby frowned. "I can explain later. Right now what I need is for you to tell me where Finn's postcard is."

Ruby's mother blinked, hearing the question and understanding it, yet looking mystified, nevertheless.

With a small shake of her head, Ruby's mother said, "Finn's postcard? What is this all about, Ruby? Who are all those people outside?" Twitching her head around to look at me, she asked "Who are you?"

I felt that I ought to extend my hand and introduce myself, but I wasn't entirely convinced shaking hands with her would be sanitary.

Compromising, I gave a little wave. "Hi, I'm Patricia Fisher."

"She's that sleuth we saw on the news in the summer, Mam. Remember?"

Clearly she did; I saw the recognition in her eyes when she looked at me again.

"Helen," Ruby's mother extended her right hand, giving me no option other than to shake it unless I felt like slapping it away. Dropping her hand back to her side, she said, "I still don't know what this is about."

"The postcard, Mam," Ruby reminded her. "And have you seen or heard anyone around here today?"

I could see Helen was about to start asking even more questions, so I cut in before she could.

"Finn was found on board the ship on which I live and work as a detective, Helen. He had treasure in his possession. Yes, treasure. Like gold and diamonds and stuff," I clarified so she wouldn't question what I meant. "I think it's what got him killed. Sorry for your loss," I added quickly.

"Damn fool probably brought it on himself," growled the father.

Dressed as he was in a frilly lace dress and French knickers, I'd been happily pretending I couldn't see him. Now I had little choice because Helen was upset and he was the focus of her ire.

"Maybe he did!" Helen snapped, rounding on him. "Maybe he was a toerag and a layabout no good swindler. He was our son, Kenny! He was *my* son, and I miss him!"

Kenny backed away, his wife's wrath enough to stifle any further comments.

Getting back to what I was saying, I touched Helen's arm. "I'm trying to catch the person behind your son's murder, Helen, but there is more going on than my investigation now. Your son found a priceless horde of treasure from a Spanish ship that supposedly sank more than three hundred years ago."

"I'm sorry, what?" Unsurprisingly, Helen had a few questions."

"There's no time," I implored her to just go with it. "There is a man who will do anything to find it and he has taken one of my friends because we got too close. I need to see that postcard. If you know anything about where your son was or what he found, it could help us to get our friend back."

Ruby cut over me, "There were two men outside the pub earlier today, Mam. They claimed to be Cathy and Michael's boys …"

"But Liam died years ago," Helen voiced her confusion.

"Exactly," I seized control of the conversation again. "I think they have been sent by the same man who has our friend. I might be wrong … I hope I'm wrong, but if I'm not …"

I didn't get to complete my sentence because the lights abruptly went out. Not like someone flicked the switch, but very much like someone cut the power.

Escape in the Dark

"**M**adam!" Jermaine burst back through the door before I could blink.

"I'm here," I replied.

"What's going on?" asked Helen.

From the hallway, Martin reported, "There are figures outside. Looks like half a dozen or more. We should expect them to be armed."

I cursed that we were not. Well, not me. I fired a gun once when I was really pushed to my limit and beyond, and hope to never repeat the experience. I willingly left the firearms handling to other, more capable persons, and cursed they were not loaded for bear right now.

Grabbing Helen's arm, I said, "Are there any guns in the house? Shotguns for vermin control or something?"

"Of course," she replied. "It's not my house though, so wherever Tom keeps his shotguns, I don't have a key."

I swore inside my head.

In the hallway and beyond, I could see Sam, Molly, Schneider and all the others moving stealthily. They were staying away from the windows while making sure they could see what was happening outside.

Deepa darted back into sight, sounding a little breathless when she announced, "I don't think they have anyone covering the back of the house. If we are going to make a break for it, we need to go now."

There was no discussion, no need to debate the idea. Ahead of me, Deepa was already gone, Martin, Molly, and Sam all following. Martin, Hideki, and Jermaine paused to let me catch up, ushering that I should turn right and head to the back door in silence when I passed them.

I was in the farmhouse's kitchen, next to an old, solid Aga, its gentle warmth spilling out to make the room toasty when we all heard the loud hailer.

"Patricia Fisher. It is time to give yourself up," the voice boomed. It was a man's voice and came with an Irish lilt. "There is no escape, but this does not have to end with bloodshed."

He continued talking as we snuck out the back of the house.

"We need you along with Helen and Kenny Murphy. Everyone else is free to go. I will give you to the count of five. There will not be a six. I will not be responsible for the lives that are lost if you force us to come in to get you."

I didn't know who they were or how they found us given that Helen and Kenny were staying at a friend's farm, but the how of it didn't matter. They were armed and would come for us. We might have slipped out the back of the farmhouse, but what now? Escape on foot over the pastures behind the farm?

Well, apparently, yes.

Sort of.

Tractors

- -

"Tractors?" asked Hideki.

Behind the farmhouse, which sat at the edge of the farm and close to the road, were several large steel-sided barns. Two looked relatively new. The McCaffrey's kept sheep, that much I knew, and I guess rounding them up and taking them food required farm machinery, because we were being led into a barn where Kenny, still kitted out like a French maid complete with black and white feather duster, promised there were vehicles we could use.

He wasn't wrong.

I didn't bother asking for an explanation, but there were far more tractors than any one farm could ever use. Even in the dim light I could see they were all shiny and well-looked after. Loved even.

"Tom's a bit of a tractor nut," Helen explained. "He buys them, fixes and restores them, and keeps them in here. It's another reason why he hasn't taken his wife on their honeymoon until now – he kept spending what the farm earns on his hobby."

That was all very well and nice, but how were we supposed to escape armed mercenaries using tractors?

"They'll not be able to follow," Ruby explained, climbing into the driver's seat of a bright green and yellow John Deere. I'm no tractor enthusiast, but there a few brand names I think we all know and recognise. "If we can get out the gate and into the pasture, we'll be halfway up the hill before they know where we've gone."

As plans went, I thought it to be terrible, but I had no alternative to offer.

We loaded onto four of the pristine tractors, picking ones close to the doors while Hideki and Jermaine swung them wide open to let the moonlight flood in. There was barely a cloud in the sky outside and it was cold, our breath forming clouds of vapour in the air above our heads.

The voice on the loudspeaker had given up talking which meant we couldn't have long before they were in the house. They would soon realise we were not in it, but I doubted it would get to that because the moment the first engine started they would know where we had gone.

Beyond the barn doors, we needed to turn a hard left where a gate leading to the fields blocked our way.

Hideki and Jermaine got to it just as the lights started to come on in the house.

"Now," said Kenny. He was getting us away from the danger and taking charge. Given his costume it was about as out of place as it could be. Somewhere along the way, I noted, he had managed to swap out his heeled ankle boots for a pair of wellies. However, the man had to be freezing in his tiny lacey underwear, his arms and legs exposed, plus most of his chest and back. If he stayed outside for too long, he would suffer hypothermia or worse.

With a roar, the engines came to life. Ruby's parents, accustomed to a life of farming, had a tractor each. One of my friends was seated behind each of them with two more hanging on to the sides. I was behind Ruby on the John Deere she promised was probably the fastest in the barn, and a fourth was being driven by Sam, who knew how to operate it from a summer camp activity thing he'd taken part in before he came to work for me.

Kenny's tractor lurched forward and then took off. It moved faster than I expected which made me question how fast a tractor could go. I knew I'd seen them on the road with traffic overtaking them; that had to mean they were capable of thirty or forty at least.

Failing to take sufficient grip, I almost flipped off the back of Ruby's steed when she started moving. The next thing I knew we were whipping through the open air, sweeping out through the gate, and racing up the hill.

I twisted in my seat to look behind; I wanted to make sure Hideki and Jermaine were able to safely clamber on board Sam's tractor. I got a wave from Sam and a big, goofy grin when he saw me looking.

It was nice to see he was having fun, but my focus was not so much on him, but the dark, shadowy figures running from the house. They were giving chase, the ugly outline of their weapons visible as the shiny metal caught the moonlight.

The crack, crack, crack sound of automatic fire filled the air, but only for a moment. The shooter was knocked to the ground by another of the team amid shouts that I had to be taken alive.

It chilled my blood to hear them express their intent so clinically, but would they catch us now? We were away, churning up the land as Tom's vintage tractors showed what brilliant pieces of engineering design they were.

Our cars were behind us and lost, but if I had my geography right we were heading back to the pub or, at least, in that general direction. There we would be able to get a phone signal and call for help. The only problem I saw with that scenario was the likely response time. How far away were the nearest cops? Would they be equipped to handle a gang of highly trained armed gunmen? Probably not. This was rural Ireland, not a major city.

With those worrying thoughts echoing in my head, I realised the thing we had all forgotten: Tom had lots of tractors.

Barbie's Research

The wealth of artefacts, materials, studies, and books owned by Xavier and pertaining to the San José was staggering. In different circumstances, Barbie would have been in her element and overjoyed to be locked away where she could immerse herself in history and research.

The fact that she was 'actually' locked away took the shine off the experience, but Xavier wasn't really giving her a choice about whether she dug in or not.

The twinge of hope she felt when her eyes alighted upon a powerful looking computer in the corner of the room. If he left her alone, even for a couple of minutes, she would be able to contact the outside world and send messages to her friends.

It was hard not to look at it, but she forced herself to look at the collection laid out for her to inspect.

The physical artefacts drew her instantly; they were so tactile and exciting. Knowing they were hundreds of years old gave her chills when she reached out to touch them. She curled her fingers inward though, her hand stopping short. The artefacts were interesting, but contained no information. There was nothing to be gained by inspecting them.

Led into a library of sorts, Barbie was standing before a long wide table on which the many seafaring artefacts were arranged. To her right, reference books lined the shelves of an entire wall. To her rear, another shelf held boxes. They were labelled in Spanish, which created no barrier for the Californian gym instructor. She was fluent in several languages, but she grew up speaking Spanish almost as often as she spoke English.

The boxes were filled with more delicate artefacts – letters Xavier collected over the years, plus journals and diaries. They were not necessarily written by persons who had been on the San José, but could be from relatives of those who sailed or important persons who might have had dealings with the ship.

"Where do you want me to start?" she asked, looking at the collection and not the man standing behind and to her right.

"That is entirely your choice, Miss Berkeley. I shall not bias your instincts. If you will excuse me, I have other tasks to which I must attend, but I will return to check on you shortly. When I do, I believe we should review the files on your laptop. I have some questions for you."

Barbie didn't respond other than to give a slight nod of her head to show she heard what Xavier said. He was back to being super polite, but she wasn't going to allow herself to be fooled. He believed he was going to acquire Patty, and the 'other tasks' he mentioned could be arranging to kill people for all she knew.

He left the room, locking the door from the outside so she could not leave and wander the house.

She counted to three, staring at the door and listening for his footsteps to fade away. The moment she felt she might be able to get away with it, she raced to the computer, grabbing the mouse with a shake to see if the screen would come to life.

Her heart skipped when it flashed into life a moment later and she heard the oh so familiar sound of the computer's cooling fan beginning to whir.

There wasn't even a password!

Dropping into the seat, she planned to navigate to log into her emails. It would take seconds to fire out a message and she could send it to multiple recipients to be sure someone would look at it. She would also need to find a program that could identify her location. She thought there might be something she could do with her IP address but wasn't sure.

Convinced she would figure it out, her brow began to crease because she couldn't access her emails. Blinking in confusion, she realised the odd-looking search engine the computer brought up in lieu of what she asked for was not an internet but an intranet – an enclosed controlled version of the same. The architect behind it was able to provide internet search functionality, but in a limited manner where they determined what types of websites could be explored.

She had a computer at her fingertips, and it was useless to her. Maybe, if given enough time, she could figure a way around it, but after twenty minutes of fiddling, Barbie accepted that she just wasn't going to get a message out. Xavier was too clever for her.

With a sigh, Barbie sucked on her teeth and looked about. There was no point wasting further time on the stupid computer; it wouldn't get her anywhere. However, Xavier would return sooner or later, and she wanted it to appear as though she had been working since he left.

Ten minutes later, she had the contents of several boxes spread out on a portion of the central table. The artefacts that previously covered it were pushed to one side to give her space and she was reading the diary of a man called Samuel Cristobal with great interest.

His father sailed on the San José as the bursar. One of the senior men on board, Henri Cristobal was remembered fondly by his son, but the odd thing about the diary, and presumably why Barbie found a small red flag poking from between two pages, was that he mentioned travelling to see him. He spoke about it in the future tense: it was something he planned to do.

Some pages later another red flag attached to the page revealed a further key clue - Samuel was lamenting his father's death. The date listed was August 12th 1710, two years after the San José sank.

Barbie read on, fascination drawing her through the pages. Samuel Cristobal missed the chance to see his father again, yet wrote about the prize that waited for him if he could retrace his father's steps.

Barbie's eyes flared. She was reading about a man who supposedly died when the San José sank, but clearly didn't. He didn't return home because he was supposed to be dead, but wrote to his son in Spain to arrange their reunion somewhere else.

The door behind her opened, Xavier coming through it.

"Ah, I see you have found the diary of Samuel Cristobal."

"It's incredible," Barbie admitted, the tide of emotion pouring off the page sweeping her up, so she momentarily forgot she was talking to her kidnapper. "I think Samuel's father knew the location of the treasure. I found three separate references to a 'prize'."

Xavier nodded and came to stand at the end of the table just a couple of yards from his captive.

"Yes. If you continue to read, you will discover that Samuel planned to travel to join his father. Henri hints that there are 'great rewards' and that Samuel alone cannot collect them. He writes that it will take a team of men to recover what he has. Henri is careful to never use the words 'treasure' or 'gold' and though Samuel questions the nature of the 'prize' and its location, Henri never provides that information."

Barbie frowned, looking from the thin parchment paper in her cotton glove-clad hands, and back to Xavier.

"Wait, what am I missing? There's nothing from Samuel's father, only that he references what his father has told him. His father is somewhere – he never says where and I got the impression Samuel didn't know, but he couldn't travel to meet him because he wasn't safe. However, you're talking about Henri as though you read the letters he sent to his son."

"That's because I have, my dear." Xavier went to the wall of boxes behind her, retrieving one to place it on the table to her left.

Opening it, he removed a bundle of very old, very faded letters. Barbie's heartrate tapped out a staccato beat at seeing the wax and stamps where the author once sealed them.

"I'm afraid I do not have every letter. It is clear when you read them that some in the sequence are missing. Indeed, it may be that Samuel never received them all, such was the efficiency of mail in those days."

Barbie wanted to take the letters from Xavier, and had to tell herself to hold back as the man continued to explain what he knew.

"The Spanish had enemies everywhere, most specifically England at this point in history, but Henri could have been almost anywhere. I believe he chose not to return home because he was injured – his ailments, of which there appear to be many, are mentioned more than once in the letters and his son enquires about them in return. Then there is the inconvenient fact that Henri Cristobal was supposed to be dead. The San José sank with all hands when it exploded. That is the report the British filed, so Henri needed to stay away from Spain or face some very uncomfortable questions."

"You've been through this in detail," Barbie tried to shortcut the conversation. "Is this a dead end? I mean, other than it proves the San José didn't sink with all the treasure on board."

Xavier, his eyes on the small pile of ancient letters, placed the one he tenderly held back on top.

"This is as close as I have ever come, Miss Berkeley. I believe Henri knew he was dying. You will read it in the words of his final few letters. However he sustained his injuries, he never fully recovered from them, and his health deteriorated. He wrote to Samuel telling him he would have to recover the 'prize' by himself. That he should arrange a team of trusted friends and to tell them they would all be rich beyond any fantasy they could ever imagine."

Barbie gasped. "Then he *did* have the treasure's location!"

Xavier met her gaze. "That would appear to be the case. You are undoubtedly thinking that he must then have surely told his son and he did."

Barbie stopped breathing. Only for a tantalising moment though. It occurred to her almost as soon as the excitement struck, that there had to be a missing part of the puzzle. Were that not the case, Xavier, crazed murderer that he is, would have found the treasure already.

"For many years I allowed myself to believe the treasure was in England. It made a lot of sense for that to be the case. Henri would be trapped there, living a life on the run or as a vagrant. There is a code, you see? It is in a letter that Henri sent towards the end of his life. When he accepted he was never going to claim the treasure for himself, he needed to provide his son with a way to do so, but had to do so in code so that anyone who might intercept his letter, or subsequently read it, wouldn't be able to understand it."

"But you haven't been able to crack it." Barbie stated what was obvious.

Xavier nodded, his eyes staring ahead at some point in the past.

"The code is gibberish, I'm afraid. In another letter he provides the key for it: the Bible. I assumed it would be the current Bible in circulation at the time, but it was not. Deferring to other Bibles that might have been held in the Cristobal household, I performed the same task. I employed scholars and experts, religious men, and academics, setting them all the task of cracking the code to reveal a location, but none of them were able to find a start point. Samuel Cristobal died at home in Spain shortly after his father and never completed the quest. Though I have not been able to ascertain a cause for his death, I do not believe it was foul play."

Barbie was listening, unwilling to interrupt, and found that she genuinely felt some sympathy for the man who had made finding the lost ship and its treasure his life's work. Her empathy lasted for as long as it took for her to remember the explosive cuffs on her wrists again. If asked, she would admit that she too wanted to solve the mystery. It felt tantalisingly close, but what she knew she needed to do was find a way to get the cuffs off or deactivate them. Silvestre said he had an app on his phone, but where was it? Did he have it on him?

If she attacked him now, Barbie was sure she could overwhelm him – she was a good deal stronger than most men. What then though? If the phone wasn't hidden about his person, she would find herself in serious hot water. And could she take the cuffs off or was there an anti-tamper device? What if she escaped with his phone but still had them on? Did he have another way to set them off?

There were too many unknowns for Barbie to risk doing anything – precisely what Xavier wanted.

"I'm afraid, my dear, the Cristobal correspondence is a dead end. You must find another approach."

Barbie watched Xavier replace all the letters and Samuel Cristobal's diary back into the box. He treated it all with the reverent care it deserved, returning the box to the shelf once everything was inside.

Pointing to the computer, he said, "Perhaps there is more to be gained by revisiting Finn Murphy's details. I had the files from your laptop transferred to it already. Soon we will be able to quiz his family about where their son was in the days leading up to his death. We need to be ready to ask them the right questions."

Barbie said nothing, wondering quite what that could mean for Mr and Mrs Murphy.

Tractor Chase!

From out of the barn and through the gate came six more tractors. Each appeared to have a lone rider which meant they would be lighter. Did that mean they would be faster? Were we about to be caught in our cross-country race, or did that come down to engine power and strange mechanical terms like torque?

I had no idea, but I shouted to be heard over the roar of our engine.

"What?" asked Ruby.

"They are in pursuit!" I repeated, tapping her arm and pointing to make her look back the way we'd just come.

Ruby uttered several rude words before shouting, "Mam! Mammy!"

Helen's head jinked around at the sound of her daughter's alarm-filled shouts, and she tracked my pointing arm to see the danger too.

I didn't know if they were gaining or not, it was too dark out here on the field. The moon shone down but all it really did was turn an invisible blob into a slightly more visible blob. That worked in our favour, of course, for had they been able to see who was on which tractor, I think they would have started shooting.

At the rear, Sam was doing his best to keep pace, but his tractor simply wasn't as fast as Ruby's. The men in pursuit would get to him first and I was starting to freak out. What was my way to save this situation?

If I surrendered, they might take me and leave my friends alone. Not willingly, I suspected, but if I got off now and everyone else kept going, I could lead the chasing group in a different direction to buy my friends a little time.

It sounded like a crazy idea in my head, but I was giving it serious thought, nevertheless. They would take me to Dr Disguise and I would finally learn his name. I hoped. I mean, I didn't know for certain that the man chasing us was here because of the treasure, but it was a sensible assumption to make. I could be reunited with Barbie and the two of us would be able to work together to get free.

I won't claim I liked the plan or that it felt like a winner, but it possessed certain merits; my friends not getting shot being one of the big ones. Making my decision, I was about to swing a leg over and jump off when Ruby shouted something. I had to ask her to repeat what she said.

"We're not far from the pub!" she shouted. "We've got a locker full of shotguns there!" She checked over her shoulder. "We're going to make it. Don't you worry."

A locker full of shotguns and a position from which we could defend ourselves? It sounded like a wish fulfilled. I looked to our rear again. The chasing pack were closing in, but only on Sam and I didn't think they were going to get close enough to know the people on his tractor were expendable.

Gambling with lives yet again, I settled back into the seat and held on.

The next three minutes ticked by far too slowly, yet as we continued to hurtle over the rough terrain, the tractors all going as fast as they could, I began to make out the outlines of the little hamlet again. The streetlights were shrouded by the trees around them, or we would have seen it all so much sooner, but a sigh of relief fell from me when I accepted we were going to get there in time.

Only just, but that was a whole lot better than not quite.

Just ahead of me, Kenny didn't bother to slow down when he got to a fence that bordered the field behind the pub. Instead, he barrelled through it, his tractor's mighty wheels smashing the steel posts and plastic mesh out of the way and squishing them into the ground.

Helen whipped through the same spot a moment later with Ruby right on her heels.

Ruby screamed, "Hold on!" as she hit the brakes hard. The tractor slewed when it bounced down a bank and onto the tarmac of the carpark right next to the bogs.

It was abandon ship at that point, everyone leaping from their seats with the exception of Kenny. Not dressed for the temperature outside, he'd managed to race all the way up the hill and back down the other side, but he was more or less frozen in place now and had to be helped from his tractor.

"Get him inside! Quickly!" commanded Martin, grabbing one of the large man's legs as Deepa, Molly and Schneider all jumped in to help out.

Helen was already at the door, getting it open with a key.

"Hurry! All of you!" she urged. "Ruby, take them to the shotguns. Get them armed. No one is taking me anywhere I don't want to go!"

Sam was fifty yards back, the chasing pack only another fifty behind them. It was going to be hard for them to get here, get off, and get inside before the gunmen could see who they were.

I wanted to get inside, but I couldn't risk it. I couldn't risk the chance that someone might open fire. If I was visible, maybe they would think twice about it and we could all run in together.

Rooted to the spot, my breath caught in my throat when I heard Sam's engine cough. It caught again, but then died completely! We were so close, and he had run out of fuel!

I heard them shouting at each other. Sam couldn't get the tractor to start again, and the guys were smart enough to know they needed to go the rest of the way on foot. I watched their silhouettes leaping from the ailing farm vehicle, their arms and legs then nothing but dark blurs as they sprinted headlong to get to me.

I made urgent motions and I shouted for them to hurry; a redundant instruction if ever there was one.

Behind them the chasing tractors fanned out, the six men riding them communicating without using the need to shout. I assumed they had radios of some form, probably the type that strap to a person's throat and is voice activated when they speak. Whatever the case, they were spreading out so they could come in from all sides.

Thinking it was time I got inside – the guys were going to be with me in seconds – I turned to find Martin and Deepa coming back outside to cover Sam, Jermaine, and Hideki's final yards.

Only they weren't.

"Where are the shotguns?" I gasped. How could they fire off warning shots to push the gunmen back if they still weren't armed?

"There isn't any," Deepa told me, glumly. "The locker is there, but it's empty."

"They've been robbed?" I blurted, shocked at the irony of it. In the short period since we left the pub someone had broken in and emptied the place.

Martin tugged at my arm. "Come inside, Patricia. There's no time left."

Go inside? What for? Without the promised firepower I hoped my team would find here, we were defenceless. The race across the hill was for naught. The gunmen on their tractors would be able to do as they pleased. My only option now was to surrender and hope my friends and Finn Murphy's family would be able to get away.

I yanked my arm free with a look of apology.

"I'm sorry, Martin. This has to end here. I'll not risk anyone being hurt on my account. They are not going to kill me. They will take me to … him. The man behind it all." I met

Martin's eyes. "Promise me you'll get everyone to safety. Once they have me, I think they will leave."

Jermaine arrived, Hideki by his side as they ran through the busted fence. The pair were dragging Sam along rather than slow to his pace.

"Madam, I believe it is time for you to evacuate this area," Jermaine remarked in his usual understated manner. He was a little out of breath and there were flecks of dirt all over his clothes. Like Martin, he wanted to get me somewhere safe, but it was too late for that.

In fact, it was too late for anything.

A volley of shots rang out through the night, the bullets stitching a line in the brickwork four feet above my head.

I spasmed with fright, but held my ground.

"Go! All of you. Get away now!" Jermaine was about to argue, so I said, "Take Sam and get him to safety, Jermaine!"

Maybe he would have complied, and maybe he wouldn't, but the gunmen on their tractors were arriving and they were too close for anyone to go anywhere. Those who swept around to the sides had arrowed in again to cut off the road in both directions.

My stomach tensed when I looked to my left to find the way blocked. To the right was blocked as well and the remaining four gunmen were closing in on the farmhouse from the rear. We could probably get inside via the backdoor but what then? They would follow us in and if we barricaded the doors they would smash the windows and come in that way.

I raised my hands and stepped forward.

"Madam?" Jermaine warned. "I will not let them take you."

He tensed his body, pulling his arms into a fighting pose while Hideki did the same just a few feet away. The idiots would fight to protect me using their martial arts against automatic weapons. I'm sure that worked in the movies, but I wasn't willing to find out how effective they could be in real life.

I placed a hand on Jermaine's arm and tugged at it until he met my eyes. The gunmen were closing in, their weapons held confidently. They knew they dominated the environment, and no one was coming to save us.

"Sweetie, they are going to take me to Barbie. Nothing else will change other than Barbie will have some company. The rest of you will need to figure out the mystery, find the San José and come get me. I will be fine, but if you try to stop them, they will hurt you and they might hurt Sam or Molly or anyone of the others here."

He knew I was right, yet what I wanted him to do, to accept was happening whether he liked it or not, went against every fibre of his being.

Turning to face the approaching men, I said, "There's no need for any violence. You don't need to hurt anyone. I will go with you. I know where the San José is," I lied.

The man I was speaking to, the one nearest to me, glanced at a colleague.

"The San José?" he questioned, checking to see if that meant anything to the other man. When he got a shrug in return, he looked back at me. "Sorry, lady. You *are* coming with us, you got that part right. We're taking Mr and Mrs Murphy too. I'm afraid we're not leaving anyone behind though. Not alive anyway." He raised the muzzle of his gun, aiming it at Jermaine standing right next to me.

He was going to shoot him!

They were going to take the people they came for and leave no witnesses.

I threw myself in the way of the gun, buying an extra second on impulse. How could it have come to this? How could we beat the odds so many times, defeat so many enemies, only to lose now in a nowhere hamlet that was barely a speck on the map to a gang of gunmen who probably didn't even know or care who they were killing?

My friends were being rousted from the house, brought outside where they could be accounted for and the gunmen could be sure they had the ones they were instructed to take before they started shooting.

I felt sick. I thought I might genuinely vomit.

"Here, lads, what do you think of the cleaning staff?" joked one man, shoving Kenny roughly from the house. The sight of the heavyset, hairy man in the French maid outfit drew a laugh from most of the armed men, but a cannon blast of sound shut them up again.

The sudden noise jolted me, and terrified I looked around to see who had been shot. Had I not scanned the group, looking for one of my friends to fall, I might have missed Greg and Bertie popping up like jack-in-the-boxes from behind the garden wall.

They both held shotguns, their barrels aimed straight at the nearest gunman. It wasn't just them though. Too stunned even to breathe, I saw the other men from the pub revealing themselves as they stepped out of their hiding places. That would have made it six on six but the guys from the pub had clearly been busy because there were new faces coming from every direction and every last one of them had a shotgun.

The team of men who chased us were looking around, their motions frantic – were they going to start shooting their way out?

The fear I held made my heart beat so hard I thought I could hear it in the brief silence that followed the locals' appearance.

Then one of the gunmen dropped, keeling over forward to hit the ground with his face. The shotgun blast I heard went into his back. It acted as a catalyst, like a starter's gun going off.

Jermaine exploded into action, launching his body forward. I was right next to him and couldn't tell you how he did it. One moment he was stock still, the next he was a human missile, his arms and legs scything out to strike the two men nearest me as though they'd been asked to catch a running lawnmower.

To my right, Martin, Hideki, Deepa and the others were tackling another of the gunmen. In their confidence, they came too close and in so doing reduced the effectiveness of their weapons.

I heard a volley of shots going off. They struck the ground and the wall of the pub as the man holding the gun had it torn from his grip.

The remaining gunmen found themselves surrounded by locals pointing shotguns. Recognising the situation for what it was, they surrendered.

It all happened so fast. My friends had been about to die and now they were all safe. Not only that, we finally had some advantage.

Forcing courage into my legs, I managed to get my feet to move.

"Is everyone okay?" I begged to know.

Greg nudged the injured gunman with a boot. "This 'uns not feeling too clever," he sniggered.

The man on the ground groaned, proving he was still alive at least.

Helen, her coat wrapped tightly around her, stormed across to where Greg stood, her face filled with thunder.

Greg glanced at her, his smile still in place until he saw how she looked. The mirth dropped from his eyes, replaced with a touch of panic.

"Greg Flannery," Helen growled. "Did you break into my house and then my shotgun cabinet, empty everything inside and form a militia out of your drunken reprobate friends and their relatives?"

Greg looked around for help. Any help. No one was saying anything.

"I'm waiting," Helen snarled.

Pinned to the spot, the shotgun in his hands became nothing more than something to twiddle nervously.

"Well?"

Unable to avoid Helen's glare, Greg winced when he finally said, "Um, yes?" His response came in the form of a question; he was asking if his actions were acceptable or not.

We all got Helen's answer a moment later when she threw her arms around the old man and pulled him into a hug.

The gunmen were secured on the ground, disarmed and tied up by the time Helen released Greg. Bertie and some of the other old men from the bar came over to get their hugs too and the 'how' of it all came to light.

"We overheard what that lady and her friends said about you being in danger," Greg revealed. "Ruby rushed off, leaving us to drink up and let ourselves out, and we got to talking."

"Did you now," questioned Kenny, who'd nipped inside to quickly change his outfit. Now attired in trousers (thank goodness) and a coat with a flat cap on his head to ward off the cold, he wanted to know why they thought to arm themselves and how they managed to open his cabinet.

"Oh, that part was easy, Kenny," Greg chided. "You keep the key on the wall, and it's even got a label on it."

Helen narrowed her eyes at her husband. "I told you it was supposed to be placed somewhere secure."

Spokesperson for the group, Greg continued to explain, "We heard some shots being fired when we were leaving the pub ..."

"That was half an hour after I told you all to drink up and get out," Ruby interrupted to point out.

Greg nodded to acknowledge her point. "Aye, but like I said, we got to talking. So, we heard the shots coming from the direction of the McCaffrey farm and figured maybe it was time to act."

"Then we heard the tractors," Bertie chipped in.

"Aye," agreed Greg. "Then we heard the tractors and it was soon obvious you were heading our way. So we called everyone, and Young Neil ran around knocking on doors."

"And we hid," added Bertie, a wide grin plastered across his face.

While the local Irish people were reliving the experience and Kenny was reopening the bar – he felt tots of whiskey for all were required at the very least – Jermaine, Martin, and the rest of my security team searched the gunmen and Hideki took Molly to tend to the one who got a barrel full of shot in his back and buttocks. He was going to survive just fine, Hideki assured me, but needed a hospital.

The police were coming, but before they arrived in however long that took, I wanted some answers. Taking it as red that the gunman who did the talking was the one in charge, I placed one knee on the ground next to his head.

"What is the name of the man who hired you?" I demanded to know.

He smirked and a small snort of derisory laughter left his nose. "You'll get nothing from any of us, sweetheart. Don't waste your time."

"He kidnapped a friend of mine ..."

"That's no concern of mine."

"What do you have to gain by protecting him? I just need a name."

He laughed again. "I'm sure you do, but you'll not get it from me. Besides, I don't know it. This is the kind of business where transactions take place in a bidding room. I've no need to know who is paying, only that they have."

Jermaine looked like he might hurt the man if he didn't start talking. He wanted Barbie back as much as if not more than me.

Rising out of my crouch, I asked, "Did he have a phone, sweetie?"

"Yes, madam." Jermaine held out his hand to Sam, who produced a modern iPhone from a plastic, supermarket carrier bag.

The man's eyes flared in panic, and he tried to bury his face in the ground. Moments later he was hauled to his knees, and I was able to hold the phone in front of his face to activate the facial recognition.

Phone unlocked I scrolled through his contacts. If he was here on a job, the person who hired him might or might not have been in direct contact, but if he had there would be contact in the last twenty-four hours.

The text messages revealed nothing, other than he had two different women on the go. There were messages of affection and sexual promise to Jessica and Elaine. I forwarded messages from each to the other with a simple explanation of what they were seeing.

Ok, so I have a vindictive streak. Treat women better, dirtbag.

The phone's call log showed only one international number. The code was for Spain, the same country to which the plane's tailfin was registered. Flicking my head to take the hair away from my left ear, I thumbed the button to make a call and waited for a voice to answer.

It rang for several seconds and I thought it was going to switch to voicemail when the tone changed and I heard a man take a breath.

"Is it done?" he asked. "Do you have them?"

A smile teased at the corners of my mouth. It was the voice of the fake Professor Noriega. Since he first came into my suite weeks ago when the Aurelia was docked in the Canaries, he'd had the upper hand. He still had Barbie, so it was not the case that all the power had just shifted, but I was getting there.

"Do I have them?" I asked. "Yes. Yes, I do. I don't suppose I could convince you to swap them for Barbie, could I? They are mostly unharmed."

The response when it came was not immediate, the man at the other end taking his time to adjust mentally to the unexpected shift. I would have preferred him to have started shouting and swearing. That would have told me I could upset him and get under his skin. A person like that would make mistakes and act rashly.

My opponent was cool as a cucumber instead.

"Very good, Mrs Fisher. It is you, yes?"

"It is. You can call me Patricia though. What can I call you?"

I severely doubted he was going to give me his name, and was surprised when he said, "Xavier. You should call me Xavier. It will give you something to scream when I cut out your heart."

A cold shiver passed through me accompanied by a wave of nausea.

Gritting my teeth, I replied, "And you can write Patricia on the walls of your cell, Xavier. If we can dispense with the unpleasantness, perhaps we can get down to business. You have something I want. Give her back to me and I will leave you alone. You can have the treasure – if you can find it – I just want Barbie back."

There was no pause while he considered my offer, no need for deliberation. He snapped back, "Too late, Patricia. Miss Berkeley has already worked out where the San José is. She is alive for now, but if I catch the slightest sniff that you are near, I will send you a piece of her on your birthday for the rest of your life." The line went dead, the call terminated before I could say another word.

"Madam?" Jermaine wanted to know what had been said. "Madam, what did he say? Is she all right?"

How did I answer that question? Xavier told me enough for me to feel confident Barbie was still alive, but beyond that my head was filled with terrible images. I needed a moment to gather my thoughts, and when my brain recalibrated, I focused on one singular thought.

The postcard.

Barbie Figures it Out

While Patricia might hope Xavier was lying about knowing the location of the San José, Barbie knew that he was not. Not exactly. For more than an hour they had scrutinised every facet of Finn Murphy's life. What was instantly clear from the wealth of information available was that Xavier had already conducted extensive research into the Irishman.

"He found the treasure, Miss Berkeley," Xavier replied when she questioned where it all came from. "He is perhaps the most important person in my investigation for he has done what no one else has been able to for more than three-hundred years. Of course, had it not been for Mrs Fisher's strange need to report his death and the uncut gemstones in his stomach on such a public forum, I might never have known he existed." He was silent for a moment, before saying, "Actually, that is something that has bothered me since I first read it. Can you tell me why Mrs Fisher chose to send such sensitive information to the press? Her employers cannot have been pleased by the attention it garnered."

Barbie snorted a tired laugh. "They were not. Not one bit, but Patty didn't leak the information, someone else did it to embarrass her."

"Oh?"

It was clear to Barbie from the way Xavier posed his response that he hoped to know more. So far as she was concerned, he could go on hoping. She wanted information too – like why couldn't he just drop dead?

When she gave him nothing, Xavier chose to let it go. It made more sense that the woman he'd come to respect as an adversary would not do something so careless as to release sensitive information.

Barbie had a pen held lengthways between her teeth, a habit she often fell to when researching. She didn't use the pen for anything, unlike Patty who would make notes on actual paper, but it was one of those odd quirks she'd picked up somewhere.

Finn Murphy had no criminal record, not much of an education, and no family beyond a sister and his parents. His career employment record was bleak with huge swathes of time when he simply held no job at all. Barbie found herself questioning if he had been deliberately aiming to achieve nothing with his life.

Excusing himself, Xavier left the room – to visit the restroom, Barbie guessed. The moment the door closed behind him, Barbie was out of her chair and across the room where she reopened the Cristobal box.

It took her more than a minute to find the letter she wanted; the one Xavier described. It was a series of numbers with dots to separate them and then spaces to separate the sequences of numbers.

"It looks like words," Barbie murmured to herself.

Far from being a cryptologist, Barbie wanted to have a crack at the code not because she believed she was any cleverer than the people who came before. In fact, she wasn't even going to try to break it herself.

Instead, she intended to use artificial intelligence (AI).

Xavier didn't say when he last had people look at it, but the advances in AI had exploded in the previous twelve months, the potential applications seeming to double almost every week. Finding a site she wanted, Barbie checked over her shoulder, listening for Xavier's return before committing to the task of entering the code.

Barbie's experience with AI software was limited – it fascinated her, but as a gym instructor on a cruise ship there was little call to employ it. Regardless, when the program made a soft beeping noise a few seconds later, her breath left in a whoosh of surprise.

It had been a random, silly guess, nothing more. Xavier revealed the page of the Bible from which the code was supposedly crafted, and admitted trying multiple Bibles without success. Had he used Bibles from a language other than Spanish though?

By his own admission, Xavier believed Henri chose to stay away from his native Spain, so where was he? Well, that was hard to guess, but since Xavier suggested he believed the San José's former bursar might have been in England, Barbie started there.

One question aimed at the internet confirmed the most popular Bible in circulation in the early seventeen hundreds: the King James Version, later known as the King James Bible. Giving the AI program the right text to use and the code it needed, Barbie got a short paragraph in return in less than a second.

In Rochester Cathedral, where James Draper lies, you will find the first marker, and the directions to take you onwards. Good luck, my son.

Barbie was still staring at the screen when Xavier came back through the door five minutes later.

An hour after that, they were in his helicopter and heading for his plane. He refused to wait for morning and cared not that Barbie was tired. He was impressed and even said so in words. Barbie doubted that meant he would choose not to kill her if she was right and he found the treasure. Xavier was keeping her alive for now in case he needed her. Nothing more.

The translated instruction made it clear they were going to find the *first* marker, which meant there had to be more. In turn that meant they were far from finding the treasure. Resting her head against the cool glass of the helicopter's window, Barbie closed her eyes and prayed her friends were already ahead of her.

The Unexpected Clue

"I'm not telling ye where I keep the things that I don't want ye to find!" snapped Helen Murphy, the tone of her voice enough to silence her husband who foolishly chose to voice his opinion on their son and his postcard.

After they fought about it and Kenny threatened to destroy it if he found it stuck to the fridge door again, Helen removed it to a keepsake box. Where she kept that was a secret from her husband and looking to stay that way.

We were gathered in her kitchen with a good dollop of the locals back in the bar where Ruby was once again serving drinks. Helen turned to leave the room, leaving her husband behind, but spun around to glare at him again in case he thought it wise to follow her.

"Just you wait there, Kenny Murphy," she warned. With a final dagger from her eyes, she flounced upstairs, muttering about her 'mammy being right about that boy she wanted me to marry' the whole way.

Kenny turned to face the other people in the room, a fake bewildered look plastered to his face.

"I swear being a married man is like being in Alcoholics Anonymous." His eyes focused on nothing as he adopted a pose and started to act like he was in a meeting. "Hello, everyone. My name is Kenny and I'm a married man. It's been six months since I made a decision."

Martin sniggered until a look from his wife, Deepa, silenced him.

"I almost voiced an opinion a few days ago," Kenny continued his act, "but I was strong. I kept it to myself. I know one opinion only leads to another."

I couldn't help the smile that crept onto my face. He was being funny, and I knew I wasn't the only one who needed an outlet to relieve my tension.

"What is it that they say?" He'd dropped the AA act and talked as himself. "Happy wife, happy life? Anyone heard that."

"I have," Sam volunteered.

"Me too," bragged Martin proudly, raising his eyebrows at Deepa. "That's how I live my life."

"Mm-hmm," grunted Kenny. "What's the opposite saying?"

His question drew blank looks.

"There isn't one!" Kenny provided with a semi-roar. "If there was it would be 'Happy husband, what's he been up to?' or possibly 'Happy husband, we'll soon see about that!'"

"Got something to say?" asked Helen, re-entering the room.

Kenny tried an innocent expression. "Nothing at all, my petal. Just keeping our guests entertained."

Blanking him completely as though he were not there and hadn't spoken, Helen walked by her husband, her right hand reaching out to offer me what she held: the postcard.

Everything else in my head went on hold so I could stare at it. The picture on the front wasn't, as I hoped, a big fat clue. In my head it would be a photograph of Athens or Gibraltar, Southampton maybe or Venice. It was none of those, it was one of those 'saucy' postcards with a man employing an unintended innuendo.

Okay, so it didn't give me a place, per se, but it was from England. I couldn't tell you if saucy postcards are limited to distribution in Britain, but since it was in English …

I flipped it over, checking the stamp to confirm it held the Queen's head. King Charles was on the throne now, but the postcard was months old and the new stamps with Charles' likeness on them were only just coming into circulation.

The postmark was from somewhere called Lymington. I glanced around to see if anyone knew where that was.

"On the south coast," said Molly. "My granny used to have a holiday cottage near there. I remember watching the ships going past."

Jermaine's fingers were a blur on his phone. "It's right next to Southampton, madam."

There was a date on the postmark too. It was hard to make out, but with a little squinting and some mental calculation I blurted, "This is right before the Aurelia was in Southampton!"

Jermaine, Hideki, Deepa, and more were crowded in around me, some of them forced to read the postcard upside down.

"Does that mean he boarded the ship in Southampton?" asked Sam.

"Possibly," I replied. I wanted to be certain. I wanted to *know* things, but all I knew was that Finn Murphy was in the Southampton area right before it last left there. That it was also where he boarded the ship was an easy conclusion to draw and could very well be right. All we had was a postcard though.

The message, scrawled in patchy blue ink on the back, was to Finn's mother, Helen. If it contained a hidden message ... well, let's just say it was very well hidden. There was no nod to suggest he'd found something extraordinary or was excited about anything in particular. His message, twenty-seven words in total, let his mother know he was alive and doing well.

Looking about as I let my mind work the problem, I handed the postcard to Anders, who was yet to have a proper look, and caught sight of a photograph on the wall. It was a family shot; Helen and Kenny with their two children. The kids were both adults in the shot and Ruby looked little different from now.

"How old is this?" I asked, pointing.

Helen had to turn her head to see what I was asking. "Oh, um, about a year."

"It was taken six days before we found out he'd gambled away the pub," Kenny remarked, his tone surly. "As you well know, dear."

"We got the pub back," Helen replied without deeming it necessary to look Kenny's way. "That's not something I'll ever be able to say about Finn."

It was clear she was hurting still from the unexpected loss. I suspected Kenny was too, but hiding his pain behind a façade of anger. Kenny's last words to his son were bound to be ones he now regretted and could never repair.

What drew me to the photograph was how full of life Finn seemed. In death he was emaciated, his ribs jutting from his abdomen. In stark contrast, the man I saw now was athletic and well-nourished. He'd hidden in the bowels of the luxury cruise liner and lost a decent percentage of his bodyweight before he died.

From the corner of my eye, I could see Hideki on his phone. He was speaking quickly, talking to someone in an animated fashion.

"Hey," he called to get our attention. "Everyone, listen to this." Hideki pressed the button to activate the speaker on his phone. "It's Dr Davis."

"David?" I enquired, wondering why the Aurelia's senior physician might be calling.

"One and the same," his voice boomed over the airwaves. "Good evening, everyone."

He got a chorus of "Good evenings" in return. Even Helen and Kenny offered their salutations though they shot questioning looks at me because they had no idea who Dr David Davis was.

"I thought perhaps I would call to see how things were going, though I can guess you are yet to locate Miss Berkeley, or I would know about it."

"That's correct," I replied, shooting a look at Hideki. I wasn't about to be rude, but we really didn't have time for people to be calling for updates. Where would that end?

Hideki held up an index finger, begging a little patience, and said, "Tell them what you just told me, David."

"I found a clue in Finn Murphy's clothing."

I gasped in surprise and surged across the room to get closer to the phone in my eagerness to hear what massive revelation he might have to share.

"He bought a shirt from a shop not too far from Southampton. Well, they have a Southampton postcode, but the address listed is a place called Boxley Abbey. I went back through his autopsy notes to see if I could find anything we might have missed the first time around. I'm not sure if that's helpful or not; from memory you were trying to establish where he might have snuck on board."

"Dr Davis this is brilliant. Thank you."

"Hold on," he begged, "There's more. I called the shop earlier today ... I would have called you sooner but there was a heart attack on board and that had to take priority. Anyway, I begged them to tell me when they sold the item – I made it sound like I was part of an official investigation – and that's where I hit a snag."

I blinked. He'd called to give us incomplete information? I had thought he was about to deliver something crucial.

"You see," Dr Davis continued, "The shirt wasn't sold, it was stolen. Shoplifted is a more accurate term, I guess."

"Of course it was," grumbled Finn's father.

Dr Davis had been teasing us; making us think he didn't have the answers when, in fact, he did. That the shirt was shoplifted from the store in Southampton was just the key piece of evidence we needed. Not only did we have a postcard placing Finn Murphy in the area, we knew for certain he was in Southampton.

"I thought you would want to know Mr Murphy stole the shirt the day before the ship left Southampton."

The back of my skull itched, and I punched the air. That was good enough for me.

"Gather your things, people," I announced to the room. "We have a flight to catch."

Helen's eyes flared, "But you've got to wait for the police, surely," she complained. "They'll be here soon enough, and they'll want to talk to you."

I shook my head. Hideki's phone was off speaker and back at his ear where he was winding up the conversation.

"Sorry, Helen, we have a friend to save and that's all I care about. Your friends have the mercenaries under control?" I knew they did. The six men had been searched, their weapons removed along with anything they could feasibly use to get free from the binds holding their hands and feet. Half a dozen of the villagers watched over them still, shotguns at the ready. Only the injured man was inside the house where the cold wouldn't exacerbate his injuries.

"What are we supposed to tell them, Patricia?" Helen continued. "They'll want to know what happened here."

"So tell them," I invited, slipping my arms into my coat when Jermaine held it for me. "Tell them everything and tell them why. Tell them Patricia Fisher was here and she's about to solve another giant case."

I grabbed Helen's hand and pulled her in so I could deliver an air kiss to her right cheek. I whispered once more that I was sorry for her loss and wished her luck for the future.

Afterward, I worried that I came off as big headed with my confident attitude, but in that moment I felt certain we were going to find where Finn Murphy had been in the days before his death and that would lead us to the treasure. We were going to get there ahead of Xavier, and I would lure him in to get Barbie back.

Rochester Cathedral

T he plane jolted when the wheels touched down, waking Barbie from a dead slumber. Had she been snoring, she wondered, blinking and stretching while a yawn split her face. Sleeping was deliberate on her part, grabbing the chance to catch a few hours during the flight. The constant change in time zones over the last two days was playing havoc with her brain and she was not only tired but also physically sluggish.

It was something close to four in the morning now, UK time, according to the Rolex clock set into the bulkhead next to the cockpit.

Barbie yawned again, doing exercises in her seat to get her body working.

"Where are we?" she asked, raising her voice slightly so Xavier would hear her. He was sitting in a large rotating chair near the front of the small cabin. Everything about the aircraft spoke of luxury and wealth, but none more so than the oversized captain's style semi-couch supporting Xavier's body.

A folding table attached to one arm held a laptop which in turn held Xavier's attention.

Without looking up, he said, "Rochester airport. It is a small commercial airport, but sufficient to meet our needs and close to where we are going next. I have arranged for a car."

His matter-of-fact attitude masked the excitement he felt. Many years ago, Xavier Silvestre chose to make the San José his life's work. Obsessed with the possibility of the treasure from the first moment he heard the tale, he'd never been so close to fulfilling his dream as he was today.

That the attractive blonde woman figured out what so many scholars and theologists could not was so improbable Xavier felt like he might wake up from a dream. Yet he knew it was real. She used modern AI technology to decipher the message; something that simply didn't exist the last time he had someone look at the letters. More than that, she possessed the vision to question if the Bible they needed to use might be one from a different country – something that had never once occurred to Xavier.

Her feat was impressive, and he found a need to contain his excitement lest it boil over and cloud his weariness.

From the aircraft they walked to a hanger and from there, via the simple expedience of using hefty bribes, the party from Spain exited without the flight information being logged and without the foreigner's passport details recorded.

So far as the world was concerned, Xavier Silvestre's party was not in England.

Walking to the car, another black Mercedes, Barbie zipped up her jacket, thankful she'd been permitted time to change before they left Xavier's house. Decked out in jeans and a top with a thick hoody and then a jacket, the winter air was still crisp and cold.

The drive into Rochester's ancient heart took less than ten minutes, the spire of the cathedral visible long before the rest of the building came into sight.

The area was familiar to Barbie, yet she chose to keep that small fact quiet. If there was any home advantage to be had, she needed to keep it a secret. She didn't know Rochester well, but for almost three months she lived and worked in the area when Patricia chose to move home and start a detective agency.

Apparently Mike Atwell, a detective sergeant they all met and got to know, had taken the business over now with Patricia's blessing. Barbie idly wondered how that was going.

Gomez stopped the car on the old cobbles of the road outside the cathedral. To their front, the headlights illuminated North Gate, the old, fortified entrance to the city. To their left, the ancient castle, long since abandoned by its residents, but preserved in a semi-derelict state by the National Trust. To their right, the cathedral sat bathed in light from a series of spotlights set into the ground.

Excited by the chance to explore the castle, she and Jermaine paid the fee to climb the stairs inside and roam the history-dripping hallways not long after they first moved in with Patricia. The cathedral, however, was a building she had never entered.

"You're really planning to break into that place in the middle of the night?" Barbie questioned. She didn't care either way, she just hoped Xavier would get caught. The place was bound to be alarmed; they would trigger it, the police would come, and if she got lucky the police would shoot Gomez. Except they wouldn't, Barbie realised, because British police do not carry guns.

Xavier nodded to Gomez who exited from the driver's seat to come around to Barbie's side of the car. His opening of her door was not a chivalrous act, but one of control. Swivelling her legs around and out, she ducked away from the giant brute before he could attempt to grab the back of her neck – his favoured method for steering her.

"I can walk by myself," she insisted. Lifting her explosive cuffs, she added, "It's not like I can run away."

Gomez took a step toward the blonde woman only to be called back by his master.

"Leave her be, Gomez. Miss Berkeley has earned a few small privileges."

Barbie wasn't about to give thanks to her captor – she wanted to punch out a few of his teeth. A few small privileges? She practically solved the mystery of the San José treasure and he acted as though she'd helped him with a tricky crossword clue. He wasn't paying her any attention though. His eyes were turned upward along with his face, a look of intense scrutiny in place as he took in the Cathedral's architecture.

"Magnificent," he remarked, talking to no one but himself.

Barbie could feel Gomez's eyes boring into her as she made her way around the car to join Xavier in front of the cathedral doors.

"Remind me of the message, please" Xavier requested.

Barbie recited, "In Rochester Cathedral, where James Draper lies, you will find the first marker, and the directions to take you onwards."

"*In* Rochester Cathedral," Xavier echoed. He looked around, turning on the spot as he looked for a graveyard. They wanted the body of James Draper, and the clue said he was *in* the cathedral. He'd hoped it wasn't literal and the grave was to be found outside in the grounds as one might see in many old churches. That did not appear to be the case though.

Stepping back, he called out, "Gomez!" The command, though unspoken, was quite clear. Gomez came forward, ready to break down the doors.

Barbie could only guess how they were secured, but they looked like thick oak with ironwork fittings. It would need a battering ram to get them open.

From his jacket, Gomez withdrew a stick of what Barbie instantly realised was plastic explosive. As a gym instructor by profession, it ought to be the case that she would never see such a thing in her life. Spending time with Patricia Fisher had changed all that.

Automatically, she stepped back; she wanted to be well away and protected by a big, stone wall when Gomez set the charge off. However, in moving back a yard, she gave herself a better view up the street.

"Cops," she warned, the word bypassing her brain on its way out.

Xavier said but one word. "Gomez."

What did that mean? Was it short for 'Gomez put the explosive away, we shall reconvene later when this danger has passed'? Or did it mean 'Gomez please kill these officers and dispose of their bodies'?

Barbie got her answer when Gomez withdrew a pistol from another pocket.

"We can come back later," she begged. "The cathedral is open to the public. You can be here at ten when they open it. That's just a few hours away, Xavier. What if you kill the cops and we can't find John Draper's grave? The whole area will be crawling with cops, and this is England – they've got CCTV everywhere. You might be getting recorded right now."

A snort of frustration left Xavier's nose before he said, "That is not how we do things, Miss Berkeley. There will be no cops here tomorrow, they will still be looking for these two."

Gomez started screwing a suppressor attachment to the muzzle of the pistol.

The squad car pulled up next to their black Mercedes, the window rolling down as the driver looked out.

"Everything all right here?" he asked. The question wasn't directed at Barbie, but the young man was looking her way when he said it.

"Yes, thank you, officer," replied Xavier.

Barbie checked her position relative to Gomez and stepped into his path; he would need to make his intention obvious before he could aim and take fire. Would that give the cops enough time to realise what was about to happen and hit the gas?

The cop in the driver's seat said, "This is your car, yes? You're stopped on double yellow lines."

"We are just leaving," Xavier replied. "Thank you for your concern."

Barbie heard the second cop, the one in the passenger seat, murmur something. They were becoming suspicious and it came as no great surprise. To Barbie's mind, anyone seeing Gomez would be suspicious; the man was a walking threat.

Acting fast, she broke out her best smile and went to the squad car – if the cops chose to exit their car and ask more questions they were as good as dead.

"Miss Berkeley," warned Xavier, his voice loud enough for her to hear, but not the cops.

Twisting her head, she flashed the same smile at the Spaniard. "I'm helping, okay?" Halfway to the cops, she started talking. "Hey, do you guys know Patience Woods?"

The cop in the driver's seat lifted his right eyebrow and the one in the passenger seat leaned forward and around so he could get a better look.

Barbie heard him whisper, "Hubba, hubba," and chose to use that to her advantage.

"Yeah, we know her," admitted the nearest of the two cops. "Do you need us to contact her?" he asked. Patience Woods was well-known for her stance on women's rights and even better known for handing out street justice when men were acting in a less than polite manner towards her or other ladies in her vicinity.

Barbie could see the cops craning their necks to look around her now – not something men usually did. They were concerned her companions were causing her bother; that's why they asked if she wanted Patience.

"No, she's a friend," Barbie said. It wasn't a lie exactly. They knew each other but only in passing. "I've been away recently, but I'm back now and she's always telling me how many cute guys there are at work."

The cop's attitude changed in a heartbeat. The drop-dead-gorgeous blonde girl was looking for cute guys and they were ready to fit the bill.

"Maybe the two of you want to double date with us sometime?" she teased. Seeing the guys twitch their eyes at Gomez and Xavier again, she added, "Oh, don't worry about them. That's just my stepdad and his bodyguard. He's seriously rich. He owns like half of Europe or something. He won't go out without his protection." Dropping her voice to a huskier, more flirtatious tone, she said, "I carry protection with me all the time too."

For Barbie it was fun to watch the men's eyes dilate although she did feel a little guilty. She asked them about dating, then dropped in that she was loaded and topped it off with a casual sex reference.

"Hi, I'm Tony," said the cop in the passenger seat, leaning right across his colleague to shake Barbie's hand. "This is Nigel. He'll date Patience in a heartbeat."

"Oh, I will, will I?" questioned Nigel.

"Yeah. he's been lusting after her for years."

"Well, she is a cute one," Barbie grinned.

Nigel had, in fact, once asked Patience out on a date only to get knocked back. She was nice and all, but this blonde woman was in a whole different league.

"Na, I think you'll do better with Patience," Nigel voiced his thoughts. "I'll take out this nice, young lady. What's your name, angel?"

"It's Barbie," said Barbie, leaning down to shake Nigel's hand and making sure he got a good view of her cleavage as she reached into the car to pluck a pen from the front of his tunic.

"Hand, sweetie," she encouraged with a wink.

She wrote her number on Nigel's hand and then Tony's, whispering, "Maybe we can double date without Patience." It was about the sluttiest thing she could think of to say – she wanted them thinking about her and only her, not the seven-foot goon standing five yards away. She badly wanted to write a message on their hands, but if they reacted they would die and with Xavier standing just a few yards behind her, there was no chance to explain. Better to send them on their way and wait for another opportunity when she felt less likely to cost two men their lives.

"Call me tomorrow," she faked a yawn, covering her face with a hand. "I'm tired now and I can't very well distract you from your duties."

Nigel and Tony were not so sure that was the case. They would have been more than happy to be distracted. Barbie was walking away though, heading for the back door of the Mercedes into which she disappeared with another wink.

The cops pulled away, their squad car cruising down the street and out of sight before Barbie allowed herself to breathe a sigh of relief.

The car's other rear door opened, Xavier sliding in with his eyes firmly fixed on Barbie.

"We shall return in a few hours, Miss Berkeley. If you try another stunt like that one at any point, I will have Gomez cut off your ears."

Barbie cringed inwardly, the worry that he might make good on his threat enough to churn her stomach. Swallowing hard, she forced herself to sound calm when she said, "I understand."

"I hope that you do."

Gomez slid into the driver's seat, his eyes flicking into the rear-view mirror to meet Barbie's. He looked upset at missing the chance to kill a couple of cops.

Barbie refused to avert her gaze. "I understand," she repeated, "that you are holding all the cards, Xavier. I am helping you not because I want to, but under duress at the threat of terrible injury. Despite that, if I have the chance to save someone from dying at your hands, I will do so."

It was a bold statement, a challenge even, and Barbie held her breath waiting for a response that never came. Did Xavier chose to let it go? Or did he not care what she said because he was going to kill her soon enough anyway?

The First Marker

Barbie slept a lot better than she expected. Xavier had a suite for them at The Castle, which isn't actually a castle at all, but a rather plush hotel on the outskirts of Rochester. The suite had only two bedrooms, but there was no need to worry about being forced to share with Gomez because he chose to sleep in front of the door.

The lumbering ox picked up a couch, carrying it under one arm like it weighed nothing. He set it down to block the entrance/exit, fluffed a couple of the throw cushions and settled onto it, his knees pulled up to his waist so he would fit.

There had been umpteen opportunities for Barbie to alert someone to her plight just in the few hours since they landed in England, but she knew the most likely outcome was the death of whoever she involved. She couldn't have that on her conscience. It would be the same today, she already knew.

Xavier preferred to operate in secret, keeping to the shadows when possible, yet through her actions, they were going back to the cathedral in daylight. There would be people everywhere; enough to ensure she could create a diversion and get away. Or enough to help her overwhelm Xavier and even Gomez.

That she could do neither for fear Xavier would detonate the explosives strapped to her wrists was all the deterrent she needed. In bed last night, she tried to focus her mind on finding a solution – a way to get the cuffs off safely, but sleep claimed her before her brain could even begin to devise a solution.

Barbie wasn't convinced there was one.

Exiting her bedroom once she was dressed for the day, Barbie found herself momentarily stunned to find a new man talking to Gomez. He wore a baggy, faded hoody displaying a surfer motif, ripped and bleached jeans and brand new, designer label sports shoes that cost several hundred dollars. Sunglasses with an iridescent lens covered the new man's eyes and his mass of blondish hair had been formed into dreadlocks that hung in a huge, matted mess down between his shoulder blades where they were pulled into a tight wad by a pair of rubber bands.

"Ah, Miss Berkeley. I was beginning to think I would have to send Gomez in to rouse you."

Barbie's jaw dropped open to hear Xavier's voice coming from the unkempt bum.

Seeing her expression, Xavier looked down at himself, spreading his arms wide as he took in the outfit he wore.

"I take it you find my disguise convincing?"

Barbie shook her head slowly from side to side. "It was you on board the Aurelia. You were Professor Noriega," she stammered, barely able to believe it.

"Yes, my dear, of course it was. The ability to change one's appearance is a skill more people should learn. It doesn't take all that much to fool humanity; they go through life with their heads in the clouds, only rarely focussing on what is in front of them. Anyone who sees me today will remember the stupid shoes," he used a sweeping hand to draw her attention to his feet. "Or perhaps it will be the hair. Giving them something that stands out, that makes them focus their attention, pushes everything else into the background, you see. I will be seen, but no one will actually see me."

"What about him?" Barbie nodded her head in the general direction of Gomez. "Where's his disguise?"

Gomez's eyes bored into her, his expression unreadable but far from pleasant.

"Such a tactic would be a waste of time, Miss Berkeley. Gomez is too tall to be hidden. For tasks such as the one we propose to undertake this morning, he will remain out of sight."

Barbie's pulse skipped a beat. If they were out of the giant's sight, would she be able to incapacitate Xavier? It was a long shot – she still didn't know if there was a backup device to trigger the cuffs – yet this could be her best chance so far. If she had to keep Xavier in a headlock until the bomb disposal people figured it out, so be it. Anything to get out of her current nightmare.

A knock at the door made her jump, but it was just breakfast being delivered. They ate in near silence – nothing unusual for Gomez – each keeping their thoughts to themselves as they dined on the selection of fresh breads, pastries, fruit and more. It was nothing Barbie would normally pick for her first meal of the day, but reminding herself she was being held captive still, she knew she had it pretty good.

No sooner had they eaten than they were leaving. It was light out, the sun creeping into the sky behind a wall of grey cloud. The air felt moist, like the clouds were all around them even though there was no mist to be seen.

Returning to the cathedral in the middle of Rochester's central tourist area took only a few minutes though slightly longer than the previous night due to traffic on the road. Obviously, they were not going to park in the street as they had a few hours ago, but finding a parking spot not far from their destination proved easy enough.

Gomez stayed with the car much to Barbie's quiet joy. He could see the cathedral from where he was, but once they were inside and out of sight, she could change the game.

Maybe.

The thought of taking such a risk made her insides perform acrobatics. She couldn't just stay in Xavier's custody though. He was never going to let her go, so making her best play in a public place was the only sane option no matter how terrified she might be.

There would be things she could grab inside the cathedral – a weighty candlestick or something similar. It really didn't matter so long as she could use it to knock Xavier out. But not kill him. Barbie was quite certain about the last part; she did not want to take his life even though she knew he was a killer. It would weigh her down and affect her conscience for the rest of her life. If there was a way to avoid it, she would.

They crossed the road together, Xavier staying just a foot away. If he reached out, he could take her hand. It gave her the creeps to have him so close, but it worked in her favour if she planned to brain him.

At a donation box in the cathedral's doorway, a woman with glasses and a hairstyle thirty years out of date smiled and welcomed them inside.

Xavier made a point of stuffing a ten pound note into the box as he passed.

"Would you like a tour?" she asked. "It's free."

Expecting Xavier to decline, Barbie was startled when he did the opposite.

"You know, babe," he was imitating a Californian drawl and not doing a terrible job of it, "I think that sounds great. I have all kinds of questions."

The woman wasn't offering to take them around the cathedral herself, but had a colleague to hand who was raring to go.

Xavier impressed Barbie with a slick cover story that he delivered in such a convincing manner she almost began to believe it herself. He was a final year art student at UCLA having ditched his career as a sports journalist when he suffered a heart attack from the stress of perpetual deadlines. He was in England to trace his family's roots and that brought him to Rochester where he was assured one of his earliest known ancestors was said to be buried – Xavier told the tour guide he paid one of those online ancestry firms for information.

Their tour guide was a man in his late seventies called Ian. His bushy beard needed a trim in Barbie's opinion and was grey going to white at the edges. He was fifty pounds overweight, all of which sat on his belly which mimicked that of a pregnant woman in her third trimester. He used a walking stick to overcome a tricky leg or hip – Barbie wasn't going to ask which, but moved with a sprightliness that belied his years.

Ian listened dutifully, pointing out the features of the old church and rattling off facts and figures such as age, cost, how long it took to build, and showed he was paying attention to Xavier when he asked, "What is the name of the ancestor? There aren't all that many people interred inside the cathedral."

"John Draper." Xavier waited for the man to show he recognised the name and had to still his disappointment when it was evident he did not.

"Hmm," Ian scratched at his chin. "I'll have to phone a friend on that one," he remarked, looking about.

"Phone a friend?" Xavier repeated, his question-filled eyes aimed at Barbie.

"It's from a game show," she explained. "It just means he needs to ask someone."

Satisfied, Xavier waited patiently while Ian returned to the entrance and the woman still standing there to greet visitors on their way in. They were too far away across the echoey cathedral with its high, vaulted ceiling, for Barbie and Xavier to hear the exchange, but in less than a minute Ian was coming back. His face bore a hopeful expression and they'd both seen the woman pointing to one corner of the building.

"It seems you were correctly informed," Ian remarked as he approached. He didn't stop, but went right by, gesticulating as he passed. "I believe we will find what you want over here beyond the nave."

Following behind, Barbie could not help but question what Xavier planned to do when they found John Draper's grave. The coded message suggested the next clue was to be found inside the coffin. Was he going to break into it? How was he going to achieve that? What would he do about Ian?

They reached the front row of pews, angling toward a corner where a door led behind the choir seats set up either side of the altar.

"It should be just through here," Ian advised, continuing to lead them.

Ian explained how the grave of John Draper was one of only a handful within the cathedral and that he was a former verger who was tragically murdered in 1710 – Ian had just learned all this from Dierdre, who Barbie guessed to be the woman they met on the way in. As a member of the bishop's supporting staff John Draper was interred within the ground of the cathedral. Of course, Ian went on to say, his actual body wasn't here at all, just a commemorative plaque set into the floor.

The clouds outside made the sky grey, the stained-glass windows made the interior of the cathedral dim, and passing into a corridor with no natural light and only a low watt bulb overhead left Barbie squinting to see. That's why she missed Xavier's strike.

The moment Ian pointed to the brass plaque laid into the floor ahead, Xavier hit him. The blow was as fast as it was vicious, the butt of a handgun driven into the base of Ian's skull enough to render him unconscious with one blow.

Barbie ran to the man, catching him just as he collapsed and saving his head from further injury on the unyielding stone floor.

"You didn't have to do that!" she snapped.

Xavier paid her no mind, continuing forward to examine the brass plaque.

"You are far too sentimental, Miss Berkeley. How do you ever get anything done?"

"I have friends," she snarled through gritted teeth.

"Sentimental," Xavier remarked again, his tone dismissive.

Barbie laid Ian's head against the cold floor. He was breathing and was probably going to be okay when he came around. The back of his head bore a terrible swelling that grew larger as Barbie watched. In the centre where the gun struck, his skin was torn. Blood leaked onto his shirt collar but no more than a few drips.

She saw when Xavier found what he wanted.

"Here! It's here!" he said the words with barely contained excitement. To Barbie's ears he sounded like a child on Christmas morning.

With a final check to make sure Ian was okay, Barbie came out of her crouch and went to help Xavier. The sooner she got him out of the cathedral, the less likely it was they would be discovered with the unconscious body. Xavier would kill to ensure he got away, but in thinking about escape, Barbie's brain hammered with an insistent message: this was her best chance.

They were out of sight and away from Gomez. She could get Xavier's phone, figure out if there was a way to make her cuffs safe – there had to be, right? Then she could call the cops and end her nightmare.

Quietly wrapping the fingers of her right hand around the shaft of Ian's walking stick, she hefted it. As a weapon it wasn't all she could have hoped for, but swung with enough force, it would do. Violence was not her natural state. In her life she'd only intended to hurt a person once or twice, but now was not the time to be timid.

Xavier didn't even look her way when she took a step toward him, but as she raised the walking stick above her head, his right arm folded out from his body with the handgun still held firmly in his hand. It lined up on her face, halting Barbie's approach instantly.

"I warn you, Miss Berkeley, I grow bored of these foolish attempts. I will release you when I am ready and not before. Any more of this and I think perhaps I will blow off your left hand just to prove a point. I suspect that will quell your need to rebel, don't you?" he turned his head to meet her eyes when he posed the question.

Barbie lowered the walking stick, saying nothing as she placed it back by Ian's side.

"You need to stop hurting people," she remarked, her voice wobbling even as she tried to force the fear from her body.

Hiding his gun again, Xavier said, "And you need to get with the program. That is how the Americans say it, yes?" He didn't wait for an answer, shuffling to his left instead. "Here, help me with this. I need you to grab the edge when I lever it out."

Xavier placed his phone on the floor by his knee, a call going through to Gomez. Using a blade he withdrew from the sleeve of his baggy hoody, he cleared away some of the dirt wedged into the gap between flagstones.

The call connected, but no voice came.

"Gomez?"

Barbie heard the phone beep once; the sound it makes when someone keys a number.

"I have found the first marker. I expect to be out shortly. Come to the cathedral entrance. I may need you."

The sound of a key being pressed came again – one for yes.

Xavier thumbed the red button to end the call and used the knife to get under the edge of the flagstone. The brass plaque set into it showed only the name and the years of birth and death though the numbers and letters were almost completely worn away by the passage of feet over the centuries.

The flagstone measured no more than fifteen inches square, but it demanded a goodly amount of grunting and straining to get it to move.

Ian groaned softly at one point, sending a shard of fear through Barbie's heart. Would Xavier finish him off if he came around?

Mercifully, she didn't get to find out because the flagstone finally accepted defeat and when it started moving it almost popped from the hole it must have occupied for more than three-hundred years.

Barbie slid the fingers of both hands under the edge as it rose, levering the stone back as though hinged. Questioning if there would be bare dirt beneath and whether this was a false trail or someone might have got here first, she felt genuine relief when she spied a hole.

Crudely cut into the substrate beneath the floor, the circular pit measured twelve inches across. The size didn't matter, only what the hole contained was of interest.

Xavier snatched at it as though it were the treasure itself. Plucked from the ground, though it was clearly heavy, a small wooden box free from decoration or adornment had withstood the ravages of time with remarkable resilience.

Unable to contain his need to get it open, Xavier wedged the knife into one edge only to find the wood simply crumbled away. The unmistakable shine of gold came from within, explaining why the small box weighed so much.

Ian groaned again. He was definitely coming around and they both heard one of his shoes scrape across the stone floor.

Xavier still had the knife in his hand.

Barbie growled, "Don't you dare."

Xavier's eyes locked on hers. "Dead men cannot talk, Miss Berkeley. He will identify you and I cannot have that."

"You are not killing him!" she snarled, getting to her feet and positioning herself between the two men. "Blow my arms off! Kill me if you must, but if you try to kill that sweet old man, I will scream this place down and you *will* be caught here."

Xavier folded his arms. He'd never had much use for a conscience and was finding it odd to now have one walking around beside him.

"You have five seconds, Miss Berkeley. Get the stone back in place and let's go."

Barely daring to believe he was going to let Ian live, Barbie made sure to stay between them when she crouched once more to put the flagstone back where it came from. When she yanked her fingertips out of the closing gap and the stone square slid home, she snatched at Xavier's arm – the one holding the knife.

"Come on, let's go," she pleaded. If she could just get him out into the open where people could see, he wouldn't dare hurt anyone. Barbie wished she could do more for their guide, but told herself Ian would be found soon enough.

Xavier gave the old man a final reluctant look on his way out of the door that led back into the cathedral proper. They skirted the pews, taking the aisle on one side of the building all the way to the far end where they turned toward the exit.

Dierdre was gone, replaced by another, younger woman who was doing her best to speak with some Chinese tourists.

Still gripping Xavier's forearm, Barbie begged they excuse her as she squeezed past them and into the daylight. Xavier had the box held securely under his left arm, though he handed it to Gomez the moment they got outside and with a yank pulled his right arm from Barbie's grip.

"To the car," he insisted, his eyes locked on the carpark across the street.

They were out and no one had died. Barbie cursed that she hadn't been able to do something about her own situation, but ignoring that compromise, this was the best scenario she could have hoped for. Whatever the box held, she hoped it would take them far from Rochester and on to the treasure rather than another location which might lead them to another location ...

"Barbie?"

She froze. She knew who the voice belonged to without needing to look. They were in Rochester and though she told herself the chances were slim, there always existed the danger of running into someone she knew.

"Barbie, it is you," the voice chuckled, "I'd recognise that figure anywhere. What are you doing here? Who are your new friends? Where's Patricia and Jermaine?"

Cringing, her heart banging in her chest at what she felt was, quite frankly, an unhealthy pace, she swivelled around to face Big Ben.

The Church in Farnham

"**M**rs Fisher?" Sam handed me a cup of coffee, which I gratefully received.

Our private jet got us into Southampton airport just a little after one in the morning. We were all running on empty by then and were lucky to be able to secure rooms at the on-site airport hotel. It wasn't a flashy place, as one might expect to find at most major airports, but the rooms had beds and the hotel served breakfast – that was all we needed.

The sun was up now, and breakfast was done and forgotten. We could race off and attack the day, but as much as we wanted to, we didn't have a direction in which to go. For that reason alone we were still in the hotel outside Southampton Airport.

A brainstorming session, taken slowly for once so we wouldn't rush madly in the wrong direction dictated that we only had two possible destinations. The shop where Finn stole the shirt was one option. According to Dr Davis it was located somewhere called Boxley Abbey, a village so small it didn't even show on a map. I couldn't see what advantage there might be from going there, so it got shunted into second place behind the location of an artefact Barbie turned up in her search when we first started looking into the San José.

A dagger and a cup, both displaying the emblem of the House of Asturias, a family who took passage on the San José to return home to Spain from Peru, were found in a church in Farnham, just across the Hampshire border in Surrey.

It wasn't a long drive so that's where we were going.

Well actually, the concept of splitting up got floated and was firmly stamped on by Jermaine. My dear butler politely pointed out that we came across a team of elite assassins not twelve hours ago in Ireland and barely survived. There really wasn't any way we could argue with him.

As a team, we set off, leaving the hotel behind in yet another trio of hire cars. Unlike the southern reaches of Ireland, the roads here were open and busy with flowing traffic. In many ways it felt like I had come home. This wasn't exactly my part of the country, but it wasn't too far from it and looking out the window as the miles sped past, I remembered the journey I took to get me to Southampton and the Aurelia all those months ago.

Fleeing what I thought at the time was the worst moment of my life, I still marvelled at how weak and vulnerable I was back then.

Back then.

Less than a year ago.

It turned out not to be the worst moment at all. In fact, in many ways it was the best. My life changed almost overnight and though there was stress and danger now that was never present in my previous life, I was fulfilled and happy in a way I would have never thought possible before.

Before everything changed.

The car bumped over something, Jermaine muttering an apology for the thing in the road he wasn't able to avoid.

"How far now?" I asked, thinking we ought to be near the end of our estimated forty-five minute journey.

"Another five minutes, Mrs Fisher," said Sam who among all my friends was the one who continued to address me formerly. Well, him and Jermaine, obviously. Sam was reading from the satnav which showed us coming off the Hog's Back. A road linking the A3 to the market town of Farnham.

The five minutes proved to be ten as the traffic snarled coming into the business district. That wasn't where we were going to find the church, but our route went through it. Just out the other side, as we left the furniture showrooms, garden centres, and other businesses behind, the large, packed-in-tight buildings gave way to gorgeous cottages in a wonderful rural setting.

Peering at the screen mounted in the centre console, Jermaine declared, "I believe this must be it on the right."

The hedgerow would be thick with foliage in the summer months, but in winter the leaves were gone, and I could make out the outline of an ancient stone church on the other side.

Ten seconds later Jermaine angled the wheels off the road and turned into the driveway leading up to the church. We passed through a small graveyard, the gravestones arranged on both sides of the narrow road. Some were still upright as they were undoubtedly mounted once upon a time, but most were canted over at an angle where time and subsidence had robbed their foundations.

Leading our little convoy, Jermaine pulled into a parking space. At some point in the past, someone had come up with the money to pay for the church to have a proper carpark and the tarmac was lined with boxes to designate where cars should go.

Martin parked his car to our right, and Molly, claiming the right to drive because this was her country, pulled in on the left. We were out of the cars and heading for the little church mere moments later.

In the churchyard at the back of the plot, a lady wearing wellington boots above a Paddington Bear jacket – okay, so I know that's not what the style is actually called, but it was navy blue with big, chunky toggles, exactly what Paddington wears. Anyway, she spotted us and turned to come our way. She was gardening, clearing out the weeds around another grave and I assumed she was tending the last resting place of a long lost relative until I noticed the dog collar around her neck.

"The vicar," I remarked, angling my feet to converge with her path toward us.

The rest of my crowd came too, the gang of us probably looking quite strange in the quiet, rural setting.

"Can I help you?" she asked. "Welcome to St Bartholomew's by the way. I'm Reverend Wendy Mallow." In her late fifties, Reverend Wendy had ruddy cheeks, the cold biting into them to draw the blood to the surface, and wind swept, black, curly hair shot through here and there with a little grey. Short at maybe five feet two inches, she was what some might call dumpy, but carried it well. I thought it made her look friendly and approachable.

"Hello," I held out my hand for her to shake and had to wait a few seconds for her to remove a gardening glove. "I'm Patricia Fisher." I gave her my full name since she'd given me all of hers. "I'm not sure whether you can help us. This is likely to be an unusual query."

The vicar raised both her eyebrows and said, "Is it the kind of query that is best discussed over tea and biscuits? Only I've been out here a while and could do with a cuppa."

Her plain way of talking was welcome, and the conspiratorial wink her suggestion came with sealed the deal. Besides, it wasn't exactly a suggestion; she was already heading inside.

The church had a small vestry on the side nearest us, a door leading into the warm so we didn't have to go around to the front of the church to access it.

"It might be standing room only," Reverend Wendy warned. "In fact, if definitely will be for some of you because I've only got six chairs and these old bones are claiming one of them."

Tucked away from the cold air in the churchyard, Jermaine insisted on making the tea, recruiting Sam and Molly to help.

While they got busy over at the sink and little kitchen area set against one wall, the vicar prompted me to spill.

"So what is this cryptically mysterious query, Patricia?"

I took a second to frame the question in my head before starting to speak. "Have you heard of a ship called the San José?" It was a suitably cryptic way to approach the subject. I doubted she would unless she understood the significance of the objects found in her church more than a century ago.

I got the raised eyebrows from her again. Whatever she thought I might ask, it wasn't going to be anything to do with a ship.

After a few seconds of rummaging around in her brain, she declared, "No, I don't think so. Should I?"

"The San José was a Spanish treasure ship," I began. I explained about how it supposedly sunk but clearly hadn't because the treasure had been found recently by a man who was murdered before he could reveal where he made the discovery. I told her about the dagger and cup, two artefacts that should have gone to the bottom of the ocean on board the ship yet were found inside her church in the late nineteenth century. I kept going, drawing her into the story so she knew about Barbie and why we were so motivated to solve our little mystery. When I got to the end I asked, "Can you tell us anything that might be of help? Are there any Spanish graves in the churchyard? Have you ever heard a rumour about the history of this church that might make you believe it could be linked to the treasure?"

Reverend Wendy allowed herself a few moments to think and you could hear a pin drop in the room as we all waited to hear what she had to say. Slowly, she shook her head from side to side.

"You're welcome to inspect the graves here and in the larger graveyard down the street. I'm not aware of any Spanish names, but must confess I wasn't looking for them. I'm also afraid to admit I'd not heard the story about the Spanish ship or the cup and dagger that you say were found here." She made a thoughtful face. "I suppose I could ask ..."

The next thing I knew, Reverend Wendy was on her feet and tottering out of the tiny vestry.

"I need to make a call," she called out as an afterthought having left the room without an explanation.

"This feels like a bust," griped Deepa as though she'd plucked the thoughts from my head.

Pushing up and onto my feet as well, I said, "Might as well take a good look around. Maybe this is a dead end, but we need to be sure." When I suggested we needed to take a look around I didn't mean right away without speaking to Reverend Wendy first, but my friends were up and moving almost before the words left my mouth.

"We'll check the graveyard up the road," volunteered Martin, grabbing Deepa's hand to take her with him.

Schneider took Sam, Molly, and Anders outside to scope out the grounds around the church and suddenly there were only a few of us left in the vestry.

"Oh!" said Reverend Wendy, returning to find half her visiting party missing. "Were they kidnapped by aliens?"

Her question was intended to be humorous and she brought a smile to my face.

"No, they set out to check the graves. With your permission, we would also like to have a good look around the church itself."

The vicar pulled a face along with a shrug to show she didn't mind. "I, ah, I called someone," she started to say just as Hideki was rising from his chair. "The previous vicar, in fact. He was something of a history buff and surprise, surprise he knows all about the artefacts you mentioned."

Hideki sat back down, keen to hear where this was going.

"It seems the dagger and cup caused quite a stir when someone figured out what they were. Obviously, that was long before he was the vicar here. The late nineteenth century was probably twenty vicars ago, but my predecessor had scholars visit during his tenure, and another man, a Spaniard."

I shot out of my chair, startling Reverend Wendy.

"Did he get a name? I need a name!"

Hideki was on his feet too and with Jermaine crossing the room we were crowding her.

Her eyes wide, she said, "I, um, I didn't ask. Can you give me a second to make another call?"

"Please do," I begged.

The vicar reached inside her skirt, retrieving her phone from a deep pocket. We backed away a pace to give her some room, and listened openly when she thumbed the button to make the call.

"Graham? Yes, sorry, me again. I know, I know, you're about to have lunch. Sorry, I have another question. It seems the Spanish man you met has caused some interest. I don't suppose you remember his name?"

I wasn't moving a muscle as I waited to hear the answer.

Reverend Wendy had the phone to her ear rather than make the conversation public; that was her right, but I was so invested in getting Barbie back I wanted to rip the device from her hands and beg the man at the other end to strain his brain.

Containing myself, I gasped when she said, "You think you might have it written in your journal?" She flicked her eyes my way and gave me a thumbs up with her spare hand. "You can find it after lunch."

The bow-tight energy inside me caused my feet to bounce as I fought against my urge to shout that we needed the name now.

Reverend Wendy said, "Um, Graham, I suspect the need is more urgent than I might have led you to believe. I don't suppose you could bump it up the priority list?"

There was a pause as she listened to the response.

"Yes, I'm sure your wife's special salmon and asparagus quiche is heavenly and shouldn't be allowed to go cold. There is a rather more serious matter in play, Graham. A young woman's life might be at stake."

I got another thumbs up from Reverend Wendy and had to endure another pause while she listened to Graham griping about his lunch.

When she said, "Thank you, Graham. May choirs of angels bear you to the holy father himself. Yes, yes, sorry, you're not that old yet. No one is taking you to heaven before you've eaten lunch. Yes, jolly good."

She ended the call, dropping the phone back into her skirt with a satisfied grin.

"Right, he'll call back if he finds it. I've never kept a journal myself. I tried once when I was young, but I could never remember to make the entries and by the time I did I couldn't remember what happened on any given day. Graham though, well he has a bookshelf full of them. I remember how proud he was to show it off when I took over."

"Will he be able to find the name?" I asked.

I got a shrug. Not exactly helpful.

"Should we offer to help him?" suggested Jermaine. "We can go to his house and assist with the search."

Reverend Wendy pulled a sorry face. "He lives in the Outer Hebrides."

Okay, so the remote islands at the northern tip of Scotland weren't exactly around the corner, but we did have an airplane at our disposal if we needed to go there.

"Let's give him an hour, okay?" Reverend Wendy countered. "He might be getting on, but his mind is still sharp. He'll find the name if he wrote it down."

I didn't like it, but all we could do was wait.

Fight with Big Ben

"**H**i, Ben," Barbie lifted her hand to give a small wave of greeting.

"Oh, you're not getting away with that," Big Ben remarked, swooping in close to wrap her in a hug. They kissed cheeks and parted again. "Now how about you don't break my heart this time and tell me you ditched that boyfriend of yours."

"Miss Berkeley," Xavier warned.

The tone of his voice made Big Ben's right eyebrow twitch in question. Xavier had no idea who the man was, but Barbie did. Benjamin Winters worked at the Blue Moon Investigation Agency with Tempest Michaels and several other talented individuals. He wasn't a detective like the others, but the hired muscle. At six feet and seven inches, he was a unit of a man until one stood him next to Gomez who was bigger in every direction.

Nevertheless, Barbie knew Big Ben's prowess when it came to fighting and would bet on him against anyone except perhaps Jermaine.

"These guys bothering you?" Big Ben asked, the question aimed at Barbie though he was looking at the two men flanking her.

"We are her associates," Xavier began to reply only to get cut off by Big Ben.

"I was talking to the lady, friend," he snapped, menace in his voice.

"Ben, it's fine," Barbie tried to say. "Really, I'm … I'm working is all and in kind of a hurry. Sorry, but I have to go."

Barbie's heat raced. What would they do if Big Ben didn't step away and let them leave? Xavier and Gomez were both armed. Xavier had a gun and a knife at least and given the size of Gomez he could have a small rocket launcher in his pocket for all she knew. Maybe Big Ben could take Gomez in a fair fight, but this wouldn't be one and there were people everywhere. How many might get hurt if Xavier started shooting?

"You should just go, Ben," she replied, her voice unavoidably tinged with the worry she felt. "I'll call you later, okay?"

Ben's eyebrows twitched again; he was sizing things up.

Looking into Barbie's eyes, he said, "You're sure?"

"She said so, didn't she?" Xavier remarked before Barbie could say anything.

There could be no mistake that Big Ben was suspicious, and he nodded his head and kind of skewed his lips to one side – a sure sign he was debating his next move.

Barbie felt so tense in that moment that she stopped breathing, waiting to see what he would do.

With a nonchalant shrug that surprised her, he smiled and said, "Okay, babe. You got places to be, go be there." Twitching his focus from her to Gomez, Big Ben thrust out his hand. "Not often I meet a person taller than me."

Gomez looked down at the hand showing no sign he was going to take it. That didn't matter for Big Ben had a plan for both eventualities. With the giant's attention aimed at the ground, Big Ben threw everything into an uppercut punch. His hand became a fist on the way up, his whole body getting involved as he drove his arm up through Gomez's jaw and beyond.

"Ben, no!" Barbie screamed, terrified this was going to end in someone's death.

Too late to stop the attack, she saw Gomez tumbling back and away. Rooted momentarily to the spot, she caught the shocked look on Xavier's face, but it wasn't there for long.

The giant-killing uppercut took all Big Ben's inertia in one direction which meant it took him longer than it otherwise might to tackle what he perceived to be the second opponent. He wasn't sure what was going on, but had never seen Barbie looking more worried, and he'd spent a lot of time studying the blonde woman's perfect face.

Maybe he was wrong, but there was something off about the slacker dude in the hoody's accent. That got his senses twitching, but it was the man mountain he travelled with that caused the attack: Big Ben could recognise a henchman when he saw one.

The guy with the blonde dreadlocks and the hoody was pulling something from his left sleeve – Big Ben caught a flash of something black, but was already committed to his strike by the time he realised it was a gun.

He smashed a scything boot into the smaller man's solar plexus, enjoying the outrush of air it brought. The blow doubled the dreadlocks over, presenting the back of his head which Big Ben drove into the ground with a fist that struck like a hammer.

Two seconds had passed and both men were down. If Barbie were able to breathe, she might have remarked on how incredible a display it was. The crowd filling the open plaza outside the cathedral were all turned to watch, fingers pointing to make sure everyone was looking the right way.

The fact that they were, made the gasp when Gomez growled in rage and stood back up, all the louder.

Big Ben had been about to beg Barbie to tell him what was going on, but the threat was back and that demanded his attention. Getting the first strike in was easier than expected, but the giant looked like a fighter and he was mad now.

What Barbie didn't know was that Gomez wanted to fight. Suffering from a rare genetic disease that numbed his nerve endings so he could feel no pain, he genuinely enjoyed taking on tough guys. It didn't matter how hard they hit him, he couldn't feel the injuries.

There were few benefits from his condition, which made physical contact with a woman pointless, so he got his fun where he could.

He had two guns strapped inside his jacket and an eighteen-inch-long knife along the small of his back, but he wasn't going to use any of those. Not when it was so much more enjoyable to use his hands.

Big Ben surged forward, landing a right cross, a left jab, a sweeping leg that sent Gomez in the wrong direction. Reversing his own trajectory, Big Ben ducked a haymaker from the taller man and drove a knee into his midriff.

None of it had any real effect.

Backing away a pace, Big Ben called to Barbie. "Um, babes, am I fighting a cyborg or something?"

"Ben this isn't helping!" she cried, certain he was going to get himself killed. Xavier was still on the ground, and if ever there was a time for her to seize the phone, this was it. Scrambling, she fell upon the Spaniard, searching his pockets oblivious to the problem her reply inadvertently created.

Uncertain he could have heard her correctly, Big Ben swung his head to look at Barbie, "Huh?"

It was the opening Gomez needed. Able to move surprisingly fast for a man his size, Gomez surged forward, a punch like a sledgehammer splitting Big Ben's lips in one go.

With blood coming from his mouth, Big Ben staggered back a pace only to find the bigger man was already upon him. He defended well, absorbing the barrage on his arms, shoulders, and the meaty parts of his thighs. Looking for an opportunity to create a little space so he could counter strike, his rear foot caught against the lip of a curb and he stumbled. It was a stroke of bad luck and poor timing that played straight into the hands of his opponent.

Momentarily off balance, Big Ben wasn't able to prevent the next fist. Gomez swung the punch with enough force that it knocked Big Ben's guard out of the way to land squarely on his left eyebrow.

The skin tore, blood flowing into his eye as Big Ben took another pace back. Forced to blink, the next shot got through his guard and the next one too. He was losing – not a scenario he was used to – and when a kick to the inside of his knee took him down into a crouch, Big Ben knew he was in trouble.

A shot rang out to draw screams of horror from the morbid onlookers. Watching a fight between two enormous combatants was one thing, hanging around when someone started shooting was entirely another.

Barbie screamed, "Stop! Or the next one goes in your back."

Gomez still had his hands up, fists formed and ready to deploy. Big Ben was down on one knee, battered and bleeding yet still trying to fight.

Looking over his shoulder at the blonde woman, Gomez grinned and turned back to the man he intended to kill with his bare hands.

Seeing his decision, Barbie aimed a second shot into the grass and levelled the gun at Gomez's back once more.

"I mean it," she stuttered, her voice quavering despite telling it to stay bold and confident. In that moment, regardless of all her determination never to kill, if Gomez advanced on Big Ben again, she was going to put a bullet between his shoulder blades.

"I think perhaps I should take that, Miss Berkeley." Xavier was back on his feet and holding his phone.

She had tried to find a way to deactivate the cuffs on her wrists, but she needed time, not just a few seconds in the middle of a fight. The app was unfamiliar and confusing. Too confusing for her to figure out in the fleeting moments before she abandoned it to save Big Ben.

A siren sounded in the distance.

Barbie's breathing was heavy; adrenalin making her pulse rapid, but faced with a difficult decision, she chose to take control.

"Gomez! Back in the car!" she yelled, adding, "Now!" when he didn't immediately move.

Big Ben rose to follow, and she trained the gun on him instead of Gomez.

"No, Ben. You stay here. Don't pursue me. This isn't your fight."

Gomez grinned at her choice of words, but whatever was in his head he kept to himself as usual.

Xavier nodded, "Come, Gomez. We must leave. Once again, Miss Berkeley's tactics are sound."

Xavier tried to take the gun back, but she held it away from him and moved out of reach, heading for the car.

"You can have it back when we are out of here," she spat, arguing with herself because she knew she could shoot him and Gomez both if she chose to. If she killed them no one else would die. Maybe the explosives around her wrists would go off but she doubted it. She could kill them both and be free. The police would call bomb disposal, and someone would figure out how to get the cuffs off.

She could be free.

But would she ever sleep again?

Helping Patty to take down bad guys was one thing. They never killed anyone while solving cases, although, to be fair, a few people died of their own ill-thought decisions. That was far removed from pulling the trigger herself - to kill two men just to save her own life.

With a defeated sigh, she handed over the handgun, slapping it down into Xavier's palm when the car pulled away. She got one last look at Big Ben's blood covered face as they swept by him and away from the cathedral.

The sirens continued to sound in the distance, coming ever closer but unlikely to catch them. Two feet away on the other side of the car, Xavier inspected the contents of the wooden box. The coins spilled onto the ground when Big Ben felled him, but were back in the box now. They were of little interest though compared to the piece of parchment in his hands.

"Miss Berkeley, I shall need you to decode this message now."

Phone Calls

Waiting for Reverend Wendy's predecessor, Graham, to call, we chose to go through the church with a fine-toothed comb. We didn't know what we were looking for and chose to rely on the age-old adage of 'we'll know it when we see it'.

Built in the fifteenth century, the church was as solid as it was old. According to Reverend Wendy, the pews and altar we could see were replacements for the originals and were added in the 1940's. The rest of the church was pretty much original, which meant if there was anything left here by the crew of the San José then it was probably still where they put it.

Martin, Deepa, Schneider, and the others all returned empty handed. They found nothing of interest outside in the churchyard or up the road in the little village's graveyard. Together we crawled along the floor between the pews, checked behind and around the altar, and inspected the walls. Jermaine ascended the church's tower to see if it might hold any secrets, but after an hour we were forced to admit there was either nothing here to find or it was so well hidden we were never going to find it.

I had just plonked my behind onto one of the pews to contemplate our situation when my phone rang. Each time it did that I fervently prayed it would be Barbie calling. Not from her own phone; that had been out of service since she went missing. However, my resourceful blonde friend would find a way to call me if she got free. It wasn't like it would take more than a smile from her to convince a man to hand his phone over.

It wasn't a number showing on my screen though, as it would be if Barbie were using a phone my device didn't know, but Tempest Michaels, the owner and head of Blue Moon Investigations. Why was he calling?

"Tempest, good morning," I said, checking the time because my stomach assured me it was getting close to lunch. "How are you?" I felt like there wasn't time for phone calls and could not guess why he might be calling. Regardless, there was no reason not to be polite.

"Good morning, Patricia," he replied, his very British accent always a pleasure to hear. "I'm fine. I'm at my office patching up Big Ben's face. He just got into a fight with a giant and claims Barbie then threatened him with a gun. Can I assume your friend is in some kind of trouble?"

"Barbie!" my exclamation caught the attention of everyone in the church and those in the vestry who came running to see what was going on. "Big Ben saw Barbie? Where was she?"

"Here in Rochester. He spotted her coming out of the cathedral."

I knew exactly where that was. That she was with the giant made perfect sense, but the other part couldn't be right.

"You said she pointed a gun at Big Ben?"

Big Ben's voice echoed down the line. "And told me to leave her alone. Said it wasn't my fight."

"Sorry," Tempest apologised, "I forgot to say that I have you on speaker."

"That's not a problem," I murmured, trying to make sense of the new information. Barbie had a gun but didn't use it to get free from Xavier's giant. Why wouldn't she escape if she could? I couldn't make sense of it.

Hideki, Jermaine, and all the others crowded around me.

"What's happening?" Hideki wanted to know. "Is that Barbie?"

"Tempest, I'm putting you on speaker at this end. I have all my friends with me."

"Hello, everyone," he replied. "What have I missed?"

The disappointment on the faces around me, especially Hideki and Jermaine, near broke my heart again. They dared to hope it was Barbie when they heard me cry out her name.

I took a few moments to fill Tempest in, explaining about the San José, the treasure, the murders, Finn Murphy, and Barbie's kidnapping.

Was it kidnap though? She had a gun, so unless it wasn't loaded – a possibility that provided an explanation for her actions – she was there willingly. That still made no sense though. Barbie was fast on her feet. Really fast. From Big Ben's description she could have run away at any time while he was fighting the giant in Rochester. Yet she chose not to.

According to Big Ben's account, she tended to a second man who was with them. I guessed that was Xavier though the description of a dreadlocked slacker dude failed to match my expectations. He was a master of disguise though ...

"Where are you guys now?" Tempest wanted to know.

"In a church just outside Farnham in Surrey," I let him know. "Why do you ask?"

"Sounds like you could use all the help you can get. Plus, I think Big Ben wants another round with the giant."

"I have a score to settle," Big Ben's deep bass voice rattled in the background.

"There's really no need, guys," I replied. "We'll be moving on soon and I really don't know where we are going next."

Tempest said nothing and in that moment of quiet, another phone rang. My head snapped up when I saw Reverend Wendy reaching into her skirt once more.

"It's Graham," she announced, answering the call and stepping away to speak more privately.

Getting to my feet, which forced all those around me to back up a bit to give me room, I said, "Tempest we have to go. There might be a development. I'll call you back as soon as we find Barbie."

He wished me luck, but I was already thumbing the button to rudely cut him off. I would apologise later; the call from Graham was just too important to miss.

Once again, Reverend Wendy was keeping her conversation private so even though we followed her across the church and back into the vestry, the only sound her voice and our footsteps, we could only hear her half of the conversation.

"You were able to eat the quiche *and* look for the journal entry," she said. "Your very lovely wife brought your lunch to your study. That is good."

It was a good thing Graham was a thousand miles away because had he been present I might have throttled the information from him.

"You found the correct entry," Wendy confirmed, shooting us all another thumbs up. "It was twenty-two years ago. Goodness that's a long time."

A man from Spain came to the church more than two decades ago asking about the dagger and cup. Could it be the same man? It was hard to judge Xavier's age as he was always in disguise when I saw him. He could walk past me in the street and I wouldn't know who it was, but I doubted he could be much older than fifty. That being the case, Xavier would have been a younger man twenty-two years ago, yet quite old enough to be pursuing the San José and its cargo.

"Do I have a pen?" Reverend Wendy patted her pockets and looked around.

Jermaine produced a notepad from a pocket and with a click and a flourish presented her a pen with which she could write.

The vicar spelled it out as Graham relayed it over the phone and my heart skipped the moment she did.

"X-A-V-I-E-R S-I-L-V-S-T-R-E. Xavier Silvestre?" she confirmed back to her old friend. "Okay, got it. Thank you, Graham." She continued to wrap up her conversation while all around her, the rest of us were on our phones.

"I have him," growled Hideki half a second before Jermaine declared the same.

On their screens were pictures of a man in his late forties or early fifties. His black hair was receding but not gone in what I deemed to be the most recent shots and he was handsome but not overtly so which is to say his features were pleasantly arranged, but most women wouldn't cross the room to meet him.

One of the best and worst things about the internet is the amount of personal detail available for the world to read whether you want them to or not. In under a minute we knew he was a billionaire (in Euros), single with no children, was well known for philanthropic and charitable pursuits, and lived just outside Seville in his family home.

It failed to highlight that he was a homicidal egomaniac with an unquenchable thirst for treasure, but I imagined that was a side of his personality he chose to keep private. There was also no mention of his seven-foot-tall associate, but I knew I was looking at the right man even though he looked nothing like the person who came on board the Aurelia posing as Professor Noriega.

"So that's him." Jermaine's expression was hard to read. He was looking at the face of the man who took his best friend, a man he probably wanted to hurt. Not out of vengeance, you understand, but from a sense of moral justice. To get Barbie back, Jermaine would wade through a sea of Xavier Silvestres and leave them all bleeding in his wake if that was what it took.

Now that we had a name, we could take action, but what did that actually mean? We had no evidence of his crimes. I couldn't even claim I'd seen him committing them because he looked different when he attacked me and Barbie in the ladies' restroom on the British Union Isles.

Thinking about it, we had nothing whatsoever we could use to get law enforcement agencies involved. He came to a church in Farnham more than twenty years ago – so what?

Nevertheless, I wasn't going to be beaten by my own self-doubt.

My phone was still in my left hand from the call with Tempest. I brought up my contacts list and called Captain Danvers. It would be early morning in New York; too early for him to be at work, but he would be up and eating his breakfast or getting ready for his day.

He said, "Patricia," the moment the call connected. "How did you know?"

I opened and closed my mouth a couple of times, confusion robbing my voice.

"How did I know what?" I finally asked.

"That they cracked it. I was moments away from calling you myself. They traced the money to its source, Patricia. Some guy in Spain, apparently."

"Xavier Silvestre," I said his name, but my voice was a whisper, too timid to believe we might have a tangible thread connecting him to the case.

I could almost hear the frown on Danny's brow when he spoke again. "Yeah. Hey, how do you always do that? How could you possibly know the guy's name. I only read it for the first time myself twenty minutes ago. Do you have spyware on my phone or something?" He sounded a little angry, like maybe he believed I really was that tech savvy.

"I'm in a church in England. He was here. We learned his name ourselves just a few minutes ago. He's the one who took Barbie. It's the same man who came on board the Aurelia and stole the treasure." Okay, so the treasure stealing was his giant goon of a henchman, but it amounted to the same thing. "What can you do now? What're your next steps?"

"Well, I need to get to work and see the evidence for myself. The forensic accountant guys pulled an all-nighter to bring this one home. They have a name and they can trace the payments into Hugo Lockhart's bank account, but giving someone money isn't a crime, Patricia. At best I can make some calls and see if I can get Interpol interested enough to speak with Senor Silvestre."

"Well, they won't find him at home. He was in Rochester in England just an hour or so ago."

"England?"

"Yes, a friend of mine saw Barbie and got into a fight with Xavier's henchman."

"The bald giant? Is your friend dead?"

"No. He's not much smaller than the giant in actual fact, but he did get beat up by the sounds of things. The point is, he is here and not in Spain." I chose to leave out the part about Barbie being armed and twisted the truth a little to get things moving faster. "There was gunplay involved. You know how twitchy the British are about people brandishing guns in public. Interpol won't have any trouble getting help from the police here if they can step in with information about the shooter."

I figured they would quickly find out Barbie had the gun, but once Interpol were involved they would stay the course and if they went looking for Barbie they would find Xavier Silvestre and that was good enough for me.

Captain Danvers said, "Okay, Patricia, I'm heading to work in a few minutes. I'll do what I can to set things in motion. You were right about the other crimes, by the way."

"Other crimes?"

"The ones in Rio. I think that's how the forensic guys cracked it. There was money in the account of a man called Antonio Bardem. The payments were in a different currency, but the figures match almost exactly and he started getting the payments the moment he took on the job. The guy he replaced used to get that money too. I doubt it's any coincidence Bardem is also dead, stabbed in a back-alley miles from his house just like you said."

"Just like Hugo Lockhart," I pointed out.

"Exactly. It's all circumstantial, but now we have a name ..."

"You can get warrants to check if he was in the country at the time of their deaths."

"Well Interpol can and that will have to be good enough. I'll call if I find out anything new." He paused for a second before asking, "Hey, what are you doing? You said you found out about Xavier Silvestre in a church? How did you know to look there?"

"The San José, Danny. Artefacts from the old Spanish ship found their way here. I think we are closing in on the treasure."

Bad news for Xavier

On the back seat of the black Mercedes, Xavier Silvestre continued to curse under his breath. Barbie glanced his way periodically, enjoying how angry he looked. His rage was all aimed at himself.

The second clue sent them to a church in Surrey, an English county in the south of the country. Barbie wasn't sure if she'd ever heard of a place called Farnham, but that's where they were going, and Xavier had been there before.

Not just to Farnham, but to the very church now locked into the car's satnav.

Once Barbie decoded the message they found inside the wooden box with the Spanish gold coins, Xavier all but exploded.

"Twenty years!" he roared. "Twenty years ago I was right there! I was in that church, right on the spot of the second marker."

That he'd been so close and allowed the treasure to slip through his fingers was making the man irrationally angry. From his description of talking to the vicar at the time, there was nothing to find. Unless one had the instruction from the first marker in their possession.

With it they knew precisely where to look, and it came as no surprise to Barbie that Xavier hadn't found it by accident on his previous visit.

The second marker was located inside the wall of the church. When Henri Cristobal stopped there, it was not long after a storm damaged the roof and one wall. At night, when the stonemasons effecting the repair were asleep, Henri stole into the churchyard and hid another box just like the first inside the wall. His note gave a location measured from the north-eastern corner. The message claimed his initials were carved into the rock behind which the box was hidden. In theory the box would be easy to find though it sounded likely they were going to have to employ a sledgehammer to find it.

Regardless that it had taken Xavier more than two decades to return to the site of the second marker, it could not be denied that they were getting closer to the treasure. How many markers and whether they were all still there to be found were answers they did not yet possess, but leaving the A3 just outside Guildford on their way to Farnham, they would soon be back at the church Xavier visited so many years ago.

Xavier's phone rang, the noise an abrupt interruption in the conversation and music-free interior of the car. Barbie watched when he took it out, noting which pocket he favoured for future reference. It was the same one she found it in when Big Ben knocked him out.

"Silvestre." He answered the phone then glanced at Barbie which told her he'd made a mistake. Having introduced himself as Xavier, Barbie assumed it was a false name. Now she believed she had his real name – another reason for him to need her dead when they found the treasure.

She faced forward once more, looking out at the English countryside as the car swept up and over the Hog's Back on its way to Farnham.

Barbie didn't get to hear Silvestre's phone call which was a shame because it would have filled her with hope.

The call came from a man called Joseph Tremblay who worked at Interpol. He wasn't one of their field agents, but assigned to IT support where he excelled. He worked in the basement of the headquarters building where he was assigned to a desk and rarely left it to go anywhere other than home. His position, and general indifference to his department from the rest of the agency, allowed him to carefully insert a subroutine many years ago when he was asked to do so by a wealthy Spanish philanthropist.

He almost refused, arguing with his conscience for days before finally agreeing when the man doubled his original offer.

The subroutine sat idly in the background of Interpol's computers where it would never be discovered because he was the one managing the IT systems. Its purpose was very simple: If the name 'Xavier Silvestre' ever came across a desk at Interpol, was ever typed into the database, or a file with that name was ever created, he was to check it, copy it and, if possible, delete it. He was also to call Xavier Silvestre in person at his first opportunity.

That was precisely what he was doing.

"It has happened, Senor Silvestre," he reported dutifully. "It cannot be deleted though."

"Why is that?" Silvestre asked, his voice calm for he had no reason yet to be anything else.

"Because it's being handled as a live case, sir. They are investigating you in connection with several murders." Joseph held back his desire to ask if Senor Silvestre might be guilty. Honestly, he didn't want to know. The money he'd taken over the years had paid for a summer retreat in San Tropez, plus more than one new car. If Senor Silvestre was guilty and they investigated his finances, they would trace the money back to ... Joseph didn't want to think about what that could mean.

Remaining calm, and certain there was no way Interpol or anyone else would ever be able to connect him to a murder and make it stick, he asked, "What else can you tell me?"

"Well, sir, there is mention of a woman called Patricia Fisher."

Silvestre's jaw muscles clenched.

"Do you know who that is, Senor? She's a famous English sleuth."

"I am familiar with the name," he cut Joseph off to make him move on.

"Oh, well, it would seem she is involved. I can see that an Interpol agent has been assigned to liaise with her."

"The name of the agent?" Silvestre interrupted again.

"Oh, um, its Chase Mitchell. He's from the London office. I would imagine he'll be making contact later today. There is also a police captain in New York listed in the file. He's the one who raised the case and presented the initial evidence, sir."

Silvestre absorbed the information with a huff of impatience. His search for the San José and its treasure had never been an easy one, nor did he ever fool himself into believing it might be. Were the ship easy to find, someone else would have done it long ago. However, now that he was close, the interference of law enforcement agencies and the ever-meddling Patricia Fisher were distractions he could do without.

Everything would change if he found the San José. No one would care that he'd been forced to kill a few insignificant individuals. His lawyers would muddy the water enough that even if law enforcers thought they had a case, it would drag out for years before it ever saw a courtroom which he doubted it ever would.

Nevertheless, this latest development was troubling. Was there something he missed? Did he inadvertently leave behind some small clue when he took Hugo Lockhart's life, or the lives of any of the people who came before him?

He didn't think so, but how could he be certain? The answer, he knew, was that he couldn't.

Exhaling a slow breath to steady himself, he chose to ignore the possibility the police were onto him. He was on the trail of the San José's near priceless treasure, and nothing could be allowed to deviate him from his path. Not now that he was so close.

The car slowed when they met traffic in Farnham, but they were soon out the other side and heading for the church. Silvestre remembered the landscape even though he'd only visited once so many years ago. It was summer when he first visited, and though the countryside looked familiar, it was also very different from his memory. He could see the church for a start, he realised. Looking through the window next to his head, the old stone building with its square tower and cross on top was visible through the hedgerow. So too was ...

With a jolt, he recognised Patricia Fisher's tall, black butler. He was too far away to make out his features, but his shape and hair was familiar enough to convince Silvestre. That meant the small blonde woman just to Jermaine's left had to be the woman herself. There was close to a dozen people in total, all walking away from the church.

"Gomez, slow down," he instructed, his body tense as he watched Patricia's butler open the rear door of an Audi A4. The whole party appeared to be leaving apart from a woman standing several yards behind them. She wheeled a bicycle out of the church gate just as the cars pulled away, the two-wheeled contraption carrying her away at an angle across a field that led to some houses further along the main road.

With Gomez proceeding slowly along the road, they were correctly positioned to see the cars exit the church driveway and turn to go the other way.

His mind racing to calculate the best strategy to follow, he told himself there was no way they could have found the box. Patricia Fisher's presence had to be because she knew about the dagger and cup - it was available knowledge one could find on the internet. She was here only out of coincidence, Silvestre was certain of it.

Speaking to Gomez, he said, "Don't follow. Pull into the church. The box will be there."

Next to him on the backseat, Barbie allowed a small smirk to tease her lips. Maybe the box was there and maybe it wasn't, but she was prepared to bet money Patty was at least one step ahead of her captor.

It was the second time her friend had appeared unexpectedly. Had Silvestre not spotted Patty and the others first, they might now be engaged in yet another car chase. More and more Barbie was coming to terms with the very real possibility that she was going to die before this adventure was done, but so long as Patricia Fisher won out over the man who kidnapped her, she would go out with a smile on her face.

Silvestre's Next Move

A t the church, it was instantly apparent that Patricia Fisher and friends had not found the box hidden in the wall. It was completely intact, and the stone inscribed with H.C. was exactly where Henri Cristobal's message said it would be.

"Gomez." Silvestre said the one word and stood back to give his henchman room to work.

Using the tyre iron out of the car's boot, the huge man took a rough swing and jabbed the pointed end into the mortar between the blocks. Five minutes later, when it was easy to see Gomez would need at least double that again to get the stone free, Silvestre returned to the car.

There he began to strip his clothes, removing the hoody he wore for his disguise in Rochester and replacing it with a crisp white shirt. Fighting her natural urge to look away when the man removed his clothes, she saw the devices strapped to his forearms. Two small calibre pistols sat on the inside of each arm, ready to deploy at a moment's notice like some kind of quickdraw expert.

That was how he managed to get a gun into his hand so swiftly when she came up behind him in the cathedral. Now fascinated, she watched when he removed a knife from a pouch inside one sleeve of his hoody. Like Gomez, Xavier was a walking arsenal.

Over the next few minutes, Barbie observed a fascinating transformation.

The wig of dreadlocks went, replaced with a new hairpiece. This one was mostly grey and suited his age better. The addition of a neatly trimmed grey beard and moustache changed his features completely. A tie and jacket that matched the trousers he then donned made him look like a businessman, Barbie noted before changing her mind.

No, she thought, he looks like an FBI agent. His suit was neat but functional, with a pin to hold the tie in place and sensible, yet shiny shoes in which a person would be able to run.

If he wanted to look different, he was achieving it.

By the time Silvestre returned to check on Gomez, the stone was hanging out of the wall. Moments later it fell to the ground with a muffled thud.

Gomez stepped back to allow Silvestre access – he wanted to be the one to pluck the box from the wall. He removed his suit jacket for the task, unwilling to dirty the right sleeve when he reached inside.

Expecting that he would pull the box out straight away, Barbie frowned as she watched the Spaniard rooting around. He pulled out his arm and peered inside the hole. Next, he reached for his phone, selecting the torch function to better see before launching into a tirade of Spanish expletives.

It required no translation, nor did the reason behind it: the box wasn't there.

They would never know but the stonemasons found the box the morning after Henri Cristobal placed it inside the wall. They were unhappy with how that part of the wall was sitting and chose to take some of it apart again. The presence of the box was a mystery, each of the team of three masons accusing the other two of playing 'silly buggers'. That was until they opened it and found the gold. The note with the gold received minimal scrutiny and was discarded when they could make no sense of it.

With no way to know the truth behind what happened to the box, Silvestre formed another conclusion: that Patricia Fisher had it. It must have been removed from the wall many years before. It could be centuries, but if the secrets within were there to be deciphered, then Patricia Fisher had them now. Others may have looked at the box, but only she would know what it represented.

Worse yet, Silvestre knew there was a chance, however slim, that she knew his name now. Not just his first name that was no clue at all given how popular it was. Back when he first visited the church, it had not yet occurred to him to hide his identity. The disguises and fake identities started years later when he recognised the need for subterfuge.

His hatred for the troublesome woman trebled in that instant. Patricia Fisher was ahead of him and might be on the final leg to find the treasure. He wasn't going to be denied. Not now. Not today. His choice of outfit was dual purpose. It was part of a disguise that would fool anyone who bothered to look his way. In Patricia Fisher's case, he needed it because she had already met him, but more than making his appearance vastly different from the previous disguise he wore, he wanted to look like he worked in law enforcement. The cheap suit was one he'd donned before to play the part of a police detective. Adding glasses further distorted his features and a fake ID, quickly manufactured using a portable machine he kept with his suitcase of costumes, finished the disguise.

Knowing what he did, Silvestre knew he could contact Patricia Fisher and act the part of Chase Mitchell. Gomez would need to remain out of sight, but if Silvestre played the role as well as he knew he could, the annoying woman would drop her guard and he would be able to kill her, the butler, her strange assistant with his obvious mental capacity issues, and all the rest of her friends.

Once she'd led him to the treasure, that is.

Boxley Abbey

"Half an hour, madam," Jermaine advised to my enquiry about how long it would take us to get to the shop in Boxley Abbey.

The funny thing was that when we tried to put Boxley Abbey into the satnav it failed to find it. I thought perhaps Sam might have misspelled it, but he hadn't. Using my phone, I discovered that Boxley Abbey wasn't so much a place as it was an, um, Abbey.

It was a monastery founded in the eleventh century by monks who were drawn to the area due to a natural spring producing unusually clear water. The shop was there to cater to tourists who visited to explore the old buildings and because, according to the website, they had events in the grounds such as weekly farmers' markets and vintage car rallies.

Finn Murphy went there and ... well, keep this to yourself, but when I found out it was a monastery, the back of my head itched. The odd sensation that occurred randomly during my cases to let me know I was on the right path had barely happened at any point during the last two days, so the reoccurrence now made me question how significant the location might be.

Should we have gone there first? Well, only time would tell, but visiting the church in Farnham and being able to set the attack dogs on the man behind Barbie's disappearance was worth the time it took to go there.

The abbey was a short hop along the coast from Lymington, the place where Finn mailed his postcard, and not far from Southampton – the signs for it were on every road to tell us how close we were. The clues were all tying up, but the monastery was inland, more than a mile from the coast and it was such a busy coastline that even three hundred years ago, a ship could not have been wrecked there without people noticing.

That this might be just another stop on the path to figuring out where Finn was when he found the San José was a concern I did my best to ignore. Truthfully, I believed we were getting close. Finn Murphy snuck onto the Aurelia in Southampton, of that I was fairly sure. The dates tied up so if it wasn't there, he would have needed to follow it around the Mediterranean to board it there somewhere. Frankly, that sounded improbable.

That being true, Finn Murphy must have found the treasure not long beforehand and therefore we were in the right area. I knew I ought to feel comforted by that, but I didn't. The treasure's location had remained a secret all this time because it was hard or even impossible to find. We were on our way to visit a shop where the one person in the world who found the treasure stole a shirt.

Where did we go after that? Was there anything to find there other than a retailer with an item missing from their inventory? It was the only place left on our list though, so if it failed to yield a new clue, we were going to be something close to sunk.

When my phone rang I was staring into nothingness, the barren, winter countryside flashing by outside. As always, I said a silent prayer that it would be Barbie calling and my heart skipped when the number came up as unknown.

Tentatively, I answered. "Hello?"

"This is agent Chase Mitchel of Interpol," said a man with an English accent. "Am I speaking with Mrs Fisher."

My heart rate went up a little further.

"Yes, this is she."

"Mrs Fisher, I have been assigned to assist with your kidnapping case."

I spluttered my surprise, "That was fast work. Captain Danvers only contacted you a few hours ago."

There was a good deal of smugness in his voice when he said, "Well, this is Interpol, Mrs Fisher. We are known for solving the complex cases. I was led to believe you were in the Southampton area and I have already left London. Can you give me your location, please. I think my first and best step should be to interview you and find out everything you can tell me about the history of the case. From the notes I have, it sounds like there is some kind of treasure hunt behind the kidnapping?"

"That's right," I confirmed. We talked for a couple of minutes, just long enough for me to tell him where we were going and why and give some small pieces of background information because Interpol knew nothing about Finn Murphy or the San José.

He was going to find me at Boxley Abbey as soon as he could get there and asked that we might wait for him before moving on. I saw no reason not to comply with his request.

When I put my phone away, thoughts of Agent Mitchel and Interpol went with it. My focus was on Xavier Silvestre. I took my phone out again and thumbed back through my list of calls to find Xavier's number. My thumb hovered over the screen.

Should I call him? Now that Interpol were on to him, would he get nervous and release Barbie? Or would he kill her? If I called, it wouldn't be to gloat, but to try to make him see reason. Ultimately, I decided I couldn't risk the chance that he might panic and vanish. He was in England this morning, in Rochester of all places. That we were in the same country again made me believe he was also closing in on the treasure. Why he went to Rochester I could not guess, but the bigger mystery was to do with Barbie and how it was that Big Ben came to believe she was working with the murderous Spaniard.

Jermaine turned his head a little to the left to speak to me from the driver's seat. "Nearly there, madam."

The major roads leading through the south of England were far behind us, the route to Lymington a winding one through lots of small country villages with thatched roofs and quaint names. Snatching a look through the windscreen, I saw a road sign stating it was three miles to Lymington, though that wasn't our destination.

The satnav claimed we had less than a mile to go and that the remaining distance would take us two minutes. Less than a minute later we could see the Abbey. It was a large building set in beautiful grounds. It was visible because we were above it, descending from higher ground. It looked to be two stories high with small towers at each end. Rectangular rather than square, it looked old like the church in Farnham but not a thousand years old as I was led to believe.

Telling myself it must have been upgraded or rebuilt at some point in the last few hundred years – which made sense – I made sure all my things were packed away and got ready for the next stage of our hunt.

Cruising through the abbey's welcoming entrance gate, I looked for signs that might point out the shop. Now closing in on mid-afternoon, I hoped they were open this late into the season. A spike of panic shot through me. Why hadn't I thought of that before? What if they were shut? It was low season for people to be visiting anywhere, but coming through the trees I saw my concerns were for naught. The site's carpark had three large, modern coaches in it, each there as part of a tour, no doubt.

We parked the cars in an area reserved for them away from the coach park. Reforming as a team yet again, I told everyone who wasn't in my car about the call from Interpol. It was seen as good news by all – having law enforcement on our side, especially an organisation that could cross borders without jurisdiction issues, gave us a powerful ally.

A chill breeze coming from the sea way off in the distance, forced me to wrap my coat close to my body.

"Are we going to wait for Agent Mitchel to get here?" Anders questioned, the tone of his voice indicating he didn't think we needed to.

I started walking towards the buildings. "No," I replied over my shoulder. "I'm not sure what we will find here, but I doubt it will aide Interpol in their search for Xavier Silvestre and Barbie."

There was much speculation from the team regarding why Barbie might have pulled a gun on Big Ben and chosen to stay with her captors when she could have escaped. The leading theory centred on another hostage who would suffer if she failed to comply with Xavier Silvestre's instructions and I had to agree it made sense. I certainly wasn't able to offer a more tenable motive to explain her actions.

Mostly I hoped she would be able to tell us herself soon.

The shop at the Abbey was not manned by men in brown tunics with odd patterns shaved into their heads as my imagination suggested it would. Instead, it was staffed by three ladies. One in her sixties, one in her forties, and one in her late teens. I didn't see it at first, but when they revealed they were three generations of the same family, the resemblance became obvious.

They remembered Finn Murphy when I showed them a picture and confirmed it was Maggie, the elder lady, who spoke with Dr Davis the previous day. Other than that, they had nothing to tell us.

The shop sold a range of souvenirs, toys, craft things, woodwork and pottery made on the site by the monks, and a range of garments embroidered with the Boxley Abbey logo – a silhouette of the main building.

I was about to move on when the youngest of the trio, Maggie's granddaughter, Perdita, said, "I've no idea why he felt the need to steal it. With his staff discount it wasn't expensive."

Jermaine spoke first. "Staff discount? He worked there?"

All three ladies frowned and looked at one another.

"How did you not know that?" asked Perdita's mother, Carol. "You seem to know so much about the man it never occurred to me you wouldn't know why he was here."

"How long?" I asked. "How long did he work here for?"

Carol looked at her mother when she answered, checking with her to see if she was right. "Oh, about a month, I think. He worked in the brewery. They make scrumpy when the apples are in season and two different ales. The way I heard it, he knew almost as much about brewing beer as the abbot. Apparently, he hired Finn on the spot. He lived here and worked here, and then one day, poof!" Carol made a gesture with her hands to accompany the sound to show Finn vanished like a puff of smoke.

"He came in here the day he disappeared," said Maggie. "Asked to try on a shirt and snuck out with it while I wasn't looking. I thought he would come back to pay for it later, but he never did."

I was still listening to the three ladies, but they were getting significantly less than my full attention. Their topic of discussion was no longer of any interest. Finn worked here, but he left abruptly.

"Sorry," I interrupted Maggie who was arguing with her daughter and granddaughter about something to do with prices, their conversation having veered off on a tangent. "Do you know when he left here? The date?"

All three looked at each other again. It was months ago now and they were struggling to be exact.

"I can tell you when Mr Murphy left us," said a voice from behind me. I twisted around to find a short, petite man standing just inside the shop's doorway. He wore a monk's habit and sandals on his feet. He was eighty if he was a day, and had no hair on his head whatsoever unless one counted his eyebrows which were pure white.

Meeting my eyes with his own, he smiled warmly and stepped forward. "Hello, I'm Father Cyril. I'm the abbot here. Perhaps I can be of assistance, Mrs Fisher."

Caught off guard when he addressed me by my name, I said, "You know who I am?"

He released my hand and stepped back a half pace. His smile stayed in place. "Of course, Mrs Fisher. We have television here. And newspapers. We even have the internet. We devote our lives to God, and support our simple lifestyles through the products we produce and by the revenue we are able to generate through visitors coming to our humble residence."

The three ladies working in the shop went largely forgotten as the abbot's charismatic manner drew me in.

The shop door opened, the little bell above it ringing to signal fresh customers arriving. It struck me as odd that the abbot managed to enter without making a sound. The newcomers had to be from one of the coach parties and were coming en mass into the shop.

His serene smile still aimed at me, the abbot asked, "Perhaps you would like to accompany me to my chambers. We can talk in private there."

Obviously, I agreed, following the abbot outside with half of my team going ahead of me and the other half trailing behind.

"Mrs Fisher!" Yet again someone was calling my name and I looked around to find a gentleman in a suit coming my way, his hand up to identify who to look at. He had neatly trimmed grey hair and a surprisingly good tan for this time of year. Assuming he'd recently returned from a holiday in the sun or was perhaps one of those persons who like to hit the sunbeds and keep that year-round glow, I ventured a guess.

"Agent Mitchel?" How had he gotten here so quickly? He told me he'd already left London when he called, but to arrive twenty minutes after us? There was no reason to question it, but it felt ... off.

I'm not sure why, but I expected someone younger. He sounded younger on the phone. The man coming my way looked close to fifty. Spectacles with a thick black rim dominated the top half of his face while a thick beard of equally grey hair covered the lower half sandwiching his mouth between it and a moustache.

"Yes. One and the same," he announced, producing ID to show me. It was the first time I'd seen an Interpol badge and had no reason to doubt it was real.

"Have we met before?" I asked, certain we had not, but finding something familiar about the man. My skull itched, a tickly feeling to tell me I should be paying close attention.

Agent Mitchel cocked his head to one side, a curious expression on his face. "I'm fairly sure I would remember if we had. I've been working out of the London office for the last five years; have you had any business with Interpol in this country prior to today?"

I shook my head. "No. I'm sure it's just me."

"I guess I just have one of those faces," he remarked. "Now, time is important in a kidnapping case, Mrs Fisher. I'm sure you already know that. I need to interview you as soon as possible. I have a car waiting and there is a field office not far from here if you can come with me ..."

"Sorry." I shook my head again. I wasn't ready to get into that stuff yet. There was more to learn here and while Interpol might throw their impressive resources into finding Xavier Silvestre, I believed finding the treasure before he could was still my best shot at getting Barbie back. "I'm afraid the interview will have to wait. For a short while, at least. We can walk and talk, Agent Mitchel, but I have some questions for the Abbot before I leave to go anywhere else. The answers we get here could expedite the capture of Xavier Silvestre *and* ensure the release of Barbara Berkeley."

I thought the man from Interpol was going to argue for a moment. Something dark passed behind his eyes but it was gone in an instant, replaced by a nod of acceptance. My skull itched again. I was missing something.

"Very well," he gave a congenial reply.

The abbot started walking again, leading my group, which now included one Interpol agent. He was leading us across a wide gravel path toward the main building.

Agent Mitchel fell into step beside me.

"What is it that you hope to learn here, Mrs Fisher?"

I sucked in a breath and asked, "What do you know about the case so far, Agent Mitchel? What do you know about Xavier Silvestre's motivation for taking my friend?"

"Very little," he admitted with an apologetic shrug. "I read what was in the case file, but that was only created a few hours ago. It's my reason for being here really. You clearly know what is going on. There are other agents involved in tracking down the whereabouts of Senor Silvestre and yet more trying to determine if he has indeed committed any crimes."

"Oh, he has. You can trust me on that."

We reached the large door set into the centre of the abbey and went through it following our host. He climbed a set of three stone stairs and turned left, gesturing with his right hand that we should follow.

"This way please, nearly there. We can talk in private soon."

I paused to let Agent Mitchel go through the door ahead of me. We were walking almost shoulder to shoulder and could not get through like that. Of course, he tried to do exactly the same, the pair of us creating a bottleneck as both stopped short of the door, both apologised, and both then tried to move at the same time.

I held up my hands. "You first," I insisted.

Agent Mitchel went inside and I was about to follow when I noticed Sam had fallen behind.

"Everything all right, Sam?" I called. He was down on one knee looking at something on the leaf of a holly bush.

He looked up at the sound of his name being called.

"I found a bug," he said.

I fought the urge to roll my eyes and made an urgent gesture.

"Come along, sweetie, let's get inside where it's warmer."

Sam was still looking at the bug when I turned to go through the doorway, but when I looked back he was jogging to catch up. I waited for him just inside.

Jermaine, as always, waited for me, never wanting to be separated from me by more than a few yards. Agent Mitchel likewise chose to hang back from the crowd who were now ten yards down a wide hallway and turning left to go through a door.

Agent Mitchel continued to bug me about what actual evidence I believed I could provide with regard to Xavier Silvestre and the back of my skull continued to itch.

Reaching the same door my friends followed the abbot through only seconds before, I found myself in a large room. It was plainly decorated, which was to say it wasn't really decorated at all. I must confess I don't know a great deal about monks, but believed their chosen lifestyle eschewed all personal belongings. The plain, wooden furnishings inside the room stood testament to that and the desk, which I guessed was where the abbot worked and wrote letters, or whatever it was that an abbot was supposed to do, was as sparse and spartan as any I'd ever seen outside of a showroom.

The abbot, wizened old man that he was, offered to have refreshments brought to us, though when we unanimously declined, he got the message and got to the point.

"You may be wondering why I chose to lead you away from the public areas and refused to say anything more until now."

He was quite right, and I hoped he was going to tell me something that would be worth my while.

"Mrs Fisher," Sam hissed, tugging lightly at the sleeve of my coat.

"The fact of the matter," the abbot continued, "is that I know what it is that you seek."

Sam tried to get my attention again. "Mrs Fisher, look at this bug."

Bug. The word echoed inside my skull.

"Furthermore, I know where it is," the abbot was being deliberately cryptic, I felt, but the itching at the back of my skull had just returned and though I dearly wanted to pay attention to the abbot's grand revelation, something about the way Sam said 'bug' made me turn my head to look.

Betrayal

M y eyes just about popped out of my head. In Sam's hand, a little beetle looking thing wriggled its body as it walked across his palm. I had never seen a live one, but I saw the pictures and knew without a shadow of a doubt Sam held a lucanus punctatum, the rarer than rare beetle that existed only on the island of Asreb off the coast of Melilla.

I gasped, "Sam, where did you get that?"

He grinned at me. "It was in the garden, Mrs Fisher. Is it the same one we were looking for in Africa?"

I wasn't going to correct him on his small error just because we were technically in Spain at the time, and I couldn't talk anyway because my mind was racing. Finn Murphy never went to Melilla, he got the bug in his hair from when he was here at the abbey.

That answered a question that had been bugging me for months, but it created a much bigger one: what were the bugs doing here? Better yet, how did they get here?

The abbot was still talking, saying something about the history of the abbey and how they once cared for an injured Spanish sailor.

Like a blinding light exploding inside my head, I saw why the treasure had never come to light.

"It's here!" I blurted. "It's been right here all this time."

The abbot met my wide eyes with a smile.

"I knew you would come, Mrs Fisher. The moment I read about Finn Murphy's death and how it was you who found him, I knew it was only a matter of time before you came knocking on our door."

Agent Mitchel blinked in his confusion. "What's here? What did I miss?"

The abbot said, "Can I ask how you figured it out?"

I took hold of Sam's hand and held it aloft, using his strength to keep my own arm from shaking.

"It was the bug," I managed to say, my knees feeling weak. "Well, it was a lot of things, actually, but those things just led us here. The bug sealed the deal."

"Mrs Fisher, please," complained Agent Mitchel, his tone terse and annoyed. "I want to know what the abbot was telling us about the Spanish sailor. Your assistant's bug is irrevolent."

Irrevolent?

Time slowed down and seemed to come to a stop. My head and eyes were moving around and to the right, shifting away from Sam to look at Agent Mitchel. Not that he was Agent Mitchel. His attention was back on the abbot, who was, in turn, looking at me.

The treasure was here in the abbey somewhere. Don't ask me how it got here, that part would remain a mystery until the abbot provided the full explanation. I couldn't guess where it was either, but Finn found it and took as much as he could carry when he left in an almighty hurry.

Finding the location of the San José's treasure was enough to create a shockwave that made my brain feel like jelly, but I'd been given no more than a few seconds before the next mind-blowing revelation: Xavier Silvestre was standing only a few feet from me.

Lifting a shaking finger to point at him, I had to rally my senses to get my mouth to work.

"Him," I stuttered. "It's him." It should have come out as a roar of accusation, but I was so stunned my voice was almost conversational.

The abbot held the focus of the room, all eyes converging on him with only mine looking elsewhere. He was saying something about a storm in 1708 when he noticed I wasn't paying attention. Only when he stopped speaking did the rest of the room hear what I had to say.

"It's him," I managed to blurt again, my right hand and index finger still aimed at Agent Mitchel/Xavier Silvestre.

"Him who, Patricia?" asked Deepa, her head cocked to one side as she tried to make out what I was trying to tell everyone.

My lips felt numb. Silvestre was turning his head to look my way again and now I could examine the features I could see behind the disguise, I knew for sure I was absolutely right.

"Sil …" I tried to say his name, but with the devil himself staring straight into my eyes, the word died in my mouth. Mustering every shred of indignant anger I could find, my fear for Barbie's life, how close his henchman came to dragging me over the side of the ship when he emptied my safe, the way Xavier almost shot me in Rio, and I converted it into volume. "Silvestre!" I bellowed. "That's Silvestre! Grab him!"

My outraged cry caused confusion more than anything else, but Jermaine reacted the way I hoped everyone would. The echo of my command was yet to fade away and he was already moving. Seeing him burst into action, others were doing likewise. Hideki, Deepa, and Molly to name three, but Silvestre was moving too.

From his sleeves, and activated by a flick of his shoulders, two pistols appeared, one in each hand. They were up and raised, the threat they represented instant and deadly.

Jermaine is fast, but no one could have closed the distance in time to prevent Silvestre winning the race.

"Stop." His command was simple and delivered in a calm voice that betrayed only one emotion: anger. His pistols, acting like extensions of his arms, were pointing directly at Jermaine and Hideki. He needed to spread his arms wide to achieve that, and was shifting them to aim the guns at anyone else who dared to move. "All of you, back up. Now!" he barked.

We complied. What else could we do?

When he had a couple of yards space and we were all gathered in one place near to the abbot's desk, he lifted his left arm to tear at his face. The glasses went first, followed swiftly by the wig. His eyes never left mine when he teased one corner of the beard and began to peel it away from his face.

"All these years, Patricia Fisher, no one had ever figured out who was beneath the disguise. Tell me how you did it." The timbre of his voice suggested he would start shooting if I didn't. The wig, beard, and glasses gone, he looked just like his picture. Finally we were seeing the real man.

"Irrevolent!" I spat with a terror-filled laugh. "You said 'irrevolent'!"

Silvestre looked confused.

"There's no such word, you idiot! It's irrelevant! Irrelevant. You said it wrong when you attacked me in the ladies' restroom on the British Union Isles and you said it wrong again just now."

Silvestre pursed his lips, annoyed with himself. The pistol in his left hand hung in the air now that he wasn't gripping it. It poked from his sleeve on what had to be a spring-loaded mechanism. I'd seen something like it once in an old cowboy film though never since and certainly not in person.

With his free hand, he took out his phone and held it to his ear.

"Gomez, bring her in. I have been made, but the treasure is here." He twisted to point the weapon in his right hand at the abbot. "Isn't it, old man?"

The head monk nodded his head. "Yes, it is. But I cannot let you have it. My brothers kept it hidden all this time because they understood what evil such a treasure would attract."

Silvestre's mouth twitched into a smile. "Cannot let me have it? You imagine I am going to give you a choice." He returned to his phone, speaking to someone called Gomez – his giant henchman most likely.

Jermaine shifted his feet, tensing his body. Now that he held only one gun, did my butler believe he could get across the room before Silvestre shot him? I snaked a hand around Jermaine's forearm, unwilling to let him try.

Maybe he would get there. Maybe if we all went we could overpower him. Honestly, I knew such a mass attack would almost certainly work, but at what cost? Silvestre would get a shot or shots off before he was taken down and the chance that he might shoot one of my friends was too great to risk the strategy.

I understood that our situation and the chance to improve it might only get worse if we didn't act, but before I could finish arguing with myself the sound of someone approaching outside drew Silvestre to the door.

He opened it to reveal the bald-headed giant and I confess I didn't know what emotion to feel in that moment for he had Barbie with him too. My blonde friend had been missing for days, held by the murderous Spanish treasure hunter. Now she was back, the joy I felt made me want to cry despite the fear of imminent death I harboured.

"Hideki!" she squealed. "Guys!" Released from Gomez's grip she ran to us, throwing her arms around Hideki and Jermaine and holding tight for a moment before doing the same to me and then some of the others, thanking us all for trying to find her.

"Enough, Miss Berkeley. I'm afraid your reunion is over, and your usefulness is at an end." Without taking his eyes away from my group, he spoke to Gomez, "Kill them."

Gomez removed a large calibre handgun from inside his jacket. It looked tiny in his hand yet probably weighed so much I would struggle to lift it.

Threatened with impending death, Jermaine, Martin, Schneider, and more were moving. The all-at-once-charge tactic I didn't want them to employ earlier had become our only option, but they all froze again when Gomez fired his first shot.

The hand cannon's bark sounded like thunder to my ears. The explosion of noise in the confined and enclosed office made my ears ring, but it was my eyes that were struggling. Gomez didn't shoot one of my friends or even the abbot.

He shot his boss.

Silvestre stared down at the bloody stain spoiling the front of his shirt. It was spreading fast, the hole Gomez put in him right over his heart.

He sank to his knees, a disbelieving look on his face.

"What?" Silvestre spluttered. "Why?"

Gomez glared down at Silvestre, his gun hand cocked into the air when he said, "Ten years I've been doing your bidding. Ten years. Pretending to be a mute. Taking your orders, doing your bidding. Killing for you when necessary. You don't even pay me, you idiot. Did you ever stop to question my motivation?"

Silvestre was losing. His wound was fatal and no one was coming to save him. He looked up at his henchman.

"I thought you were happy," he wheezed, sinking further toward the floor.

"That's because you are a self-absorbed fool, Xavier. You told me about the treasure. For ten years I have been waiting for you to find it. Now that you have, you are of no further use."

It was cold hearted and merciless, but no less than Silvestre deserved.

With a final sigh, the Spanish treasure hunter's head flopped forward to touch the floor and he stayed there, utterly dead within touching distance of the treasure he spent his life trying to find.

Gomez stepped forward, reaching down to check his former boss's pulse and that was when Jermaine leapt.

The big fight

The door to the abbot's office was closed; Gomez shut it behind him when he came in, and now blocked the only exit with his body. It might sound like a cliché, but the only way out was to go through him and that was precisely what my friends were looking to do.

They ran. All of them, leaving me and the abbot behind when they seized the slim opportunity they'd been given and launched their attack.

Jermaine got there first, his aim not to put Gomez down with his first strike but to disarm him. A stiff arm, striking the larger man on his forearm to shock the gun free, sent it shooting across the room. I tracked its trajectory to see where it went – under a large chest of drawers set against the wall to the right of the door.

Spinning in place, Jermaine delivered a punch to the giant's throat, acting strategically by aiming for the soft targets that would rob Gomez of his ability to fight.

Sam bellowed a rage-filled war cry as he rammed the giant, driving his head into Gomez's gut. With both fists he pummelled at Silvestre's henchman only to have a clubbing two-handed blow land between his shoulder blades.

Jermaine was trying to land another blow, but with Sam in the way he was severely hampered. Worse yet, when Sam collapsed under the strike to his back, grunting in pain, a kick sent him sprawling into Jermaine who had to grab him and try to roll out of the way.

Hideki arrived, leaping past Jermaine to deliver a two-footed kick to his target's midriff. Gomez staggered backward, hitting the door only to bounce off and come out fighting.

An arm the size of a small tree trunk swept the smaller Japanese doctor aside like he was swatting a fly, the energy generated by such a large mass was enough to send Hideki flying into Deepa as she attempted to lend a hand. The pair of them created a barrier for Martin and Schneider, a duo of highly trained security officers who ought to have no trouble dealing with someone the size of Gomez.

They jumped over the tumbling bodies only to be met with one of Gomez's giant boots. The kick took them both out.

Jermaine hammered his elbow into the giant's upraised thigh before reversing to drive the same solid piece of bone into his face. Gomez must have seen stars from that one, but even though I could see blood coming from his mouth, he showed no sign that he felt any pain.

Anders Pippin, a much smaller and slighter man than any of the others on the team didn't waste his efforts trying to knock the seven-foot man mountain down with a punch that would have been as effective as a fly headbutting a Volvo on the motorway, but picked up a solid wooden chair and smashed it down on Gomez's head.

The chair splintered and blood began to pour from a cut on the giant's head, but yet again he brushed the blow and his wound off as though it were no more than an annoying itch. Gomez whipped his head around and with a hand that would dwarf an orangutan's, he grabbed Anders by the throat. Ripped off his feet, Anders could do nothing but claw at the hand squeezing the life from him.

Jermaine lashed out with a leg, his foot parting atoms it was moving so fast when it collided with the side of Gomez's face, but all he got for his effort was Anders, thrown roughly away like a ragdoll.

Unable to avoid the collision, Jermaine fell backward under the smaller man's body.

In many ways the numbers we had to fight Gomez with worked against us. They couldn't all attack at once and his ability to ignore pain allowed him to convert their close quarters attacks against other members of my group.

Martin and Schneider were getting back to their feet, but never got the chance to get back into the fight. Having created a gap around himself, Gomez kicked out with a boot that took the breath from Schneider and probably broke several of his ribs. Martin managed to shift at the last moment, catching a glancing blow instead of the full destructive impact Gomez intended.

Across the room to the right of Gomez, Barbie and Molly were fishing under the chest of drawers for the gun. Silvestre had guns too but his were not only attached to contraptions fitted to his arms, but his body was firmly within the circle of danger Gomez represented.

Jermaine was getting back up, but he looked winded. Schneider was out of it and Sam was hurt. I could only watch in horror, certain I would only make things worse if I tried to get involved, when Deepa pushed herself upright and faced off against the giant again.

A sneer twisted his ugly mouth – he thought her choice to fight him was laughable. Anders screamed a battle cry, picking up two pieces of broken chair, he too faced the seemingly invincible man.

Blood ran from the cut on Gomez's skull, staining his jacket and the collar of his shirt. A cut to his left temple likewise leaked blood down his face and his lips were puffy and swollen on one side, but he didn't care about any of his wounds.

To his right, Barbie and Molly had given up trying to reach the gun and were now engaged in heaving at the heavy piece of furniture, doing their best to lever it away from the wall. I ran to help them, skirting the room to lend a hand. However, the chest of drawers was impossibly heavy. Even with our combined weight and strength, it wasn't budging.

"We need a lever!" Barbie yelled, looking around to find something we could use.

With Jermaine also back on his feet, there were three of my friends facing off against Gomez. Sam limped over to make it four. Four against one and I already knew they didn't stand a chance. What choice did we have though? We had to buy enough time for help to arrive or for Molly and Barbie to get to the gun.

Gomez might be some kind of mystic master who could lock away the pain of his injuries, but I was fairly sure he wouldn't be able to ignore having his kneecaps shot out. Half the people in the room were used to carrying firearms on a daily basis. Any one of them would gladly pull the trigger.

With a grunt of effort, Deepa attacked, feigning right to draw the giant only to reverse course and drop to the ground by his feet. The move confused me for a second until her right leg shot upward to kick Gomez firmly between the legs. The ol' smack in the pants move was one I'd been forced to employ myself on occasion and it never failed to work.

Except this time. Gomez didn't even blink.

He raised a giant foot, aiming to stomp it down on Deepa's head or chest. Would he drive her straight through the floor? Would he crush her in an instant? Anders launched his pieces of wood, throwing them at Gomez's head and landing what had to feel like vicious blows. He was wise enough not to get too close less Gomez grab hold of him again, but the hurled objects, while enough to put Gomez off so Deepa could roll away and escape, did nothing else to stop the titan.

In what looked like an all-or-nothing move, Jermaine threw himself at Gomez. Putting all his weight into it, he tried to bear him to the ground where together everyone might be able to pin him down, but though Gomez staggered, he managed to catch the Jamaican and stay upright.

Now trapped in the giant's grasp, Jermaine grunted in pain as Gomez began to squeeze. It was a bear hug; the kind that breaks a man's ribs and squishes his internal organs.

I cried out in fear.

"Hey, dirtbag," said Big Ben, throwing a punch that echoed around the room like two manhole covers being clanked together.

He was still coming through the door, entering behind Gomez so the giant never saw him coming until it was too late. I swear I almost cheered.

The blow caught Gomez on the right of his jaw, sending a spray of blood across the room. I saw why a moment later. With Jermaine tumbling free and Tempest piling into the room behind Big Ben, I noticed the glint of metal on Big Ben's hand – he was wearing a knuckle duster.

I guess the previous encounter encouraged him to add some extras to his arsenal. Both the Blue Moon boys were wearing their usual black tactical gear complete with Kevlar vests. They entered the room like a freight train: unstoppable and unyielding.

Gomez staggered away but turned to face them, his arms coming up. Big Ben threw another punch, this one going wide of the mark when Gomez jinked out of its way, but the punch was a ruse, a distraction to send him into Tempest's path.

Gripping the wrist of an enormous right arm, I watched as Tempest twisted, ducked, and took the arm behind Gomez. I couldn't perform such a move, but I knew what he was doing. The joints of the arm only go one way and Tempest was forcing them to do precisely the opposite.

Normally, the move was intended to force a person to submit, the pain the arm bar caused enough to make them go to the ground where they could be fully subdued. That didn't work on Gomez.

The giant henchman lashed out, ignoring Tempest's instructions to stop fighting and we all heard the crack when something in the giant's right arm broke.

A look of shock and disbelief crossed Tempest's face right before Gomez punched him with his other arm. Tempest reeled from the hit and let go the arm he had which flopped to hang limply at Gomez's side.

His right arm was broken, his jaw looked to be broken too from Big Ben's first hit, but Gomez was still on his feet and needed only a fur coat to complete the look of an enraged grizzly bear.

As he faced off against Big Ben once more, I questioned how anyone could possibly defeat him. Big Ben swung a punch that Gomez swatted aside, and a kick which he parried.

Barbie and Molly were using a walking stick they found to try to lever the chest of drawers from where it sat refusing to move, but it snapped, the sharp end cutting Molly's hand when the wood splintered.

All around the room there were injured people; my friends who on the cusp of victory couldn't defeat the one last barrier that stood in our way.

When the abbot cried out, I thought it was because he too had been hurt. I'd paid him no attention since the start of the fight. The little old man had backed away to one side to watch, wise enough to know he could add no value to our efforts.

How wrong was I?

His shout wasn't one of pain, but a cry announcing his decision to end the fight. He ran across his desk, leapt to the chest of drawers above Barbie and Molly's heads and bounced as though his feet were spring loaded to land on Gomez's shoulder like he was taking part in a parkour tournament.

He wrapped his arms around the giant's face and his skinny legs around his neck.

For a moment I thought it was a suicidal move, but Gomez couldn't get his massive left arm high enough to dislodge the tiny monk. When it looked like he might be able to grip the abbot's leg, Big Ben waded in to secure the one good arm Gomez still possessed.

Jermaine, wheezing with pain but determined to finish the job, gave Big Ben a nod of thanks as he kicked out one of their opponent's knees. Gomez went down, a second kick taking out the other leg to make him a more normal height.

The abbot was squeezing off the blood supply to Gomez's head, pinching at the main arteries delivering oxygenated blood to his brain. In less than thirty seconds, the fight went out of him. Ten seconds after that, the ageing head of the monastery released his grip and allowed Tempest to help him to the floor.

Gomez slumped, his broken body out cold for now.

From their pockets, Tempest and Big Ben both produced thick, plastic cable ties; the kind they used to secure prisoners. The boys set to work and I think we all breathed a sigh of relief when Gomez was finally hogtied and unlikely to resume fighting when he came around.

I looked about the room. My team were a mess. They had cuts and bruises. They were holding their ribs and nursing their jaws. Medical attention was needed and it looked like only me, the abbot and Barbie had managed to get through the ordeal unscathed.

I wanted to hug everyone. I wanted to know how the abbot pulled off his incredible stunt. I needed to ask Barbie a million questions, but what I said first was aimed at Tempest and Big Ben.

"How did you guys find us?"

Tempest shrugged. "I'm a detective."

Wrapping Things Up

- -

Big Ben went to the door, opening it with a swish and leaning out, he shouted, "Do you monkeys want to come in now?"

A head peered around the door.

"Come in, Brother Mark," invited the abbot.

Brother Mark entered the abbot's office followed by another, then another ... I'm sure you get the picture.

"Were they outside the whole time?" I wanted to know.

"They sure were," replied Big Ben, his arms folded across his chest and his eyes narrowed at the berobed men filing through the door.

"Brothers of our order are not permitted to enter the abbot's private chambers without verbal permission."

"They could have knocked," I stressed, bewildered that they chose to leave us to fight Gomez without their assistance.

"No, that is not permitted either," the abbot countered. "If the abbot is inside and the door is shut, they must wait until he exits."

"What if it's something important," questioned Molly.

Father Cyril chose not to answer that one, opting to duck it by giving instructions to his brothers. They fetched first aid equipment and called for the emergency services. They had an unconscious man with broken bones and a corpse that needed to be removed. That the corpse was at the centre of a police investigation involving multiple agencies including Interpol was going to get people moving fast.

The law enforcement people would get here soon enough – I no longer felt in any danger, but there was still the small matter of the treasure to discuss though that was entirely secondary to having a proper chat with Barbie.

"Are you all right, sweetie?" I asked.

She was leaning into Hideki, her head resting against his chest with one hand stretched out to hold Jermaine's.

At my question, she let go of Jermaine's hand and pushed away from her boyfriend. There were tears welling in her eyes from relief that she was finally safe, and she reached out to take both my hands in hers.

"I'm fine," she sighed, "but I do have a little problem." She let go of my hands again and rolled up the sleeves of her winter coat.

Jermaine, his face screwed up, asked, "What are those?

Barbie bit her lip and winced when she said, "Would you believe they are explosive cuffs?"

The odd garments that looked a bit like shin pads for a person's forearms extended from her wrists to her elbows. They were leather on the outside which reminded me of Roman armour or something a gladiator might wear.

"How do you get them off?" Hideki asked, taking Barbie's left arm and turning it about to inspect the device.

"Is this why you didn't escape in Rochester?" I guessed.

I got a tearful shrug from the Californian blonde – she had been through a lot recently.

When she found her voice a moment later she was looking at Big Ben.

"Ben, I'm so sorry."

He gave her a thumbs up. "If I'm going to get beaten up, it might as well be for the most perfect woman in the world."

Hideki grunted, "Does he ever give up?"

I suspected the answer to that was probably 'no' but chose to return to the more pressing matter.

Barbie was looking at Xavier Silvestre's body. It was covered by a blanket now, the monks providing it, but had not been touched or moved since Gomez shot him.

"There's an app on his phone he can use to detonate one or both cuffs. I tried to fight him several times, but he always had a weapon stashed somewhere. He said he would blow my hands off if I tried to get away and I believed him." Her voice cracked a little when she made the terrible revelation. No wonder she stayed with her captors when she could have otherwise gotten away.

Hearing what she had to say, Tempest and Big Ben took it upon themselves to search the body. I knew they were both former soldiers and could only imagine this wasn't their first time handling a corpse.

The abbot came to me while they were looking for Silvestre's phone.

"In all the excitement, Mrs Fisher, we seem to have gotten distracted from the reason for your visit here today."

I had not forgotten the treasure; it was very present in my mind. It was not, however, as important as the people in my life, especially when they needed medical treatment. Plus, it had been here for three hundred years, it could wait a few more minutes.

Nevertheless, I asked, "How is it that it comes to be here?"

Father Cyril looked around for a chair and when one of the brothers saw what he wanted, one was swiftly deposited under his bottom.

Comfortable once more, he took us back to 1708.

"A monk called Brother Fidelius liked to take walks along the cliffs. They are about a mile from here, but inside the boundary of our land. On this particular day, there had been a terrible storm the previous night. The abbey suffered some damage from the wind, and taking a break from the repair work, Brother Fidelius ventured to the cliffs to see whether the storm might have altered the coastline. His route took him past a small blow hole which he'd discovered could send jets of seawater shooting into the sky when the tide was high enough and the conditions were right. He knew to look out for it because an unwary man might fall down the hole into the cavern below."

Listening to the abbot talk, I looked around the room. Most of the brothers present were still performing their duties, but a few had stopped to listen even though I was sure they must have heard the tale before. My friends, though, they were silent, hanging on every word of the story.

"The blow hole wasn't as Brother Fidelius expected it. The storm had caused the roof of the cavern to cave in, widening the hole significantly. Staring down into the chasm, Brother Fidelius heard a voice. It was weak and sounded to be in pain, but whoever had fallen into the hole was still alive and that demanded a rescue be attempted."

"The San José was in the cavern!" gushed Martin, earning a slap from his wife.

"Let Father Cyril tell it!" she scolded.

Falling silent, his cheeks flushing, Martin nodded that the abbot should proceed.

"Brother Fidelius ran back to the abbey to fetch help and the entire order gathered ropes and materials they could use. When they lowered the first man into the cavern, he expected to find a lost traveller had fallen in by mistake. I can only imagine his surprise when they found a ship. It was wrecked and almost devoid of crew. The roof of the cavern, eroded by centuries of weather and tide, was dislodged by the ship's central mast, the rocks falling to the deck below where it killed or injured those who remained on board."

"But it was the San José?" I could contain my need for confirmation no longer.

Father Cyril smiled benignly. "No, my dear Mrs Fisher, it was not."

My face crinkled in confusion as did many others in the room.

"To explain that I need to continue from where I was."

I muttered an apology and tried to stay quiet.

Father Cyril restarted, explaining how the monks in 1708 found a Spanish ship in the cavern and among the many dead, they found three survivors. Their injuries were terrible: broken bones and deep cuts from the falling rocks that were made worse in the struggle to bring them back to the surface.

The monks did what they could but two of the survivors perished within a day of being rescued. The third man clung to life and though they expected him to lose his battle, he recovered. The man's name was Henri Cristobal. He remained at the monastery for more than a year, learning to walk with a stick to support a leg that had been badly broken and though reset, was never going to be the same as it was.

The monks discovered the treasure, of course, and despite the dangers, made hundreds of trips back down into the cavern to recover it all. Not for their own gain, obviously, Father Cyril was sure to point out, but because the abbot at the time believed it should be preserved.

"Where is it now?" asked Barbie, the one amongst us who had done the most to find it. Big Ben and Tempest had Xavier's phone now and were trying to figure out the app that supposedly controlled the cuffs fitted to Barbie's forearms.

Father Cyril said, "Beneath us. There was so much of it the brothers carved out new sections of cellar to store it. Knowing he was dying, one of the initial survivors insisted that he needed to confess his sins before God. He gave a full account of how they plotted and murdered, creating a deception that allowed them to steal the treasure with a plan to keep it for themselves. It is all chronicled in an account recorded at the time."

Tempest raised a hand to interrupt, waiting until the abbot stopped speaking before he started.

"I believe we have figured this out," he announced, looking intently at Barbie's wrists.

Barbie pulled a worried face. "Are you guys sure? I mean, what if you're wrong?"

Rather than answer, Tempest popped open a pocket on his right hip, taking out a butterfly knife which he extended with a flick. He moved closer, holding out his free hand for Barbie to give him one of hers.

"Let's just take a look."

Clearly anxious, Barbie extended her right arm. Being unhelpful, Molly mimed a large explosion going off with her hands and put her fingers in her ears.

"What are you going to do?" asked Barbie.

Tempest said, "Well ..." in a sudden move that caught Barbie and everyone else by surprise, he slipped the tip of the blade under the cuff and sliced upward from her wrist to her elbow.

Barbie squealed in fright and tried to recoil, but just as everyone around him flinched and tried to back away, the cuff came free.

With a grin over his shoulder at Big Ben, he said, "Told you they were fake."

Big Ben gave a nod of acceptance, but poor Barbie, who looked about ready to faint before Tempest made the cut, was hopping mad now.

"Fake! They were fake! I've been willingly staying with those two Spanish -" she employed a descriptive word a lady shouldn't even know, "and the cuffs were fake!"

Tempest offered a shrug of apology. "Sorry. The app doesn't do anything. I mean, it looks convincing, but I doubt there are even any explosives in these things."

Barbie tensed her body and released a scream of outrage. Had she been ten years younger she might have stamped a foot.

I felt sorry for her, but at the same time, it was genuinely funny. I wasn't the only one who thought so. Most of us were chuckling, including Tempest when he cut off the second cuff.

Barbie rubbed at her forearms, massaging the skin and examining the slight tan marks she had from wearing them in the sun of Melilla.

"It's not funny," she growled at the room in general, narrowing her eyes as she glared at me and everyone else.

Despite the mirth, which was a welcome relief after days of tension and stress, I looked at the abbot and said, "The treasure? Can you show it to us?"

Father Cyril eased himself back to upright and started towards his office door.

"Of course."

The abbot led us around the Abbey, talking all the time as he continued the story. The San José had been sunk by the British just as history described, but the treasure wasn't on it. The great heist, as we came to think of it, was conducted at sea with a plan for the sailors left on board the San José to sail into waters where they would likely encounter the British with whom Spain was at war at the time.

Placing a man on board dying from what was probably undiagnosed then, but sounded like cancer now, they blew out the bottom of the ship, thus murdering their own men. The treasure, now safely vanished like a modern-day money laundering scam, was taken across the Atlantic, but a storm crippled their ship and with too few men on board to control it in such heavy seas, they were probably lucky to run it aground.

The cavern they sailed into collapsed around them, sealing the ship inside for all time.

"Wait," interrupted Tempest, "it's still there?"

Father Cyril nodded. "Indeed it is."

"But how has no one else ever found it?" I questioned.

The abbot had an answer for that one too. "We are on private land, my dear Mrs Fisher. The cavern is invisible from the sea, the cliffs drop directly into the sea so there had never been any danger of people accidentally finding a way in along the shore, and there are fences around our land, which is quite remote, to ensure no one goes near the opening above."

At the bottom of a set of stone steps, the abbot stopped talking and stepped to one side to let one of his brothers through. The monk produced a large key from inside his robes and used it to unlock a large oak door.

Now, I'm not going to say the smell of gold rushed out to fill my nose, but when the door swung inward there was definitely something in the air that made me think of money and treasure. Expecting to see shelves lined with gold coins and maybe some old wooden chests like props from a pirate movie, nothing could have prepared me for the sight dazzling my eyes when the monk stepped through the door and flipped a light switch.

There was gold stretching into the distance. On the floor, on shelves, row upon row of it. Coins and ingots, plus items of jewellery such as necklaces and crowns.

I heard several muttered expletives and Big Ben said, "Is this all you could find?"

There are no words to describe the emotions running through my brain at that point. I was, to say the least, overwhelmed.

A report that the police were on site came just a few minutes later and a good thing too because standing in the presence of all that treasure and walking among it was making me feel a little odd.

As a group, we returned to the ground floor of the abbey where uniformed officers accompanied by a pair of detectives were just entering the building. We met them in the hallways leading back to the abbot's office where monks guarded Xavier Silvestre's body and the still bound Gomez.

They were going to have questions for us. They would want to take statements, and I knew this was going to turn into a global news story, just like the missing sapphire of Zangrabar, just like the Maharaja's coronation, and just like the downfall of the Godmother and her Alliance of Families.

I didn't want the press coverage. It was invasive and ugly, but it wasn't going to be possible to duck it all.

Jermaine called the crew of the Bombardier private jet to confirm we would not be needing them again. Our plan, once the police allowed us to leave, was to return to Kent and my house in East Malling where we could all take a day to recover. Tempest and Big Ben would likewise return to Kent and their homes where they lived not too far from me.

Barbie had some rather intense questions to answer regarding her part in the attack on an old man in Rochester Cathedral. It didn't help that she was filmed firing a gun, albeit into the ground, in public at the same location. The police wanted to arrest her for they had no record of her kidnapping nor any knowledge of the Xavier Silvestre case.

In fact, it was only when the real Agent Mitchel of Interpol arrived that we were able to clear things up.

The monks brought us food and some of their beer for those who wanted it. I'm not a beer drinker and my hopeful enquiry, "I don't suppose you have any gin?" was met with an apology. Disappointed, I drank water and told myself it was the healthier choice.

The Aurelia, having left New York was backtracking down the eastern coast of America on its way to the Panama Canal. I called Alistair to let him know Barbie was back with us, safe and unharmed. I told him about Xavier Silvestre, the treasure, the monks, and everything else.

In turn he assured me my dogs were not only fine but loving all the attention they got when the captain of the ship took them for a walk.

All in all it had been a hard couple of days, and I could scarcely believe it was over. Not just over, but successful. We got Barbie back, which was the aim, but we also found the San José treasure, and figured out who was behind the murders of Hugo Lockhart, Professor Noriega, Antonio Bardem, and others.

Sucking a little air through my teeth, when I realised there was still one loose end, I unintentionally drew Jermaine's attention.

"Madam?" he asked. "Is there something I can help you with?"

"Finn Murphy's killer," I replied wistfully. "This all started when we found his body. I was supposed to figure out who killed him so we could bring the murderer to justice. My sole purpose in choosing to investigate the treasure was to find Finn Murphy's killer. Now that this is all over, I still don't know who did it."

Swallowing the bit of apple she was chewing, Barbie said, "Someone called Carlos Ramirez did it."

We were in the monastery's dining room, sitting on old, yet solid wooden chairs arranged on either side of long tables. Barbie was just across from me and nestled protectively between Hideki and Jermaine.

We all looked at her and got a lazy shrug.

"Xavier told me. Xavier found out about Carlos from Antonio Bardem when he took an artefact, a cross, I think, to the museum in Brazil. Carlos got the cross from Finn when he killed him. I think Carlos was some kind of conman or something. Anyway, Xavier found out about Carlos, tracked him down and killed him which is how he knew about Finn Murphy being on the Aurelia. Xavier liked to brag." She took another bite of her apple.

Just like that the whole thing was concluded. As the ship's detective it was my job to solve any crimes occurring on board the ship. Finn Murphy's murder was an unsolved blemish I would be happy to erase.

Bernadino Alvarez

Bernadino Alvarez needed four months to properly recover from his injuries. He understood the miracle of his survival; the storm swept him ashore, somehow avoiding the rocks on which he could so easily have landed. His body ought to have been smashed, but his cuts, bruises and other injuries all healed.

His plan at the start was to escape from the people who nursed him back to health, but over the weeks that became months, Mary wormed her way into his heart.

He wrote to his sweetheart back in Spain, but held little hope that she would answer. He could not go to her, and begged that she might come to England. It was a fool's request. Spain was at war with England, and even if they hadn't been, he had nothing to offer her.

His chance at incredible fortune went down with the ship, leaving him a penniless foreigner behind enemy lines. Why would his intended bride come to find him?

Oh, they could go somewhere else. If he left England they could settle in France or any one of a dozen countries, but even as he wrote the letters imploring her to accept such terrible compromises in her life, he already knew she would not.

In his sadness, both at the wreck his life had become and the loss of the woman he knew and loved, Bernadino came to see Mary, the simple farmer's daughter, as a willing alternative. He knew she held feelings for him, that she found him attractive, and felt much the same about her.

For three months, he feigned the inability to speak in the presence of the family who took him in. He understood most of what they were saying though their accent tripped him up for a while. His own English, which he used to write them answers and notes, enabled him to communicate while he quietly practiced and mimicked their way of talking.

He lied about where he was from, claiming to have grown up in London, and about how he came to be in the water, opting to develop a simple story about surviving on a raft after his ship was sunk by the Spanish. In his tale, he'd drifted for days, hoping to spy land only to have the terrible storm claim him before he could.

When finally he began to talk, the family, and especially Mary, reacted as though it was a miracle. They gave thanks to God, and though they questioned his accent, it was because to them he sounded more like he was from Cornwall than London, they showed no sign they believed he could be Spanish.

It was not the life that he might have chosen, but the simple life he now found himself in bore a certain attraction. It was safe, for one, and when Mary chose to visit him in the barn one night, he chose to maintain his pretence.

He'd told them his name was Earnest Smith from West Ham in London. His family were all dead and he was never returning to sea. He made a life with Mary, marrying her the spring after they found his battered body on the beach. She bore him six children, and he took his secret with him to the grave.

Epilogue

- -

T wo days after the events at the monastery, the media frenzy was coming into full force. Coverage was on every channel and the news was dominated by the investigation and revelations about the history of the Spanish ship and how the captain and his officers chose to steal it all for themselves.

It was a truly remarkable tale and one that tickled Justin Masters.

Petting his cat, a four-year-old tortoiseshell called Bobbins, he pursed his lips and sucked on his teeth.

"You know, Bobbins, I rather think I might have to come out of retirement."

If Bobbins had an opinion, he chose not to voice it and continued purring, content to have his fur stroked by his human's hand.

At eighty-seven Justin was bored. That was the crux of the matter. He lived a life of relative luxury in a grand house just off London's Pall Mall, but though he had staff, he didn't really have any friends. Oh, there were plenty of them back in the day, but they were all dead now.

A career criminal specialising in highly planned heists where jewels and large amounts of cash were stolen, he would put together a new team for every job, disbanding them afterwards as part of his plan to never ever get caught.

It worked too because they never had.

Justin Masters was thoroughly proud to have stayed one step ahead of the law for as long as he had and they weren't even looking for him now. In many ways, that was the problem. His last heist was more than a decade ago, a jewellery theft from a vault that took weeks of planning. He didn't do it for the money – the thing about never getting caught is you amass a stack of cash – and when it was done and yet again the police were utterly bamboozled, he chose to hang up his crowbar, so to speak, and call it a day.

Then Patricia Fisher came along.

He read about her finding the missing sapphire of Zangrabar and then how she foiled the Maharaja's assassination. Justin followed with interest every little snippet of news that emerged and was stunned when she was named as the person responsible for dismantling the Alliance of Families. Her achievements were astounding.

But could she catch him?

That was the question Justin Masters needed to answer. Lifting the cat from his lap – not the simplest of processes since the cat was happy to stay where he was and had an abundance of claws with which to anchor himself – he used his phone to find Purple Star Cruise Lines.

He was going on a cruise.

"One last adventure, Justin, old boy. Let's see just how clever Mrs Fisher really is."

The End

Author's Notes:

H ello, Dear Reader,

It is a sunny Friday morning in June as I type up this final note. This is my eighty-second novel (I think). I have genuinely lost track of how many it is now and it then depends if we count novellas, short stories, and the growing number of collaborations.

This took me about three weeks to write and would have been less had I not got so many plates spinning. Among the plates is the possibility of my books becoming TV shows. I had a lengthy meeting in London just a week ago during which we discussed Blue Moon Investigations, Patricia Fisher, and Albert Smith with his dog Rex Harrison.

All three were of interest and a week later there are people at the firm reading my books to figure out the viability of proceeding. Honestly, I doubt it will come to anything, but when opportunity of that magnitude comes knocking, one has no choice but to stop writing and pay attention.

Also on the cards is a contract with one of the big publishing houses and there have been multiple meetings regarding that too. They want me to write a trilogy of hardboiled crime thrillers with my usual comedic slant. The story concept is one I devised five years ago. It has been rattling around in my head ever since, growing in depth and complexity.

Whether I sign the contract or not, whether they offer me a fat advance and sell millions of copies is yet to be decided. I question whether I am actually clever enough to write the book that's in my head, but will be finding out shortly as it is next on my list.

You may already realise that this means a departure from the usual service and that the next Patricia, Felicity, or Blue Moon book will be delayed, and you would be right.

My next meeting is with the literary agent in London on July 10th. Between now and then I have two conferences to attend. I am a busy man.

In this book, I brought to an end the San José/Xavier Silvestre dual storyline and hope it satisfied your mystery desires. It was a lot of fun to write, but with that subplot finished, a new one must begin. That's where Justin Masters comes in and I can promise you a whole new series of adventures coming your way soon.

I mention Artificial Intelligence (AI) systems in this story when Barbie uses programs to solve the riddle left behind by Henri Cristobal. In the last year AI has become a regular tool for me in my work. I generate images for advertising using AI image software and have another tool that helps me create plot ideas and characters.

In theory, the developing AI systems could be used to write books and perhaps one day they will. Some of my associates are worried about being replaced though it is not something that keeps me awake at night.

Patricia and friends use a map entitled 'The World Described' when they are looking at where the San José might have gone in 1708. This is a real thing and was widely circulated at that time.

I also mention saucy postcards and feel I should explain what they are just in case the concept is confusing. Maybe they exist the world over, I simply cannot say, but I have travelled a lot and have no recollection of seeing them outside of a British seaside resort.

Basically, they are cartoonish depictions of men and women with a euphemism or lewd line being exchanged. One I recall involved a group at an ornithological meeting where a young lady with a heavy chest is about to give a talk on 'great tits' – a well-known English bird.

They visit Farnham which used to be my local town. Almost twenty years ago when I was first dating my current wife, I was still in the British army and based just across the Hampshire border, Farnham being in Surrey. We would visit there if we wished to go out for a meal and poke around the shops. It is surrounded by the lush, green landscape of the region.

Lymington is a delightful seaside resort I visited once when sailing a yacht. The south coast of England is littered with such villages and should you ever be in the area and wish to see chocolate box cottages, you should aim your car at the coast.

Gomez suffers from CIPA – Congenital Insensitivity to Pain and Anhidrosis – which is a real thing. It is rare, but it served as a neat way to explain his ability to beat the likes of Big Ben and Jermaine.

Finally, I mention the Hog's Back which is a road connecting Farnham and Guildford. In my research I was not able to determine where the name came from, however it appears to have been coined at the end of the 19th century. A track or road, which runs across the top of a one hundred and fifty four metre high ridge in otherwise flat countryside, has existed there since Roman times.

That's all for now. I need to wrap this book up and get on with the next one.

Take care.

Steve Higgs

What's next for Patricia?

What she doesn't know won't hurt her, but when she finds out will she hurt you?

Arriving home at her quiet village in the English countryside, Patricia is disturbed to find a glut of police cars outside the house of a person she knows.

The church treasurer has been murdered in his own home. The result of an illicit affair? Or something far more sinister?

There's no need for Patricia to get involved, but when another friend, a person of high standing in the community is accused and arrested, locals beg her to investigate. But

Patricia Fisher isn't the only sleuth in the village. There is a certain older gentleman and his German Shepherd dog who feel inclined to poke around and the victim's niece works for a rather well-known wedding planner.

With a super team of sleuths involved, this one should be easy to solve, right? Well, not if someone is lying about what they know and when a second victim is discovered, the casual enquiry becomes a race against time to prevent the death toll escalating.

Can they work together to uncover the truth? Or are they about to learn one brutal fact:

Some secrets are best left that way.

Free Books and More

Want to see what else I have written? Go to my website.

https://stevehiggsbooks.com/

Or sign up to my newsletter where you will get sneak peaks, exclusive giveaways, behind the scenes content, and more. Plus, you'll be notified of Fan Pricing events when they occur and get exclusive offers from other authors because all UF writers are automatically friends.

Copy the link into your web browser.

https://stevehiggsbooks.com/newsletter/

Prefer social media? Join my thriving Facebook community.

Want to join the inner circle where you can keep up to date with everything? This is a free group on Facebook where you can hang out with likeminded individuals and enjoy discussing my books. There is cake too (but only if you bring it).

https://www.facebook.com/groups/1151907108277718

Printed in Great Britain
by Amazon

40102111R00139